Other Books in the Destiny and Darkness series

Daughter of Fire: Conspiracy of the Dark
Daughter of Fire: The Darkness Rising

Karen Frost

Destiny's Choice

Dedication

For Zee, the greatest American hero. Strength and honor.

Chapter 1

"Not all stories have happy endings, Lady Asher," the nursemaid says.

"For me they will! I'll make sure they're always happy," the small child replies, her chubby arms crossed.

"And what if you can't, my lady? Hmm? Come to bed now."

"I inherited a graveyard, Bronwen." Queen Alea looked out the window, her expression mournful. "Our spies in the north report Northmen are massing at the border. Tell me how I save my people. How do I pull us from the jaws of a giant beast? How do I push back invasion from the north without bringing about catastrophe in the south?"

Asher, tucked discreetly into a corner, winced. All her life, Ilirya's capital had stood as an unchallenged bastion of law and order, but since the coup against the queen's brother, King Hap, it was a pale facsimile of itself, half broken and limping as it tried to put back together the pieces that had been blown apart. Most of the city's leaders, including the king, were dead, and the confidence of its people was shattered. Worst of all, Ilirya's northern neighbor was expected to attack at any time, and Ilirya had nothing left with which to defend itself. Its troops were tied down on the southern border, fighting the same grinding war that had lasted forty years. Absent a miracle, Ilirya was helpless to stop its impending destruction.

Knight Commander Bronwen, the queen's most trusted confidante, had an answer. "We have to recall the troops from the south. It is the only way."

Her face was drawn and pale. To an outsider, she must have appeared an unlikely commander of Ilirya's knighthood. More than half her body was paralyzed, and she was reduced to relying on others for all her most basic needs. But her injury was recent. Only weeks ago, an assassin sent to kill her had cut her with a blade poisoned with insidious Dark Magic. According to a healer mage from Windhall, Lyse, the wound would never heal. Eventually, it would kill the knight commander. Yet one more casualty of the coup.

The queen frowned and crossed her arms, shaking her head gently. "But then we'll be overrun in the south!"

Asher silently agreed with her. The Southerners, mortal enemies of her people since long before she was born, were like a team of draft horses, pulling with all their strength in a slow, unrelenting churn. All that kept them from overrunning Ilirya was the presence of the Iliryan army at the border. If the queen moved troops away now, the line would break almost immediately. It was not an option.

"We must find a way to end the war with the Southerners, and fast." Commander Bronwen motioned with her head to Asher, whose duty it was that day to escort her.

Following her indication, Asher wheeled her chair to the window, next to the queen.

Queen Alea pinched the bridge of her nose. "Do you think the Southerners will agree to peace?"

"They must. We will send a delegation under a parley flag to negotiate with them. I will lead the delegation myself. We will find a way to bring peace to Ilirya."

Although the commander's voice was assertive and certain, Asher stifled a gasp.

The queen looked twice at Commander Bronwen, face full of disbelief. Surely the commander didn't intend…

Commander Bronwen's voice had a sharp edge when she spoke. "As Ilirya's knight commander, it falls to me to carry out any negotiations for peace. So long as you see fit to keep me in this office, it is I who must lead the delegation."

She paused for a moment as her words sank in. Then she continued, "You know that if peace is possible, I'm better suited than anyone else to win it. I'll leave within the week, taking a small detail with me. We'll travel as quickly as possible. Time will be of the essence. It will be a victory of ashes if King's City has already fallen by the time peace with the Southerners is achieved."

Queen Alea nodded, but her face reflected her misgivings. "If that is the only way to save Ilirya, then so be it." She motioned to Asher, who stepped forward once more and took the handles of the knight commander's rolling chair. When she looked more closely at Asher, however, her eyes widened with surprise. "You!" She pointed to Asher. "Aren't you the daughter of the late Lord Chancellor Ivar? I remember your knighting ceremony."

"Yes, my queen." Asher bowed, her face flushing. She remembered having seen the queen, then Her Royal Majesty Princess Alea, in the crowd. It made sense that the queen remembered the event. After all, her father had been the king's most favored chancellor. Still, she shunned the attention. She was a knight, not a courtier.

The queen nodded, her expression grim. "Good. Then you understand better than anyone the need to protect the knight commander. She may be a stubborn, old battle-axe, but the kingdom needs her. There is no braver, more loyal soldier in all Ilirya."

Asher nodded, her eyes lowered. "Yes, my queen. On my honor."

"It's a suicide mission." Erborn took a swig of his ale and then licked his thick lips. "Everyone knows it. Bronwen is going to the Southlands to die, and she'll take down with her anyone who goes. Peace? The Southerners will never agree to peace."

Asher's face flushed so hotly that the tips of her ears burned. How dare he say such a thing? "You're wrong! The commander knows what she's doing!"

"Does she?" Taz grimaced when Asher glared at him, then looked down at his mug. "Things have changed since the Night of the Long Swords, Asher. She's not…what she was before. You know that. She may not want to admit what's changed. Or she may think she can do something she can't anymore."

Asher seethed at the betrayal. There was no one like the knight commander in all of Ilirya, and both of them knew it. She was strong, she was brave, and she was smart. If she said peace could be achieved, it could be achieved. Who were they to question her? Hadn't she proven herself over and over again to the kingdom? Everyone agreed she was the finest knight commander in centuries.

What's more, as knights they had a duty to obey and defend her. She was their commander! Yes, she had been hurt, but that didn't diminish who she was or what she'd done. She was still the same person she'd been before, even if she wasn't physically the same. What right had they to question her now?

Asher forced herself to relax her hand gripping her mug. Her knuckles had gone white. "She's *different* from how she was before, but she's just as sharp. She knows what she's doing. She's listened to Ilirya's politicians for a decade; I'm sure she's learned a trick or two. And more importantly, she's still our commander."

"Not for long." Erborn cast his green eyes around the small tavern warily, then leaned forward. "Rumor has it Gandral is going to make a play to take command. The knighthood can't have a crippled commander, and everyone knows it. He has the backing of the new lord chancellor and a few others of the Queen's Council. This time next week, Bronwen could be out on the street."

A flush of white-hot anger washed over Asher. She balled her hands into fists against the table and ground her teeth together. It took all her self-control not to vault over the table and smack the mustache off Erborn's face. This type of talk was treason.

"The queen would never replace Commander Bronwen!"

She looked to Taz for agreement, but his face was studiously blank. Nor would he look at her. Asher's eyes widened. *Does he agree with Erborn? Does he think the commander deserves to be sacked for something that wasn't her fault?* She resolved to confront him about it later.

Erborn wiped froth from his brown mustache, which in the last year had started to sprout a few white hairs. "In any case, no one comes back from the Southlands, and that's a fact. Anyone who goes with Bronwen is riding to their death. That's why no one will do it. She can talk all she wants about a peace delegation, but she rides alone."

Asher rolled her eyes, caught between fury and disdain. "That's ridiculous! Of course people have gone and come back. What nonsense. Where did you hear that?"

She glanced at Taz, certain he would be equally dismissive of Erborn's falsehoods, but he nodded, seeming to agree.

"I've never heard of anyone doing it," he said.

"I'll tell you something more." Erborn waggled a thick finger at her. "You won't find any news of the Southlands anywhere in Ilirya. Not a peep. Whatever lies on the other side of the border, no one knows."

Asher snorted. Now she was sure Erborn was misinformed. "Absurd. We've fought the Southerners for forty years. We must know plenty about them. The royal archives must be filled with information about the Southlands. Two coppers say I find at least two books about the Southland's geography alone by midday tomorrow."

Erborn grinned, showing his broken front tooth. Asher knew he could never resist a bet, especially one he thought he would win. He extended his large hand across the table. "Polish my armor too, and you have a deal. Naftar would welcome the reprieve from his squire's duties, I'm sure."

Asher reached out her smaller hand, and the two shook on it. Asher smirked. She would relish throwing his ignorance in his face when she proved him wrong. She could already see him with her cuirass, sitting on the step in front of the armory and sweating in the hot sun as he rubbed the metal to a brilliant shine. He could stand to learn some humility, and she didn't mind being the one to teach it to him.

Erborn leaned back in his wooden chair. The large knight took up most of it, his long legs sprawled out before him like a newborn foal. He drew a sliver of wood out of his pocket and picked at his teeth with it for a moment. Then in a drawling, almost professorial tone, he said, "I reckon the Southlands are the stuff of living nightmares. There are animals, *things*, living there for which we don't even have names, with teeth and claws longer than my hand's length. And the mages! There are magical affinities there that can't be found anywhere but in the Southlands. Affinities that would make your skin crawl. Terrible, sickening stuff. I say to you: the Southlands are a death trap for any Iliryan fool enough to venture into it. There's not enough gold in all Ilirya could convince me to go."

Asher crossed her arms, unimpressed. "If, as you say, no one has come back from the Southlands, then how do you know all this? How do you know about these so-called monsters?"

Erborn looked away from the table, his eyes haunted. He shuddered, his whole body twitching. "I've been to the border, haven't I? Seen things fighting against us there I can never unsee. If they're there, they're everywhere in the Southlands."

Asher winced. Without wanting to, she saw Tayanna as she had last seen her, sitting astride her chestnut destrier Eveningsong, her armor gleaming in the morning light. Tayanna, for whom no words existed to describe what she meant to Asher. Tayanna, with her nose that hadn't healed right after being broken one too many times and her small mouth, smiling as she tossed her glossy black braid over her shoulder and squinted into the sun to gauge the time. She'd waved to Asher as she left for the southern front, so certain this was not goodbye but rather so long for now. So confident she could defeat anything. So certain she'd be coming home.

"I'll be seeing you, Ash," she'd said as she'd left.

It was what she always said when she rode away, but this time it had been an inadvertent lie. She hadn't come back. Had she encountered one of Erborn's monsters? Asher didn't know. She had refused to hear what had felled the bright star of Ilirya's knighthood, shutting her ears to any details about Tayanna's death. Knowing would have made Tayanna's death even more impossibly, insupportably painful than it already had been.

A stab of pain so sharp it took Asher's breath away landed in her gut. She forced the memory of that final view of Tayanna back into the box where she kept all of Tayanna's memories. She could live with a piece of her soul missing. She'd managed this far. She hadn't had a choice. She shook herself to bring herself back to the present and took a sip of her ale to wash away the bile that had risen in her throat, hoping that no one had noticed her momentary distraction.

Erborn, still ranting about the dangers of the Southlands, concluded, "That's why no one will go with the commander. Any knight who's been to the border and seen what's there would rather become a turnip farmer than cross that line."

Instantly, Tayanna was in Asher's memories again, her small, dark eyes sparkling. She seized Asher by the shoulders, brimming with barely contained energy and grinning from ear to ear. "No one becomes a knight who's afraid of riding into danger head-on." There was no challenge Tayanna wouldn't face. To Tayanna, life was a mountain waiting to be climbed by those with the daring to do it. Her fearless spirit was one of the things Asher loved best about her.

The memory stirred something in Asher. Tayanna wouldn't have accepted Erborn's pessimism. She would have been the first to volunteer to go to the Southlands. She would have been proud to represent her kingdom.

Asher glared at Erborn. "I will. I'll go."

Taz and Erborn exchanged a look.

She glowered at them, needled by their skepticism. "Don't you see? We're running out of time. The kingdom is disintegrating around us. The king is dead and half the King's Council with him. The Northmen could invade at any moment and, frankly, the war in the south has been going poorly for years. We need this peace. We need it more than anything right now, and Commander Bronwen's mission may be our only chance to get it."

Her voice rose, impassioned. "This is what we're meant to do: defend Ilirya. Why become knights if you won't defend your country when it's most in danger? Would you rather spend your days dodging the pitchforks of angry farmers rioting against high taxes? If we can't secure peace with the Southlands, there may not *be* an Ilirya in a few months!"

Taz had the decency to look embarrassed, but Erborn was recalcitrant. "I'll take the farmers, thank you." He drained his mug in one gulp and rose from his seat. He arched his back, pressing against it with his palms, then cracked his neck. "Going to the Southlands is a fool's errand, and besides, a week from now, someone will think of a way to stop the Northmen, and all this hubbub will have been for nothing. I don't have many years left with the knighthood. I'll happily live 'em out in peace patrolling Qarys and say 'good riddance' to this hero business. You young'uns are welcome to it if that's what you want." He flipped some coins onto the table with a practiced hand, then nodded to Taz and Asher before heading for the exit.

Once he was gone, Taz looked at Asher and sighed. "You're right about how dire the situation is, but volunteering to go to the Southlands with Commander Bronwen? I can't decide if you're brave or crazy." He bit his lip, squirming in his chair. "I hate to say it, but Erborn is right: everyone who goes will almost certainly die."

Asher shook her head. She'd thought about the problem from every angle and had found no other solution. The only way to save Ilirya was to convince the Southlands to give up on forty years of war. And even if no one else would go with the commander, *she* would go. She just wished Taz understood. "Commander Bronwen needs us. *Ilirya* needs us. If not us, then who? This is our duty."

Asher paused, then gave him a cheerful smile. "Besides, don't you want to be the first Iliryan to see the Southlands and come back to tell about it?"

Taz shook his head, his blond hair falling into his deep-blue eyes. "Haven't you had enough of adventure lately?"

Asher reflected on the last few months. She'd tracked down the father of a girl who had been kidnapped by evil mages. She'd run into a burning city guard garrison and pulled people to safety. She'd fought her way through Northmen hiding in the city to reach the castle in time to watch a rogue god trying to Gate into the king's Great Hall. But none of that made her wish for peace and quiet. It had been worrisome, true, but it had been exhilarating at the same time.

She waved her hand. "You can't help when duty calls."

The Boar's Tusk Tavern serving girl came to take Erborn's empty mug, and Asher winked at her when she caught her eye. The girl's face reddened, and she scuttled away, peeking back over her shoulder shyly as she did so. Asher smiled, her gaze following the girl's retreat. No one would ever replace Tayanna, but lately she'd found some enjoyment in casual flirtations. She still had needs, after all.

She looked back to Taz. "This is a diplomatic mission. If all goes well, there won't be any fighting. It will be quiet and boring, just how you like it. Doesn't that sound appealing to you? Just a nice ride through the countryside."

Taz licked his lips, his eyes troubled. "Do you really think the Southerners will agree to peace? After forty years, maybe all they know is war."

Asher had thought a lot about that question. It was the looming, unanswerable question that likely would determine Ilirya's entire future. She shrugged. "If anyone can get them to agree to peace, it's the knight commander. And if not, we're all in trouble anyway. Whether it's fighting in the north or fighting in the south, we're all going to fight one way or another."

"I only want to make sure you're not…going for the wrong reasons." Taz dropped his voice and eyed her significantly. His meaning was clear. He wanted to make sure Asher wasn't on a suicide mission of her own.

Asher bristled. "Taz." She didn't need to say anything more. The warning in her voice was enough. She didn't need him second-guessing her motives.

He raised his hands. "Fine. I'm convinced. When do we leave?"

Asher grinned, delighted. "You'll come?"

He smiled back at her, his grin askew. "Someone has to make sure your recklessness doesn't get you killed."

Asher clapped him on the shoulder. She knew he'd eventually come around. The two had been almost inseparable since they'd met as pages when they were seven years old, getting into playful fistfights in the stable and stealing cakes from the kitchen. Taz wasn't always brave and definitely wasn't the best fighter, but he was loyal. He had Asher's back, and she had his. Always. If Asher said they needed to go to the Southlands, he would go to the Southlands. There was no one else with whom she'd rather have gone…except Tayanna.

"Strength and honor," Asher said, citing the first half of the Knight's Creed.

"Duty and queen," Taz finished.

"Just don't make me carry your body home." Asher waggled a finger at him. "You're getting fat."

"Commander Bronwen, no!" Lyse gasped. Her hand flew to her mouth.

The young healer looked to Asher for support, but Asher only shrugged, her expression neutral. If Lyse didn't know by now how determined the knight commander was, she would soon find out without any help from Asher.

Commander Bronwen's face was set. Asher knew from experience there was no changing her mind now. "I must go." The words were simple, but final.

Lyse shook her head, her hands moving to her hips. "I can't allow it. You're too ill to travel outside the *city*, much less all the way to the Southlands. It's out of the question."

Commander Bronwen stared her down with icy calm. "I appreciate your concern, but the decision is not up for debate. Do whatever you can, but we set out tomorrow."

Lyse looked beseechingly at Asher. Asher shook her head. It was out of her hands. Only the queen could stop Commander Bronwen now.

Lyse knelt before the knight commander, her soft brown eyes serious and pleading. "Commander, there is a good chance you will die if you leave the city. While you're here, I can keep the Dark Magic that's poisoning you from spreading too quickly, but once you leave, I don't know how fast it will spread. You could die within weeks for all we know. Please, you must stay. Let someone else go."

Asher's heart skipped a beat. In all the talk of the commander's immediate condition and the Southerners' willingness to parley, she hadn't considered what the journey would mean for the Dark Magic's poison. If going to the Southlands was so dangerous to Commander Bronwen's health, then Lyse was right, she should stay. Let someone else take her place. That arrogant Gandral, for one.

Asher wished, not for the first time, they knew more about Dark Magic. A few months ago, only a handful of people in all of Ilirya had heard of it. Even now, all anyone knew was that this secret, illegal magic based on pain and death had been strong enough to tear a hole between the mortal and divine realms and that its poisoning of the knight commander's body was irreversible. Why couldn't she be healed?

Commander Bronwen's face was impassive in the face of Lyse's dire warning. "My injuries do not define who I am. I am the knight commander, and matters of war and peace are for the knight commander to negotiate."

Lyse squirmed. "Yes, but—"

Commander Bronwen looked her straight in the eye. "A soldier fulfills her duty, no matter the cost. Every day, I send my knights to die at the border. They go willingly because they believe in fighting for Ilirya. In the face of their sacrifice, how could I shirk my duties out of a fear of death? If I am not willing to face the same danger they do, I am undeserving of my title."

Lyse bowed her head.

"I am not afraid to die. But you know, life is a stubborn thing. I have seen soldiers with swords stuck through them to the hilt keep fighting long after they should have fallen. A doe with an arrow through her heart will still stagger on for miles. I may surprise you with my tenacity for living."

Lyse nodded, but her eyes were sad and uncertain. At the commander's signal, pale-indigo magic flowed from her hands, covering Commander Bronwen in a gentle healing magic like a blanket that could alleviate but never entirely remove the knight's pain. The commander closed her eyes and let out a deep breath. Moments later, her head lolled to the side as she fell into a light sleep.

Lyse stopped the flow of her magic and, standing, caressed the knight commander's head the way a mother would a child. Then she turned and fixed Asher with an accusatory stare. "She will die if you let her go to the Southlands." Her voice came out as an angry hiss.

Asher took a step backward, grimacing. She didn't know what to say. She hated the thought that the Dark Magic's poison might kill the commander, but how could she contradict the commander's will? "Are you sure?"

Lyse rubbed her hands together, looking away. "I wish we knew more about Dark Magic's effects. I don't know how fast it will spread away from the city." Reaching down, she removed the brown leather pouch she carried at her side and handed it to Asher. "Take this. You can give it to her when she wakes. It's a combination of herbs that will help dull her pain and allow her to sleep. The longer the journey, the worse her pain will get. If she insists on going, she must travel as fast as possible."

Asher hung the pouch from a cord around her neck, her stomach roiling. There was always a danger in being a knight, but it should have been from an enemy's sword, not from poison. She regretted once more the events that had led to the commander's injury. When would the repercussions from the coup finally end?

Lyse sighed. "I wish we could send a mage healer with her, but we don't have a single mage to spare. The war has decimated our ranks."

Asher nodded. Forty years of war had cost Ilirya dearly.

Lyse looked back at the knight commander slumped in her chair, her eyes soft with pity. "I hope you know what you're doing."

Asher wasn't sure whether Lyse was addressing the knight commander or herself. Changing the subject, she asked, "How is Aeryn?"

Aeryn was Lyse's partner, a war mage in training who had been the first to discover the conspiracy to topple the king and help a rogue god—called the One God—cross from the divine realm into the mortal plane using Dark Magic. Asher considered her a friend. The two of them had worked together to find the Dark mages involved in the plot, although they'd been too late to stop them from killing the king. In the process, Aeryn had almost died. Asher hadn't seen her since that night, busy as she'd been in the aftermath.

Lyse pressed her lips together, a shadow falling across her face. "Aeryn has been…different lately. I thought in time she would recover from everything that happened, but something is off. I can't imagine how it feels to have been so close to death. Sometimes I still can't believe she's alive. I…I was so sure she was dead." Her voice cracked.

"I know she still has dreams about it. She wakes up screaming in the night. Then she disappears for days at a time and won't tell me where she's been. I wish she would tell me what's wrong. I feel like I'm losing her."

Asher made a sympathetic face. "Would you like me to talk to her?"

Lyse looked hopeful. "I would appreciate that. Maybe she'll talk to you."

She checked the knight commander one last time, feeling the temperature of her skin at her forehead and in the place where the assassin's blade had struck. Finished, she turned to leave. At the door, however, she stopped, her eyes troubled. "Will you go to the Southlands too?"

"Yes." Asher's stomach twisted as she remembered Erborn's suggestion that the knight commander intended the expedition to be a suicide mission. Was this proof he was right? She pushed away the thought.

"Stay safe."

Then Lyse was gone, leaving Asher alone in the knight commander's bedchamber. Asher wheeled the commander's chair to the bed, then carefully scooped her up, laying her out on the bed with her long red hair splayed around her head like a halo. In her debility, Commander Bronwen's body was wasted away, a husk of what it had been when it was full of vigor and strength. Without her armor, she was light as a child.

Commander Bronwen smacked her lips together but didn't open her eyes. "I imagine you are thinking I should not go on the expedition."

Asher raised her eyebrows. She had thought Commander Bronwen was asleep.

The commander opened her pale-blue eyes and looked at Asher.

Asher squirmed, dropping her gaze. Well, it was true, wasn't it? The commander was too valuable to send to the Southlands. "Ilirya needs you here, Commander. Let someone else go in your place."

The commander's eyes bored into hers. "A petition for peace falls to the knight commander as the representative of the queen. As holder of that office, it is my responsibility to go. This illness doesn't change who I am or the duties that I must perform."

"But, Commander—"

"The office does not die when I do. If I should succumb to my illness, I will be replaced. The office of the knight commander will live on without me. Until such time as I no longer hold this position, I owe it to every citizen of Ilirya to strive to my utmost to defend their lives. Whatever the cost."

Asher shifted her weight from one foot to the other. There was no arguing with the knight commander. "Is it true that no one comes back from the Southlands?" Between Dark Magic and Southerner monsters, the expedition was looking increasingly like a one-way trip.

"You've heard that, have you?" The faintest of smiles traced across Commander Bronwen's pale face. "I knew some form of that rumor must have been circulating through the garrison."

"It can't be true! Someone must have done it. How could they not?"

"It's true that to the best of my knowledge, no Iliryan has crossed into the Southlands and returned to tell the tale."

"Why not? What happened to them?"

"It is likely anyone who tried to enter the Southlands was killed by the Southerners or the protective warding spells they've laid upon their side of the border. Eventually, people stopped trying."

"But we must know things about the Southlands!"

"Some things, yes. Not enough. Not nearly enough." She gave a rasping cough that racked her frail body. "Does it worry you to ride into such unknown territory?"

Asher stood taller, hand on her sword hilt. "Not at all."

"Good." She closed her eyes again. "Because no one knows what we will find on the other side of the border." She smiled. "I am glad you have decided to come. I see some of myself in you."

Asher waited for her to say more, to explain what she meant, but the knight commander remained silent. After a minute, Asher decided she'd fallen back asleep. Asher quietly slipped out of the room, shutting the door behind her. She set off down the hall with a singular goal in mind. Although she'd never visited the royal archives before, she knew where they were located. And she was determined to prove Erborn wrong. There *had* to be information about the Southlands there.

The castle, tall, rectangular, and made of brown stone imported from Rath, had been empty of its court since the night of the massacre, an abandoned beehive without a queen. Queen Alea had declared that there wasn't enough water in all Ilirya to wash the blood of her brother and his court from the Great Hall. Nor, for both superstitious and practical reasons, would it do to have Ilirya's new queen sit atop a throne in the very place where the previous ruler had been killed. Thus, a new castle was being built in another part of the city's northeast quarter, but until then, the archives were still housed next to the old castle in a long, one-story building annexed to the eastern wall.

Asher pushed open the heavy wooden door to the archives, then stopped to wait for her eyes to adjust before she entered. Thin, weak light trickled into the building through colorful stained-glass windows that ran along one wall, dimly illuminating wide wooden tables and rows of shelves containing various scrolls and parchment papers. Asher stepped across the threshold and was immediately struck with doubt. How would she find the information she needed to prove Erborn wrong? The royal archives were massive.

"May I help you, lady knight?" a kindly voice asked.

Asher jumped. To her left, a short, balding man stood next to her. A thin white ring of hair ran around his skull like a half diadem. His black tunic stretched to the floor, an older fashion that reflected a scholarly profession. Asher guessed he must be the royal archivist. Where had he come from? He'd materialized beside her like a ghost.

"I'm looking for information about the Southlands."

He frowned, rubbing his chin. "The Southlands? Hmmm. No one ever asks about the Southlands. What in particular would you like to know?"

Asher peered down the long rows of scrolls. "Anything, really. Perhaps a merchant went and wrote about his travels? Or a long-ago trade mission reported its findings?"

The archivist tapped his thick lips with his index finger. "No, I'm afraid I've never heard of any such thing. You know, the Southlands have always been very reclusive. A hermit kingdom, if you like. Iliryans were prohibited from traveling there even before the war began, and since the war began, well, you can imagine there's been no contact between our two peoples."

Asher's face fell. This wasn't at all what she'd imagined. "There's nothing? But surely there's something about the magic there? Or the terrible monsters? There must have been a soldier who strayed across the border and lived to tell the tale. Just one?" Her hopes sank as she pictured going back to Erborn empty-handed and having to polish his armor in the yard while he gloated. She didn't mind the work, but she couldn't bear the thought of Erborn winning.

The archivist shook his head, eyes mournful.

"There's really nothing at all about the Southlands here?" Asher tried to keep disappointment out of her voice. How could Erborn be right? How could the archives have nothing to say about the Southlands? They had been at war for forty years. There should be half a library's worth of material at least.

"No, I fear not." The archivist unexpectedly brightened, his hands flying into the air. "Oh my, how could I forget? There is one thing. We have the royal exchanges!"

"The what?"

"Follow me."

He led Asher through the long room, passing stacks and stacks of information collected from throughout Ilirya over the centuries. Asher was curious about what sorts of knowledge the archives held, but she didn't have time to stop and look. The archivist took a sharp left and dove down one of the stacks, stopping midway down the row to peer at a shelf of tightly rolled scrolls.

He touched them with his fingertips. "This collection of scrolls is all the communications of Ilirya's rulers with neighboring monarchs. Obviously, we can't see what our own rulers wrote since their missives are in the hands of our neighbors, but generations of archivists have found that these letters lend a keen insight into historical events. Now, let me see…"

He pulled scroll after scroll from the stack, checking the seals on each of them and then putting them back. As he worked, he talked. "As I said, the Southerners are a very isolated people, but I seem to recall a letter from the Southerner regent. Yes. Here it is."

He pulled a lily-white scroll from the bottom of the pile. It had a broken, blue seal on it stamped with what looked like a common housecat.

The archivist unfurled the scroll and scanned the writing. "This letter was sent by the Southerner King Izmar approximately forty years ago. I think he would have been near the end of his rule by then, based on the announcement of his coronation. In fact, I am certain this letter is the last letter we have ever received from the Southlands. Since then, there has been only silence." He handed Asher the scroll.

The highly stylized, looping black text was so ornate she couldn't read it. She sighed. Even her first writing tutor would have been hard pressed to understand the words, and he could read anything. She handed it back to the archivist. "What does it say?"

"Oh! We archivists are used to all kinds of writing. It comes with the job. Let me see. Well, it seems that King Izmar and King Savin were having a bit of a disagreement. In short, King Izmar warns that King Savin can't take the 'Death Stone' and would be foolish to try. And here you'll see that he finishes with his signature, that quite large bit of writing there."

He sighed mournfully. "I'm afraid this letter isn't much help to you. It has nothing like what you were looking for."

Asher stood stunned for a moment. An argument between Ilirya and the Southlands forty years ago during the reign of Queen Alea's father? The timing couldn't be a coincidence. "Is this dispute what started the war?" But how? The war began with a sneak attack by the Southerners. An unannounced land grab that the Iliryans had barely resisted in time. What would this "Death Stone" have to do with it?

"I don't know. Why are any wars begun?" Asher ignored his baleful look.

"Do you know what the Death Stone is?"

The archivist shook his head. "No. I don't believe I've seen it mentioned elsewhere. It sounds quite dramatic, doesn't it?"

Asher frowned, puzzled. The information wasn't adding up. "If there's no record of it, then how did King Savin know about it?"

"Ah, about that. I have a theory." The archivist held up a finger. "I've noticed there are some records missing in the archives. You understand, as an archivist, it is my responsibility to know what our library does and does not contain. I said that the Southerners were reclusive, but no neighbor can be completely invisible, unseen and unheard. Yet no records at all seem to exist. This absence of information is quite glaring, in fact. This deficit can only be explained if the records—however many or few there were—were expunged."

Asher cocked her head. "Expunged?"

"Destroyed."

"Why would someone destroy all the records about the Southlands? And why has no one noticed before?"

"That I cannot answer. My predecessor was long dead before I noticed the gap, so I have no one to ask. All I can say is that the destruction could only have been carried out by another archivist at the request of the king. Exactly which archivist and which king, I do not know. Nor do I know why the destruction was ordered or what, exactly, was destroyed. Perhaps once we had much, much more information about the Southlands. There is simply no way to know."

"But that scroll wasn't destroyed."

"An oversight, I'm sure. The archivist evidently forgot about it. It would be easy to forget a single scroll."

Asher ran her hand over her light brown hair, thinking. "Could King Savin have obliterated all the archive's information about the Southlands when they attacked? But why? Out of spite? Wouldn't we need that information to fight them?"

The archivist craned his neck and looked around, then whispered, "*Did* the Southlands attack first?"

"What?" Asher took a full step backward. "Of course they attacked us! Everyone knows that."

"Forgive me, lady knight." The archivist bowed deeply. "It's only…I was born near the border, where my family still lives. Early in my training as an archivist, I happened to be home when the first salvos of magic were launched. Although King Savin claimed it was the Southerner army that attacked first, I think you'll find there are many still living in the borderlands who have a different recollection of events."

Asher gaped at him. This was not at all what she'd been taught. But the archivist had no reason to lie. The hairs on her arms stood up. "Why would we attack the Southlands? Why would King Savin lie? Does Queen Alea know?"

Chapter 2

"Pay attention, Lady Asher!" Mal says, flustered.

"But it's boring," the young child whines, drawing out the long vowel. She wants to be outside playing. She's always been more interested in play fighting with the stable boys than in learning. "I don't care about politics. When I grow up, I'm going to be a knight, not a chancellor."

To Asher, possessions were mere encumbrances—anchors that would only weigh her down if she tried to carry them with her. The things most worth keeping were memories, and those were heavy in a different way. So when she packed up her room in the knight's garrison in preparation for the journey south, almost everything she owned in the world fit into a small pack that could easily be affixed to her horse Stormcloud's saddle.

The only thing she couldn't pack was a small wooden chest that was too large and bulky to carry on Cloud's back. Asher sat before it on the floor, fighting the urge to open the lid and look inside. She wanted nothing more than to see its contents one last time, but she knew it would bring her as much pain as it would bitter sweetness. She had only opened the chest a few times in the last year. Doing so was like grabbing the blade of a sword barehanded and refusing to let go. But this was the last time she would ever see the chest. She had to open it.

Of its own volition, her trembling right hand reached out and unlatched the lid. Her left hand joined it, and the two hands slowly lifted it open. She unconsciously stopped breathing as she looked inside. The chest itself was no piece of art. It was roughly made and basic, the type of practical thing a soldier would use. Moreover, it was half empty. A pair of soft brown lambskin slippers, Tayanna's one indulgent vanity, lay on top of a soft white tunic. A silver necklace lay beside the slippers, carefully arranged as though the owner would come at any moment and reclaim it.

Asher lifted the necklace out of the chest carefully, weighing it in her hand. It was light as a breath of air. She couldn't remember Tayanna ever having worn it, but it was Tayanna's and that was all that mattered. Asher undid the clasp and laid the necklace against the hollow in her neck, reclasping it behind her neck. The metal was weightless against her skin. She took a breath and closed her eyes, letting the memories come.

"Come on, you're going to be late!"

Asher jumped, her eyes flying open, as Taz burst into the room behind her. She should have heard him coming, but she had swum too deep into the pool of her memories to hear the sounds above the surface. She instinctively slapped the chest's lid shut, protecting Tayanna's last link to the world of the living. As though if Taz saw the chest's contents, the fragile link would disappear and be forever lost. The things in the chest were for Asher alone to see and no one else, at least for now.

It was too late. Taz saw the closed chest behind her and paused, pity filling his face.

She glowered at him, angry at his unwanted empathy and angry he had intruded on her final moments with these pieces of Tayanna. "I'm coming!" she snapped.

Taz's mouth twitched.

"Don't say it," Asher growled. She hated seeing the sadness in his eyes whenever he thought of Tayanna. Both of them knew that with Tayanna's loss, Asher had lost a part of herself forever. She didn't need to see her bereavement reflected on his face. She latched the chest, then picked it up, cradling it in her arms. "I'm sending this to her family in Qarys."

"Are you sure?"

Asher clutched the chest more tightly. As few things as were in it, they were all she had left of Tayanna. But Tayanna herself was not in the chest, and had Tayanna been alive to see it, she would have chastised Asher for her foolishness. "I'm not my shoes, Ash," she would have said, smiling. "You don't have to keep them forever."

Besides, if Asher didn't come back from the Southlands, as Erborn had direly predicted, it wouldn't matter anyway where the chest was. "The Majordomo will see that the chest arrives safely."

Taz took an interest in his boots. "The border…I just want you to know I'm here for you."

Asher knew what he meant. They were going to the place where Tayanna had fallen, and he was worried how she would handle it. But she wouldn't fall apart. Not again. She had a job to do. And anyway, they would only be at the border long enough to cross through.

She gave him a weak smile to show that she appreciated his support. "Are you ready?"

He puffed his chest out. "Strength and honor."

Asher grinned slyly. "Ah, so you already said goodbye to that girl you think I don't know about?"

Taz looked startled. "You know?"

"What?" Asher shrugged smugly, pleased with herself. "It's not like you were getting fat off the garrison cooking. Besides, you're not as clever as you think you are, Sir Tazamine of Parvel. I know everything about you."

Taz smiled ruefully and hefted her traveling pack to his shoulder. "Speaking of, I hope you packed food. Who knows what we'll find to eat in the Southlands. It could be lizards and tree bark for all we know."

"Still better than the garrison slop. I might have found a roach in it the other day." She chuckled, then remembering something, sobered. "The Southerners attacked *us* first, right?"

Taz blinked. "What? Of course they did!"

"Yeah," Asher said, half to herself. "I know."

But did she? If the archivist was telling the truth, then the entire war was based on a lie. One that Queen Alea's father King Savin had tried to hide. What did it all mean? What had they been fighting for the last forty years?

Taz turned to the door. "Come on. We're going to be late."

The other members of the expedition had already gathered in the courtyard in front of the stables when Asher and Taz made it outside. Commander Bronwen, mounted on her palomino paint destrier Everbright, was resplendent in her full armor. She wore intricately detailed steel greaves and bracers, black leggings, a long blue coat edged in gold trim, a shining cuirass, and large spaulders imprinted with the crest of the queen. Although she could no longer wield it anymore, she wore her longsword strapped to her side. Her red hair had been woven into a thick, long braid that traveled along the left side of her head and down her back. She made an impressive picture, and if the observer didn't know better, they might not even notice she only carried the reins in her left hand, and her legs were cinched to the saddle with thin leather straps, her torso held in place by a wide strap from the back of Ever's saddle.

It had been no small feat to return Ilirya's knight commander to riding after the attack. The knights' chief saddle maker had spent weeks perfecting a saddle that would keep her erect, while Ever had been retrained by Ilirya's Master of the Horse Ironbar himself to respond not to Commander Bronwen's legs, but to rein pressure on his neck. But there had been no question of doing it.

"A knight," Commander Bronwen had declared, "is not a knight if she cannot ride," and she'd made it clear she intended to remain a knight regardless of her physical condition. But although she could ride with help, there was no magic or device that would return her ability to fight. That was gone forever. She would never again ride into battle, a fact Asher knew pained her deeply.

To Commander Bronwen's right, Sir Henrek and Lady Jazmen readied their horses with the help of their squires, who would not be coming with them to the Southlands. Asher knew the two by reputation as experienced knights who had spent years fighting on the southern front. They would be solid additions to the group.

Asher was grateful they had volunteered to come. In the days it had taken to prepare the expedition, word had circulated in the knights' garrison that no knights would willingly accompany the knight commander to the Southlands. Too many knights shared Erborn's opinion that the journey was a suicide mission, a belief not helped by whisperings probably originating from Gandral's supporters about the mission's hopelessness. It infuriated Asher. Didn't the other knights see Ilirya couldn't afford to continue fighting in the south in the face of a possible Northman invasion? How did they expect to repel an attack from the north when the entire Iliryan army was concentrated hundreds of miles way in the south?

Asher squinted at the sixth and final member of the party. She didn't recognize him. He stood apart from the others, tightening his black gelding's girth without help from an assistant. The man was tall and lanky, with short red hair and a short beard. Although she didn't know him, she recognized his black armor, black horse, and black tack. He was a member of the King's Regiment.

Nudging Taz in the side, she said, "Who's that?"

"That's Great Mage Marandir." He didn't elaborate.

Henrek mounted his thick brown gelding Morningstar and steered him to Commander Bronwen's side. Looking toward Marandir, he grunted in a voice low enough the mage wouldn't hear it but everyone else could, "We should be bringing war mages, or at least Arvin Mage Bane. We need as much help as we can get. Could the Mages' Council spare no other mages than this one Regiment mage?"

"This is a peace delegation, not an invasion." Commander Bronwen's voice was sharp. The rebuke made even Asher wince. "Marandir is the best scout in the kingdom and, if it should come to it, a fierce fighter."

Henrek seemed to accept her answer at first, but after a beat, his voice dropping so that Asher had to strain to hear, he asked, "Can he be trusted, Commander?"

Pain and sadness rippled across the knight commander's face. The conspiracy to kill the king had reached to the highest levels, including the former Captain of the King's Regiment Vardan Ironwill, rumored to have once been a lover of the commander herself. Since he and at least two other members of his Regiment had been involved, the entire Regiment—considered the most elite of all Ilirya's fighting forces—now lived under a cloud of suspicion. Asher was glad that no knights had participated in the coup. She would have hated for the reputation of the knighthood to have been damaged by the actions of a few rogue members.

"Sergeant at Arms Gamiel assures me that he can be trusted." Commander Bronwen shut her eyes for a moment and sighed. When she next spoke, her words were quiet. "But keep an eye on him, Henrek."

"Yes, Commander." His eyes settled suspiciously on Marandir.

"Lady Asher, will you mount?"

Pip the stable boy was standing next to her, holding Cloud's reins out to her. The tall bay eyed her curiously. She patted him on the neck, telling the vain creature how handsome he was, then threw the reins over his head, checked the girth, and mounted. Pip secured her traveling pack to the back of the saddle. Asher looked around for Taz and found him waiting for his gray gelding Fleetfoot. As Jazmen's squire led him from the stable, Fleet skittered and shied from the shadows that fell across the courtyard, dancing behind the squire on light hooves. Taz settled him, cooing softly, then checked his girth and mounted. Their group of six was complete.

Asher tried not to notice how small the number was. If they were lucky, six would be more than enough to carry the queen's petition for peace to the Southerner ruler. But it was a far smaller group than it should have been. Anger competed with hurt in her chest. The knight commander deserved more loyalty from her knights. Any knight who didn't volunteer to accompany her to the Southlands was a coward, and Asher hated cowards.

As Asher gathered her reins, a small group of people entered the courtyard. She was surprised to see it was a gaggle of courtiers led by Queen Alea herself. The queen, who wore a deep red gown whose color matched the ruby in her diadem, stopped in front of Ever and patted him on his white nose. He whuffled and bumped her dark hand. The queen squeaked in delight and kissed him.

Then she raised her deep-brown eyes and looked around the group. "Danger. Uncertainty. These are the things into which I send you. Your journey will be long and challenging. You will sleep below uncharted stars far from home and your families. But you go with great purpose. If we are to save Ilirya from the peril it faces, it will only be possible through your efforts. You carry the hopes of this kingdom on your shoulders. I pray you are successful."

"We will not fail you, my queen." Commander Bronwen's chin was high and proud.

Queen Alea smiled at her. "I know you will not. I have full faith in you. Travel safely and swiftly. Come back to me."

Her blessing of the journey given, the queen bowed to the expedition, then filed out of the courtyard with her royal retinue in tow. Gandral, who had accompanied her, stayed behind for a moment. Asher stifled the urge to glare at him.

Commander Bronwen nodded to him. "Stand the watch, Gandral. In my absence, you are the acting knight commander. Strength and honor."

Gandral saluted her smartly. "Duty and queen. Safe travels, Commander. I'll keep your seat warm for you." He pivoted on his heel and marched out of the courtyard, taking long strides to catch up to the queen.

Taz maneuvered Fleet to stand beside Cloud. He muttered under his breath, "There's one person who hopes we don't return."

Asher ground her teeth together. "If we don't return, it won't matter anyway. He'll be knight commander of a kingdom of ashes. We'll have no way to stop the Northmen. Surely Gandral knows that. He needs this peace, just like everyone else."

"Riders!"

Asher and Taz stopped talking and looked to the knight commander.

She stared at each of the members of the expedition in turn, her face fierce and determined in the morning light. "It will take a week of hard riding to reach the southern front. After that, who knows how long it will take to reach the capital of the Southlands, Nyara. We have no maps, no clues to the city's location. Only a name passed down through generations of border dwellers. When we reach it, we will be the first Iliryans to set eyes on the city.

"You will all have heard the rumors. I deny none of them. They are likely all true and more. Once we reach the border, I can promise nothing. There will hardship at best, death at worst. But we represent Ilirya's last hope. The Northmen lie in wait on our northern border. If we cannot achieve peace, Ilirya will fall. Only this is certain."

"Aw, go on, Bronwen," Jazmen scoffed. Her voice was gruff. "No need to make a speech about it. We know what we're about. I've got a tenner on Henrek being the first to get offed. Let's be off then, yeah? Before I get any more gray hairs."

Asher stared at her, aghast. How dare she disrespect the knight commander? How dare she make light of the danger they faced?

Unexpectedly, however, Commander Bronwen began to laugh. "Your point is taken. And I'll take your bet, too. You attract trouble like flies to offal, Jazmen."

Jazmen snorted. "Ain't dead yet, am I?"

The Knight Commander turned Ever toward the gate, and the expedition began to trail out of the courtyard single file. Asher fell in behind Jazmen and in front of Taz, with Henrek behind him and Marandir bringing up the rear. As they left the garrison completely, Asher took one last look. It might be the last time she ever saw it. And if their expedition failed, there might be no city to which to return home.

At first, Asher thought they were heading into a massive thunderstorm. From miles away, she could see the flicker of lightning through clouds of purple, yellow, and green, colors she'd never seen before in the sky. It was as though a giant bruise was slowly spreading over the land, exactly and unavoidably on their path. She pulled her traveling cloak tightly against her, grimacing at the prospect of riding for hours in soggy clothing.

Henrek, who rode beside her, snorted. "That's not rain, youngling."

She gave him a confused look. "What? What do you mean?"

"Can't you smell the death from here? There's no smell in the world like it. Gets in your nostrils, doesn't it?"

Ahead of them, Jazmen began to cackle, leaning forward in her saddle. "There! We're almost at the front!"

A mile later, Asher began to recognize the signs of war around them: broken wagons that once carried supplies, deep ruts in the road from the tread of thousands of boots, and the waft of smoke in the distance that might either have been from cooking fires, mage fire, or both. Asher realized that what she had assumed were storm clouds full of lightning were actually spells and mage fire, thrown almost constantly by battling war mages. Magic of every color arced across the sky, a terrible and deadly rainbow at whose end lay death. She shivered. She couldn't imagine the devastation that the magic must be causing.

Farther down the road, white tents began to line their path, populated by soldiers sleeping and resting between rotations at the frontline. As Asher and her group rode past them, tired and dirty men and women, many of whom had limbs wrapped in bandages, peered out. Asher couldn't look away from their hollow faces. This was where Tayanna had slept. These were the people with whom she'd fought side by side. She could have been any of these soldiers, sitting on a small, crudely fashioned tripod and poking at a pot of stew over the fire, watching the road for reinforcements that never came. After forty years, there were none left to send. The forest had been cut down. There was no more wood to burn.

Asher tamped down visions of Tayanna being dragged from her horse, her helmet removed, and her throat cut by Southerners. Eveningsong stumbling and falling as Tayanna was incinerated by mage fire. Asher had imagined hundreds of deaths for Tayanna over the last year, her mind filling in the gaps she had purposely refused to fill. No matter how she imagined it, however, Tayanna had never given up. Had always fought until the end. Tayanna never lived a day in her life that wasn't a brave one.

Asher swallowed the lump in her throat. Though her hands shook, they were still steady on Cloud's reins. She could be here on the frontline without crumbling. She would not be sucked down into the morass of despair. She would push through the painful memories. It was her duty.

Halfway through the heart of the dusty camp, the delegation had picked up an informal honor guard as knights recognized their Knight Commander and gathered to escort her. They pushed through pockets of loitering soldiers, clearing a path all the way to the tent of General Oran. His tent, which was Iliryan blue and flew pennants bearing the queen's crest from all four corners, was situated far enough from the front line that he was in no danger of being hit by the enemy's war mages and archers but still close enough that he could issue orders for immediate execution. The way the tent swarmed with couriers relaying messages and commands to and from the battlefield reminded Asher of an anthill. She wondered how much General Oran slept each night between receiving input from the day's battle and planning for the next day. Although commanders rarely fought at the frontlines, they burned out faster than their soldiers. It was hard work managing an army of thousands.

One of the knights entered the tent to alert the general to the knight commander's presence, and Henrek and Jazmen took the opportunity to dismount, stretching their legs after hours in the saddle. Asher, Taz, and Marandir stayed mounted, unsure of what would happen next.

The tent flap opened moments later, and General Oran stepped out. He smiled broadly when he saw them, hands on his hips. "Well now, I assume you've come with the reinforcements I requested?"

The delegation members looked at each other, confused. Asher's heart sank.

"No, General. Did you not receive notice of our delegation?" There was a note of unease in Commander Bronwen's voice.

The general's face fell. "We've not received any correspondence from King's City for weeks. Surely you don't mean to tell me it's only you? No reinforcements?" He looked around the knights as though an army might be hiding behind them.

Asher glanced at the men standing near Cloud's head. The soldiers who had started to gather around them looked rough and battered. They wouldn't take the news well that no reinforcements were coming.

Commander Bronwen said, "General Oran, could we perhaps speak inside?"

The general nodded, his lips pressed firmly into an unhappy line, and retreated back into his tent. Jazmen and Henrek sprang into action, hastening to Ever's side to unbuckle the commander from her saddle. Gently, they lifted her off, then carried her between them into General Oran's tent. Taz, Marandir, and Asher followed a moment later. Asher and Taz exchanged glances. The miscommunication between King's City and the front was unsettling. Asher hoped it wasn't a sign of things to come.

General Oran sat behind a large wooden desk in the middle of the tent. Its surface was covered by a huge map on which the opposing units of the queen's army and the Southerner army were depicted as small pieces. Asher knew that in forty years, the line hadn't shifted more than a league in either direction. The pieces didn't move far. He ran his hands through his short salt-and-pepper hair and rubbed his temples as Jazmen and Henrek set Commander Bronwen in a chair in front of the desk. Henrek stayed beside her while Jazmen retreated to the side of the tent where the others stood.

"What is it now, Bronwen?" General Oran's voice was tired. "We've just lost another several dozen fighters. If I can't hold the right flank, the whole line might cave, and then the Southerners will have a direct shot to King's City. We'll be helpless to stop them, and you tell me you've brought no reinforcements."

"Is it that bad?" The commander's voice was troubled.

General Oran balled his right hand on the table. "It's been this way for months! We're one push by the Southerners away from total collapse. I've sent message after message to the capital, but there's no response. It's worse than *bad*. If we keep taking losses like we have, we won't last another month."

Asher sucked in a breath. Disintegration of the Iliryan line. An unstoppable Southerner invasion. Things were so much worse than she'd ever imagined. The Northmen weren't the only danger.

The general's face was weary. "If you haven't come with reinforcements, why are you here?"

"Peace, Oran. We're going to Nyara to sue for peace."

"Peace?" General Oran barked incredulously. "You think the Southerners want *peace*? We've been at war since you and I were holding wooden swords in our hands pretending at soldiers. Now they're a sword's breadth from finally defeating us. Why would they want peace now?"

"I'll find a way to convince them."

The general stood and paced. His boots made a soft hissing as they passed over the tent's carpet. Asher couldn't help but notice how threadbare it looked. How many generals had preceded General Oran? "If you cross that line, you will all die, every one of you. It's suicide. You won't make it five feet into the Southlands, trust me. And you, Bronwen? Look at you! How can you possibly—?"

"Enough." Commander Bronwen's voice was cold and hard as ice. "It's true we may all die tomorrow, but if we don't at least try, then Ilirya is lost. We'll be facing the Northmen at our gates soon enough, if not the Southerners too. Peace is our only hope."

The general peered at the knights in his tent. "Very well, I will have a parley flag raised, but I promise you nothing. As well you know, no one has ever tried to parley with them before. The Southerners might slaughter you all on the spot and use your teeth as jewelry."

Commander Bronwen smiled. "Have a little more faith. I'm sure they would torture us first."

The next day, Asher left their tent before the sun rose. She had hardly slept the night before, wedged between snoring Henrek and restless Taz. Her mind was filled with thoughts of Tayanna. While she waited for the camp to awaken, she walked silently among the tents full of sleeping soldiers, trying to imagine Tayanna there. Tayanna would have helped any way that she could, whether it was bandaging wounds or repairing tack. She would have listened to the soldiers' stories of home, providing a sympathetic ear in an unsympathetic place. She would have seen the camp not as a grim reminder of death, but as a reminder of the beauty of life. Could Asher ever see life with those optimistic eyes?

She caressed the necklace she wore under her tunic, feeling in some small way close to Tayanna. Tayanna would have had no doubts about the success of their mission. Asher wanted to believe in it, too, but General Oran's words had rattled her. How close was the Iliryan line to falling? Would the Southerners really kill them on the spot? What were they getting into?

"Couldn't sleep?" Taz asked when Asher returned to the tent.

She pulled a sour face. "You kick in your sleep."

He snorted. "Here." He held out a bowl of cooked oats to her. "This will make you feel better."

Asher took it and began eating, watching as the camp slowly came to life. Without magic to stain the sky, the sunrise was beautiful. The pink-red hues reminded her of the sky over the sea the morning of a storm. Henrek emerged from the tent carrying the commander, followed by Jazmen and Marandir. They all sat to eat, the air heavy with their silence. There was much to think about. Would they survive the day?

As they finished, General Oran approached, dressed in full battle armor. "The Southerners have accepted our parley request. Come now before they change their minds."

The members of the expedition swung into action with practiced ease born of a week on the road together. The horses were loaded with their traveling packs while Asher and Taz helped buckle Commander Bronwen into her saddle. The knight commander's face was determined as she took up the reins with her left hand, but blood pounded in Asher's veins. Depending on how the Southerners responded to their request to cross into the Southlands, she might have only a few hours left to live. And then Ilirya would be on borrowed time until the Northmen or the Southerners breached Ilirya's borders.

As the group commenced its march to the front line, the air was heavy with the gravity of their task. Weary soldiers who'd spent the night watch staring into the darkness on the other side, hoping not to see enemy soldiers surging forward in surprise attack, watched them with wary, uncertain eyes. Slowly, a gap opened in the line for the delegation to pass through.

General Oran stopped at the edge of the line. "You're on your own. If the parley flag is taken down on the Southerner side, we'll have to fight, whether you're still there or not. I hope you're not."

Asher's stomach lurched.

"I understand," Commander Bronwen said.

General Oran's face was grim. "Good luck."

The small group crossed the wasteland between the two armies slowly. In the quiet light of dawn, the land was still and peaceful. Asher knew when the sun rose higher, however, the space would be filled by soldiers striving tooth and nail against each other, the dead and wounded lying at their feet. Forty years of war and nothing had changed. What had it all been for? What had the lives of so many soldiers bought? Now that she knew it might have been Ilirya that attacked first, she no longer knew. She had meant to ask Commander Bronwen about what she'd learned in the archives, but she hadn't found the opportunity yet.

The closer they came to the enemy line, the more Asher's heart fluttered in her chest and her stomach twisted into a knot. They were truly on their own now. Too far away to be protected by the Iliryan army, too few to fight their way free if necessary. If they couldn't convince the Southerners to let them enter the Southlands, they would likely be killed. She looked at Taz. His eyebrows were drawn together, and he was chewing on his lower lip. *You're a knight*, she admonished herself. *Knights don't get scared! Get a hold of yourself.* But still her legs quaked.

The Southerner soldiers watched the approaching Iliryan delegation with sullen hostility and suspicion. Like the soldiers of the Iliryan army, they looked tired yet determined. In fact, but for their armor, Asher wouldn't have been able to distinguish the soldiers of one army from the other. Where were the monsters Erborn had promised? These were just men like any other.

The Southerner line parted to allow them to enter, then closed again, sealing the group in with no way to go back. Asher tried not to think about it. A tall soldier in red armor grabbed Ever's reins and led the knight commander's horse to the left. The rest of the delegation followed as dozens of pairs of curious Southerner eyes watched. Their escort led them to a large red tent and then dropped Ever's reins, ducking into the tent to alert whomever was inside to their presence. A moment later, he re-emerged and waved for them to enter.

Taz murmured, "Here we go." His voice was pinched.

Her heart pounding in her chest and her breath shallow, Asher dismounted, leaving the reins over Cloud's neck. If things went south, they might not be able to ride to freedom, but if it came to it, she would still try. Henrek and Jazmen carefully slid Commander Bronwen from Ever's back, cradling her between them. If the knight commander was scared, she didn't show it. Asher wished she shared Commander Bronwen's confidence, but at that moment General Oran's words came back to her. Did the Southerners really use the teeth of their enemies for jewelry?

Whatever Asher had expected to see when she walked into the Southerner general's tent, it wasn't a half-human monster. The creature inside was a good seven feet tall, with brown, hooved legs like a goat, a massive, muscled human chest, and huge black ram's horns that sprouted from the sides of his human head and curled around his ears. Small white tusks jutted from his lower lip and curled up toward his flat nose. Although he wore no armor at all, a massive two-headed axe was strapped to his bare back.

When Asher saw him, she froze, causing Taz to walk into her. She gasped and resisted the urge to back out of the tent. It was a primal instinct, the type a prey animal might have when encountering a predator.

"It must be an illusion to scare us," Taz whispered into her ear, his voice nervous. "Probably he's short and fat beneath the illusion."

"He's a fleshsmith." Marandir's low voice beside them was full of awe. "I've only read about them in books. His affinity hasn't been seen in Ilirya for centuries. It was assumed that affinity had died out."

Trying to be subtle and not draw the monster's attention, Asher asked him out of the corner of her mouth, "What's a fleshsmith?"

"His magic enables him to change his body at will. In this case, it appears he has taken on some of the qualities of a ram."

Asher swallowed. That didn't sound good. "Not an illusion. Can he change *us*?"

"No. Just himself." Marandir made a sound. "Well, at least that was the case in Ilirya. It's possible his magic works differently here."

Asher didn't like that answer at all. It was bad enough the creature—the fleshsmith—could crush a skull with one blow of his fist. What if he gave them all horns too? Could he turn them into rabbits? Just what could a Southerner fleshsmith do? She didn't have the opportunity to ask.

"Please be seated," the fleshsmith said. His voice was deep and powerful. It reverberated from his chest like the rumble of thunder. It set Asher's teeth on edge.

Because there were no chairs in the tent, only brightly colored pillows, Jazmen and Henrek set the knight commander down on a pillow. Jazmen sat behind her to keep her in a tolerably straight sitting position while Henrek took up a defensive position next to her, his hand ready on the pommel of his sword. Marandir, Taz, and Asher arrayed themselves slightly farther away from the knight commander, keeping as far from the fleshsmith as possible. He watched them with his head cocked to the side but said nothing. Asher noticed that the pupils of his tan eyes were oblong, like the eyes of a goat, and she shivered at how inhuman they were.

Now settled, Commander Bronwen said, "I assume you are in charge here?"

"I am." The Southerner general watched the commander curiously but without judgment.

"Thank you for granting our parley. I will get straight to the point: I am requesting safe passage through your lines for myself and my five companions. We have been sent by Queen Alea to discuss terms for peace with your regent."

"Peace?" The general smiled, emphasizing his small tusks. "Hmm. Now the Rann seek peace with the Sarsen? Have you finally given up after all these years?"

"Who are the Rann and the Sarsen?" Taz whispered to Asher.

"I think we're the Rann and they're the Sarsen." It was a guess. She had never heard either term before. Was this what the Southerners called them? Why?

"Both sides can benefit from an honorable end to these long years of war. It is hard to prosper in times of strife," Commander Bronwen said.

"So many years of war. So many Sarsen dead." The general was no longer smiling. He narrowed his eyes at the commander. "What will the

Rann give for peace? What will the Rann pay for all the lives they have taken?"

Commander Bronwen clenched her teeth briefly. "The terms of peace are for our rulers to decide. We soldiers are merely the instruments of their will."

The general smiled again, his eyes creasing at the corners. "So the Rann will beg for peace from the King of Cats?"

Asher found it hard to look away from him. How could a human be so inhuman?

Commander Bronwen held her chin high. "We beg for nothing. We come as equals."

The general grunted, turning away, and Asher worried that Commander Bronwen had angered him. What would he do if he was upset with them? Her hand unconsciously went to the hilt of her sword, ready to fight if necessary. She didn't intend to sit idly by should he use his magic on them.

"General, you know the terrible cost of war. Surely you would prefer to see it ended. Let your soldiers return to their families. Will you promise us safe passage to Nyara to present our petition for peace to your king?"

The general turned back to them and laughed, the enormous muscles in his chest and stomach rippling. Asher was taken aback by the unexpectedness of it. His smile stretched wider than ever. "Safe passage to Nyara? General Zadan can promise the lady nothing beyond these lines. Not even the King of Cats can control the five tribes of the Sarsen. But I will not stop you. Follow the road south, and you will find the King of Cats. But be warned: many things can happen on the road to Nyara." He laughed again. "And beware the dragon."

Chapter 3

The boy is bawling when the girl finds him. His face is puffy and red, his cheeks shiny with tears. She sits down next to him and puts her thin arm around his shoulders.

"What am I going to do now that he's gone, Asher?" the boy asks.

"Don't worry, Taz," the girl replies. "We'll always have each other. You and me, forever."

"What do you think he meant by 'the dragon'?" Taz scrunched his face together. His blue eyes scanned the skies around them, but there was nothing to see in them, not even a cloud.

The small group had finally stopped for a rest after hours of riding, sprawling out on the ground in a stand of trees beside the road while the horses grazed nearby. Asher was sweating heavily in the Southland sun, but like everyone else, she refused to remove any of her armor during the day. A knight had to be ready at all times. It wouldn't do to be caught in only a tunic and leggings. That was how knights died. It was better to sweat and be ready for anything than to be as defenseless as a turtle with no shell.

She lay back on the grass, putting her head in her hands, and considered Taz's question. Dragons, as everyone knew, were a myth. Probably once upon a time someone had seen a lizard and thought, "Wouldn't it be scary if this lizard had wings and was large enough to carry off a full-sized horse?" She attributed the idea that this imaginary creature should also breathe fire to the ingenuity of storytellers, who never missed a chance to make a tale more dramatic. What could be more dramatic than a creature with teeth like knives, skin like plate armor, and the ability to burn down an entire village with one breath? It was ingenious, really.

"Maybe 'the Dragon' is a person, like the King of Cats."

Taz stuck out his lower lip. "That would be a funny thing to call a person."

"So is the King of Cats. Why do you suppose he's called that? Wouldn't a king want to be called something more regal? A cat is small and unintimidating. They eat mice and sleep all day." Asher didn't particularly care what the Southerner king was called. All that mattered was that when they arrived in Nyara, he granted them the peace treaty they sought. If he wanted to be called the King of Pigs, that was his business.

Taz shook his head. "Who knows?" He pulled up blades of grass and threw them back down carelessly. "That general—I think he said his name was Zadan—wasn't very helpful. He should have provided us an escort. Or at least a map. He didn't even tell us how long it would take to get to Nyara. We still don't know anything about the Southlands."

Asher shrugged. "At least he didn't kill us on the spot." They might not have learned anything about the Southlands, but they had left with their lives and, she considered with a shiver, all their limbs still human.

"I wonder why we don't have...what did Marandir call him? A fleshsmith. I wonder why we don't have fleshsmiths in Ilirya."

Asher flicked a bug off her leg, watching it cartwheel away. "I'm glad we don't! We don't need fish-tailed women or bull-headed men in our daily life. People are complicated enough without having animal parts. Can you imagine walking down a dark alley in King's City and running into General Zadan? He's exactly the type of monster a parent makes up to scare children into behaving."

She fished a golden-brown honey oat cake out of her satchel and munched on it, contemplating her companions. Henrek was laid out on the ground, his dark cloak over his face as he snored loudly. Jazmen and Marandir were also dozing, their backs against trees, while Commander Bronwen kept a vigilant eye over their small camp. Asher considered taking a quick nap herself. Who knew how much longer they would have to ride before they found a suitable place to bed down for the night?

A twig somewhere in the forest around them snapped. Asher was on her feet in an instant, her sword half-drawn.

The commander glanced at her and motioned with her head for Asher to stop. Then her eyes returned to the tree line in the direction from which the sound had come. "You might as well show yourselves. Unless you'd like to continue following us as you have been since we crossed the border."

Asher grimaced, flexing her hand on the hilt of her sword. They'd been followed since the border? How had she missed that?

A young man, his brown patchy beard indicating he was barely out of boyhood, stepped out of the forest. He was dressed plainly in a rough brown tunic. As far as Asher could tell, he was unarmed. Marandir and Jazmen rolled to their feet and moved closer to protect Commander Bronwen, their hands on their sword hilts. To Asher's annoyance, Henrek continued to snore, oblivious to the interloper.

Commander Bronwen indicated the woods around the young man impatiently. "And the others."

From among the trees, long gray and white noses tipped with black appeared, followed by small amber eyes. There was no mistaking the creatures to which they belonged. Wolves. The animals watched the knights intently, their ears pricked forward. Asher froze, her senses screaming. The instinctive fear of a pack of dangerous predators made her body buzz with energy. Danger! She quickly assessed the odds. There were at least twelve wolves. Although they might be able to fight the pack off, it would be a bloody, deadly confrontation, and they had neither healers nor medicine with them.

Behind her, Taz drew his sword slowly. In the quiet air, the sound was loud as a bell ringing. One of the wolves growled. It lowered its head, its ears pressing back into its skull and its lips curling to reveal long, sharp white teeth. This prompted the other knights to draw their swords as well, and in an instant all the wolves were growling. The sound was awful. It echoed and built on itself in the heavy air, making the hair on Asher's arms stand up.

Asher stepped back into a defensive stance, sword held out in front of her. Her muscles were so tight they were almost shaking. If the wolves attacked, she wouldn't have much time to react. She would have to slice quickly and move even faster to avoid being dragged to the ground, where she would be helpless.

The barking and snarling finally woke Henrek. He jumped to his feet, looking with bewilderment between the wolves and his companions. "Where did *they* come from?"

To Asher's surprise, Commander Bronwen seemed unconcerned by the escalating standoff. Fixing her eyes on the stranger, she asked him calmly, "What do you want?"

The young man motioned subtly with his hands, and the wolves stopped growling, although they continued to stare down the Iliryans. In an instant, the clearing became so quiet Asher could hear Taz breathing hoarsely behind her. She shifted her weight uneasily, unwilling to lower her blade. Had the man tamed the wolves? Was it possible to domesticate an entire pack?

He said, "You are to come with me."

"We won't go a step with you! Who do you think you are?" Henrek spat, eyes narrow. He stood with his legs planted wide apart, his sword in his left hand and a dagger in his right.

One of the wolves near him stepped forward, issuing a low, tense growl. The skin around its nose wrinkled to reveal its sharp teeth and bright pink tongue. Asher's palms began to sweat. She *really* didn't want to have to fight wolves. Although she'd fight tooth and nail if it came to it.

"What if we do not come with you?" Commander Bronwen asked, ignoring Henrek's outburst.

The young man's face twisted with confusion. "But you must! The Magus has ordered it."

The knight commander stared him down. "Listen to me, young man. We are traveling to your capital on behalf of Queen Alea of Ilirya. We do not have time to deviate from our mission, not for you or anyone. You may relay that message to this Magus person. If they wish to see us, they will have to come to *us*."

"Are all Rann this obstinate?" a new voice asked.

A muscular man with midnight black hair and a fulsome mustache stomped out of the trees, glaring at the commander. He was followed by another man and two women. Surprised, Asher turned to orient her sword to them, uncertain whether they or the wolves were the bigger threat. How many people were hiding in those trees, and how had she not noticed them?

All four of the newcomers, who wore brown outfits similar to that of the young man, had called magic to their hands. It glowed with an identical green light. Asher's eyes widened. She had never seen four people with the exact same color magic. Was this another peculiarity of the Southlands? In Ilirya, every mage's magic was a shade unique to them alone.

The mustached man raised his hands, showing magic gathering there. "Will or nil, you're coming with us. The Magus demands it."

"And who is this 'Magus,' eh?" Henrek demanded.

The four mages released their magic at the same time. It formed into ropes in mid-air and then, faster than the Iliryans could move, fell upon the members of the delegation. Asher watched helplessly as her wrists were bound fast by the pulsing, deep-green magic. She heard a yelp of surprise and protest from Taz and knew the same thing was happening to him. Henrek unleashed a string of colorful curses, fighting the magic wrapping around his hands with all his strength, but to no avail. A second tendril of magic pulled fast against his ankles, and he toppled to the ground.

"Untie me, you brigands!" Henrek bellowed, rolling onto his side and wriggling his body like a fish in a net. "Or I will tear you limb from limb! You had better hope I don't get free of this confounded magic!"

Commander Bronwen's mouth quirked into a tight frown of disapproval. Of all her party, she was the only one whom the magic had not touched, but she was just as helpless as her companions. "I suppose we're your prisoners now?"

"Perhaps." The mustached man crossed his arms over his broad chest. "That is for the Magus to decide."

"This 'Magus' is your leader?"

The man motioned to one of the mages, a woman of about fifty with deep-brown skin and wavy black hair, and she released a green thread of magic that wove itself into a floating chair for the knight commander. Invisible hands lifted Commander Bronwen into the air and placed her gently into it. *So they know about Commander Bronwen*, Asher thought. Had General Zadan alerted them, or had they realized from watching the Iliryans?

Commander Bronwen growled. "If this is how it's to be, please see that the horses are taken care of at least."

The wolves turned and disappeared back into the trees. Asher was furious at herself for not noticing they'd been followed. What if their captors had been attackers instead? They had let their guard down and now they were prisoners. They were lucky things hadn't turned out worse.

"Damn mages!" Henrek roared. "Marandir, do something to stop them!"

The other Southerner woman was roughly hoisting Henrek to his feet while Henrek tried to butt her with his head like a goat. Asher shook her head. It was clear they had no hope of escaping in their present circumstances. The best they could do now was follow along until an opportunity for escape or negotiation presented itself. Henrek continued cursing until he abruptly went silent. Irritated by Henrek's ceaseless insults, the mage had created a gag that cut off his ability to make a sound.

"Ha!" Jazmen cackled. "Someone finally shut you up, you old git."

Henrek's eyes burned furiously as they glared at her. When the gag was removed, it was clear he would have things to say about it.

Their captors led them west from the road through alternating patches of field and forest. If they hadn't been prisoners, Asher might have found this part of the Southlands to be soothingly reminiscent of the Iliryan barony of Prabst, which lay immediately to the north of King's City. Instead, she focused on carefully noting everything around them. Once they escaped—or were released—they would need to know how to return to the road to Nyara, and that meant remembering key landmarks that would enable them to retrace their steps.

They walked for an hour before reaching the first signs of habitation Asher had seen since they'd crossed into the Southlands. It was impossible to guess how many people lived in the area because their houses had been built in a small forest, where they were camouflaged by the trees and the falling dusk. Even so, she could tell it was a surprisingly large settlement, likely populated by hundreds of people.

Their captors led them between the small, thatch-roofed houses and straight to a long, low building. It was a modest, unadorned hall with square holes for windows. Inside, several men and women sat on rough wooden benches along the walls, wearing the same brown clothing as the Iliryans' captors. At the far end of the hall, an old woman with a shock of white hair tied in a loose bun at the top of her head sat on a wooden throne on a small dais. As they approached her, Asher noticed with alarm that the throne moved. Thick green and brown vines slithered over and around its arms, legs, and back. Asher blinked, thinking it might be a trick of her eyes, but it didn't stop the leaves from sprouting and shriveling before her. The chair was alive.

"Magus, we have brought the Rann trespassers to you," the mustached man told the old woman, bowing to her.

"Thank you, Boaz."

The Magus fixed her captives with a fierce, penetrating stare. Her face was lined by years of exposure to the wind and sun, but her hazel eyes were sharp and clear as an eagle's.

Commander Bronwen returned the Magus' gaze. Without waiting to be addressed, she said, "We are representatives of the Iliryan government on official business. I demand that you release us and return our horses."

The Magus stood, stepping closer to them. "You are in no position to demand anything. What are you doing in Sarsen lands?"

"That is between us and your king."

The Magus waved a wrinkled brown hand. "The King of Cats has no power here." She smiled, revealing several missing teeth. "Your business is with me now."

Commander Bronwen stared at the Magus defiantly, but she was at a clear disadvantage. As the Magus had pointed out, the Iliryans—bound, outnumbered, and in a strange land—were in no position to demand anything. She nodded, then said in a clipped voice, "We have come to sue for peace."

The Magus leaned forward, peering at the knight commander with narrowed eyes. "Oh, *now* you want peace, do you? After what you've done?"

Commander Bronwen began, "Both sides have done things in this war—"

"I'm not talking about your stupid war!"

Commander Bronwen blinked. "What?"

"You fustilugs! Your mages opened a box they shouldn't have! They let all the monsters out, and now *we're* the ones stuck cleaning up your mess!"

Commander Bronwen's face was a mask of confusion. She looked to Marandir and to her knights, but none of them understood what the Magus meant either. She shook her head slowly. "I'm afraid I do not understand."

The Magus waved her hand agitatedly, her face sour. Behind her, the vines twisted and writhed over her throne like agitated snakes. "Weeks ago, some of you Rann summoned a veritable storm of Dark Magic, didn't you? Tore a hole in our world, and now we have all sorts of things traipsing around that shouldn't be here, wreaking havoc."

"But—but how could you possibly know about the…about what happened?" Commander Bronwen's face was ashen.

Asher was just as flummoxed as the knight commander. How could the Southerners know about the plot to kill King Hap and bring the One God into the mortal realm? How could they know about the Gate between the two worlds through which the god had tried and failed to pass? How could they know that Dark Magic had been the catalyst for opening that Gate? Come to think of it, how could they know about Dark Magic at all? It was an Iliryan invention, a perversion of magic by a few rogue Iliryan mages. Did the Southerners have spies in King's City?

The Magus snorted. "The Isenii know all that happens in Ilirya. Just because you Rann act like you live on an island doesn't make it so. We're your neighbor. And every time you try and use Dark Magic, it's the Sarsen who deal with the consequences. Last time you tried to use Dark Magic, it took us years to put our lands to right again!"

What? Asher blinked. *The last time?* Could she be referring to the original discovery of Dark Magic in Ilirya decades ago? Asher had only just found out about that months ago. How was it the Magus seemed to know more than she did?

Commander Bronwen shifted in her chair, grimacing. "I'm sorry. We didn't know. No one in Ilirya was aware of this problem. Obviously, you have a much better understanding of the effects of Dark Magic than we do. It seems we have much to learn from you."

A flicker of hope flared in Asher's chest. *Do they know how to stop the Dark Magic poisoning her? Can they cure her?*

Commander Bronwen pushed forward. "And yet surely you see that we must continue on to Nyara to speak to the king. We must put an end to the war that has drained the lifeblood of our two kingdoms for four decades. All else can be handled once peace is achieved."

The Magus boggled at her. "Lady knight, I have a dragon on my hands, threatening to decimate my people. Every week, it kills more of them. Peace? Your peace means nothing to me! The Isenii will be wiped out by this dragon long before the war will bleed us dry! A dragon, you understand, caused by you Iliryan fopdoodles. I don't need peace; I need someone to kill this dragon!"

An uncomfortable silence ensued while the Magus stared at her. Commander Bronwen stared back, bewilderment on her face.

"A dragon?" she said at last.

The Magus nodded. "A very large one."

"But dragons aren't real!" The commander protested weakly. "They're just stories!"

"Balderdash! I suppose you might as well go and tell *it* that it doesn't exist. I suppose it hasn't quite gotten the message yet."

"And you…desire *us* to kill the dragon?"

"Well, it's your fault," the Magus huffed.

"How does one kill a dragon?"

"The usual way: cutting off its head or spearing it through the heart."

"Oh."

"But you must take care of its ichor." The Magus waggled a finger. "And its fire, of course. Both will melt armor. Dragons are bloody hard to kill, which is why it's a good thing they only appear every few decades when you bloody Rann accidentally summon them."

"Why can't *your* mages kill the dragon?" Jazmen piped up. "They know how to create binding spells and all, don't they? Can't they tie up the dragon so it can't move, and then one of your warriors can cut off its head or spear it or whatnot? It seems an easy thing for you to do."

"Oh no!" The Magus's voice suggested the answer was obvious. "Dragons are immune to magic. They're natural mage banes."

"So you are asking us to help you kill the dragon because you cannot," Commander Bronwen said.

"Oh goodness no! No, I'm *ordering* you to try to kill the dragon. Better you than I lose more of my people." The Magus sat back down heavily on her seat, and the vines wriggled away.

"We're hardly prepared to fight a beast that until this moment we didn't even know existed!" Marandir protested. "It would take us time to study and learn more about it. We would have to observe it in its habitat and track its movements…"

"This will be a distraction from the task Queen Alea has set us to." Commander Bronwen frowned deeply. "And we don't have time to spare.

What's more, we are, as you see, a very small delegation. We are not well equipped for the undertaking you ask."

The Magus's hazel eyes hardened. "Let me express this in a way you will understand. You desire peace. The Isenii are one of the five tribes of the Sarsen. If you kill the dragon, we will support your petition for peace. If you try to shirk this duty, however, not a one of you will live to set foot outside Isenii lands. Clear?"

The knight commander pressed her mouth into a tight line. "Very."

"We're not monsters," the Magus said, looking to the knights and holding her hands up in supplication, "but fair is fair. It's your problem. You clean it up."

Without warning, Commander Bronwen gasped and doubled over. The muscles in her jaw clenched as her body shuddered, racked by a spasm of pain. Her left hand balled into a tight fist, and she slumped onto her right side. Asher's heart jumped into her throat. The Dark Magic. She remembered Lyse's words. Away from the city, the Dark Magic would spread much faster.

The Magus, who had instinctively risen at the knight commander's gasp, stepped off the dais and moved closer. She held up her right hand, and the same green magic shared by the other mages reached out and wrapped itself around Commander Bronwen's chest. "You're dying. You carry Dark Magic inside you, and it's killing you." There was an unexpected note of sympathy in her voice.

Commander Bronwen didn't answer. She was breathing heavily, her face gray.

"Can she be healed?" The words jumped out of Asher's mouth.

The Magus shook her head, pulling back her magic. "I'm sorry. No mage in the world can pull Dark Magic out of a body. It's nasty stuff."

"Why?" Marandir asked. "Why can't our magic stop it?"

Asher wanted to know too. What made it so different from the other magic?

"I don't know."

The knight commander said through gritted teeth, "Tell us how to kill the dragon."

The Magus retreated back to her throne and sat on it while vines twisted and snaked around her. "I'll send a healer with you. That will be of some help against burns. Other than that, get your pokey bits into its fleshy, soft bits and you'll be fine."

"We should slip out at night while they're sleeping." Henrek waved his hand at the door. "We can steal back the horses and be gone before they've noticed."

The group had been left alone together in a small hut with only some scratchy, thin brown blankets to lie on and a few rounds of flat, tasteless bread to eat. Dim, flickering torchlight feebly illuminated the room, creating grotesque shadows that danced on the walls. Although their magical bindings had been removed, Asher was not fooled. They were prisoners of the Isenii, not guests.

Commander Bronwen sat against a wall while Henrek paced. Everyone was tired and disheartened. Between their capture on the road to Nyara and discovering that the use of Dark Magic in Ilirya had resulted in the appearance of a dragon in the Southlands—one that now they would have to fight to the death—Asher was having trouble processing everything that had happened. How had things fallen apart so quickly? They hadn't even been in the Southlands a day.

"Oh right, that's it," Jazmen retorted. "We'll just nip off, will we? Ta, lads."

"The Isenii will have sentries around the village, no doubt, not to mention the guards encircling this hut to prevent exactly such a flight," Marandir said, ruffling his red hair with his hand. "We wouldn't make it ten feet before we were caught. Even if we managed to make it back to the road, their territory could run for days. We would be easily recaptured, and what then?"

"We fight!" Henrek said, brandishing his fist.

Commander Bronwen sighed. "There is neither utility nor dignity in running, Henrek. If what the Magus says is true and we are the cause of this dragon, then we are honor-bound to kill it."

"We don't owe them anything! They kidnapped us and brought us here against our wills, the scoundrels!"

"Could we send word back to the front?" Asher asked. "We're still close. We could ask for a combined platoon of archers, knights, and pikemen to be sent. Maybe the Isenii would let us go if they knew a larger fighting force was on its way. Then we could continue on to Nyara."

"It's a good idea, and we could offer such a proposal to the Magus," Commander Bronwen agreed, "but she has no reason to trust us. She would most likely make us wait until the platoon arrived before allowing us to leave, and that could take weeks. General Oran would need time to prepare the platoon—staffing it, equipping it, perhaps even training it—followed by negotiations with General Zadan to allow it to pass through the Southerner line. And that's *if* General Oran agreed to send a platoon at all. The army has no platoon to spare. No, we can't risk waiting."

"Do it ourselves then. Is that what you're saying, Bronwen?" Jazmen asked, watching the knight commander closely.

"I don't see an alternative. We don't have time to spare. Every moment, the Northmen draw closer to invasion."

"It's a *dragon*!" Jazmen exclaimed. "They shouldn't even exist, hey? You heard the Magus: they're more than dangerous. Giant fire-breathing lizard with skin like armor and blood that melts metal, yeah? Sound like something we should be charging at with our little swords? We're only six. We can't afford to lose anyone."

"I know." There was stress in Commander Bronwen's voice. She looked tired. Her face was ghost-white and her red hair, starting to come loose from her braid, hung limply over her shoulders. "I don't like the risk, but we have no choice."

"I'm not afraid."

The others stared at Asher in surprise. Taz's mouth even fell open a little.

Asher held her chin high. It wasn't exactly the truth. She was concerned about the idea of fighting a dragon—blood and fire that could melt metal?—but she was a knight, and knights didn't run from danger. They had come this far. They couldn't stop now. "I'll fight the dragon."

"I'll do it, too." Now all eyes turned to Taz. Asher knew him well enough to recognize the brief flicker of uncertainty and doubt that flashed across his face, but it quickly passed, leaving in its wake gritty determination. She nodded at him.

Jazmen threw up her hands. "We can't let the children show us up, Henrek. Fine, I'll go, too."

"As will I," said Marandir.

"Thank you." Commander Bronwen looked around at her companions. "You honor me with your bravery."

"I'm no coward!" Henrek protested. "I've faced plenty of danger in my time! I was merely saying that it would be faster not to waste our time fighting the cursed lizard, that's all. I didn't say I wouldn't do it."

"No, you shall remain with me, Henrek," Commander Bronwen ordered. "I will need someone with me."

It took Asher a moment to realize what the commander meant, and when she did, her stomach gave a lurch. In the event the dragon killed the other four, the commander would need a companion with whom to either push on to Nyara or limp back across the front line and into Ilirya. She was hedging her bet.

Jazmen said, "That's it settled then! Go on, to bed with everyone. Tomorrow we fight a dragon."

She plopped down onto one of the blankets and started to pull her armor off. Slowly, the others followed. Asher pulled her blanket next to Taz's. He was struggling to unclasp his cuirass, so she brushed his hands aside and did it herself.

He gave her a half smile. "Who would have known we'd end up fighting a dragon in the Southlands?"

Asher smiled. "Just think: You'll have been the first Iliryan knight to fight a dragon and all Erborn will have to talk about is his angry farmers."

"Do you think it will be like in the myths? Teeth like daggers and wings that can block out the sun?" Taz's eyes were uncertain.

Asher snorted. "Of course not! Don't be ridiculous. You'll see. That dragon will be smaller than Cloud."

Chapter 4

"I'm Tayanna," the knight says, extending her hand.

Her dark, slanted eyes dance with life and she smiles with an open, honest expression. Asher is momentarily transfixed. An unexpected lightness in her chest steals her breath away.

"I'm…Asher."

At first, Asher thinks she's dreaming. Then she realizes it's a memory. She's back in King's City in her room at the garrison. She's folding her recently laundered tunics into the top drawer of the large dresser in her room. She loves the rainbow effect they create, the way the cloth aligns in perfect, symmetrical order. Folding the clothing to her is soothing—from chaos, order.

She senses it before anything else, the feeling of a presence behind her even though she didn't hear anyone enter the room. Her skin prickles with anticipation as she freezes, waiting. As a knight, she should react to an unknown presence by immediately defending herself, but this is not a stranger. She would know this presence anywhere. Soft hands run up her arms and a warm body presses into her back. Her eyes flutter as her heart skips a beat. Her breathes catches in her chest. Tayanna smells faintly of sweat and leather and metal, of the campaign from which she's returning. She smells of home.

Asher closes her eyes and leans back. She releases tension she didn't even realize she was carrying, months of worry and fear and yearning. Tayanna drops her head and kisses Asher on the side of her neck, sending a shiver down Asher's spine that goes right to her toes. Tayanna's breath whispers against her skin like the wings of a butterfly, so soft she could almost be imagining it. Her arms prickle, charged with energy. Then Tayanna wraps her arms around Asher's stomach in an embrace that envelops her like a warm blanket. As they stand motionless that way, she can feel every breath Tayanna takes, every beat of her heart.

Asher feels safe, protected. She basks in the feeling of Tayanna's body against hers. Without her near, the world has been cold and empty. Tayanna's nose nestles against her neck, her forehead against the back of Asher's head. They fit together. They have always fit together. Two pieces of a puzzle that, in a world full of mismatched pieces, found each other.

Eventually, she turns around to look into Tayanna's face. It's a face she's seen a thousand times or more. It's become more familiar to her than her own. She thinks it's the most beautiful thing she's ever seen. Tayanna's dark eyes stare into hers, a smile playing on her lips.

She reaches up and runs her hands delicately across Asher's cheeks. "Hiya, Ash."

Asher all but shivers with emotion. She wants to shout with joy. She wants to grab Tayanna and hold her until the sun has set and the moon is high above the city. She seizes Tayanna's face in her hands and pulls her into a deep kiss. Reflexively, Tayanna's hands drop to settle at her hips, and it's as though no time has passed at all. Their bodies have not forgotten what it's like to love one another.

When Tayanna pulls away, her grin has blossomed into a full-blown smile. She leans forward, resting her forehead against Asher's. "I missed you."

Asher can hear the longing in her voice. She runs her hands lightly over Tayanna's arms, barely believing Tayanna has returned. If she closes her eyes, will she find this is only a dream? It's been months since Tayanna left for the front. Communication during that time was sparse. Asher doesn't even remember when she last heard from her. Every day was agony, not knowing if Tayanna had been hurt or killed. But she's here now, safe.

Asher rests her hands along the sides of Tayanna's neck, binding the two of them together. "Don't leave me again."

It's a silly, sentimental request. Neither of them can promise the other anything. Knights go where they're ordered. But she makes it anyway. Tayanna shakes her head gently, her forehead rubbing against Asher's. "Never." It's the same thing she promises every time she comes back.

She twines her fingers in Asher's tunic and looks into Asher's eyes. Asher doesn't know how she can love anything as much as she loves Tayanna. She didn't think it was possible. There's nothing she wouldn't do, nothing she wouldn't give for her. She belongs totally and utterly to her, from now until the end of time.

Tayanna kisses her again, sweetly. "Tell me you missed me," she murmurs.

"Every minute of every hour of every day."

"You didn't forget me? Not even for a second?" Tayanna's smile has turned playful. A light shines in her eyes.

"How could I? How could I ever forget you?" Asher has never meant anything more. Tayanna's tone is light, but emotion colors Asher's. The idea of forgetting even a hair on Tayanna's head is impossible.

The memory starts to fade, dissolving at the edges. Asher clings to it, fighting to keep it, desperate for a few seconds more. It's become a dream now, however, and in the dream Tayanna is leaving, something that didn't happen in real life. Asher is glued to the floor, unable to stop her.

"No!" she begs, "don't go. Tayanna, please don't go. You promised you would always come back. You promised!" Her voice is plaintive as a child's. Her heart pounds. In her heart, she knows that once Tayanna leaves, she will be gone forever.

Tayanna's smile is infinitely sad as she looks back from the doorway. She's becoming harder to see, as though a veil has fallen between the two of them. She says, "You can't change the past, Ash. I love you. I will always love you."

Asher was awakened by something sharp poking her in the side.

"Ow!" she exclaimed, rubbing the area but not opening her eyes.

The vestiges of a dream lurked at the edges of her memory. When she tried to reach for the dream, however, it evaporated, leaving her with only a vague sense of profound loss and sadness that was quickly dissipating. Whatever the dream, she wouldn't remember it. She let it go, allowing the feelings it generated to dissolve as well.

She felt another poke and opened a disgruntled eye to find its cause. The Magus peered down at her, preparing to jab her a third time with the tip of a spear. Asher's lingering melancholy was instantly replaced by annoyance. What was she doing?

"Wake up!" the Magus barked.

Taz groaned, rolling away from Asher and nestling tight against the wall. The Magus turned her attention to him, kicking the thin blanket off him and then walloping him in the leg for good measure. The latter did the trick of waking him completely. He rolled to his knees and held out his hands, trying to ward off his attacker. The other Iliryans were already awake and starting to get to their feet, sleep still heavy in their eyes.

The Magus declared, "The best time to kill a dragon is the morning, so eat something and then be off with you. Your horses are waiting for you outside. You'll need lances to kill the dragon, so I've left you a few. They're sharpened dragon bone from the last dragon we had to kill. It's the only thing that doesn't splinter on dragon hide. I'm sending Lan and Ulu with you. They'll be able to find the dragon wherever it's gone."

She stepped back toward the door, ignoring Henrek's glare. She grunted. "Well, good luck to you. The dragon's weakness is its underbelly. Aim there and…eh, maybe you'll get lucky." She shrugged. Then she was gone.

Asher turned to Taz to say something about the Magus but stopped short when she noticed his face was pulled tight in a mask of sorrow. She reached for his shoulder, worried. "What is it, Taz?"

"I was dreaming of my father." His voice was small and forlorn, the voice of a young boy missing his father.

Asher patted his shoulder. She and Taz had been pages when his father had died of plague, and the death had left a hole in Taz's life that he'd never been able to fill. Some wounds never healed. She would know.

"We'll always have each other, Taz. It's you and me forever."

Taz managed a broken smile. "And a dragon, apparently."

Asher reined Cloud next to Marandir's black gelding Crow as their group headed south in search of the dragon. "Marandir, why do the Isenii mages all have the same color magic?" It was only one of the many questions she had about the things she'd seen so far in the Southlands and it was only the second day.

Marandir's face was pensive as he rubbed his chin. "I don't know. All the mages we met were spellcasters too. I've been wondering if they're able to tap magic from an external source. It might explain why they all have the same magic. But…I've only read about such a thing as a hypothetical possibility. No one in Ilirya has ever seen it done."

"Isn't that a bit like how Dark Magic works? Dark mages draw power from pain."

Marandir nodded. "Yes, but this would be something else, something that probably isn't human."

"Why do you think that?"

He scratched his cheek. "Well, it's definitely not Dark Magic. You heard the disgust in the Magus's voice when she talked about Dark Magic. The Southerners don't seem to like it any more than we do. And besides, Dark Magic is always black."

"Then what could the source be?"

Marandir shook his head. "I couldn't begin to guess. Nor do I think they would tell us if we asked. They don't seem particularly inclined to conversation, do they?"

Asher understood what he meant. Their guides Lan and Ulu hadn't said more than ten words since they'd set off from the Isenii village. Lan, who turned out to be the young man they'd met the day before, had taken point far ahead of their group on a rangy bay mare while Ulu rode well behind them on a stout red roan gelding. By coincidence or design, conversation with them was effectively impossible.

Asher wondered if the Southerners were purposely trying to limit what the Iliryans found out about them. After all, General Zadan hadn't been any more talkative. She thought about what the archivist had said. The Southerners were notoriously reclusive. Whatever their secrets, they didn't want the Iliryans to know them.

Something moved in the woods around them. Asher automatically tightened her fingers around Cloud's reins as she recognized the light-colored shapes running through the trees. "Marandir, the wolves are back!"

Marandir nodded. "Oh yes, the young man—I believe he's Lan—is a Therion mage."

"A what?"

"An animal mage. They're able to influence animals with their magic. In this case, Lan shares a bond with these wolves. There are Therion mages in Ilyria, but so far as I know none are bonded to a wolf pack."

Asher whistled quietly, impressed. A moment later, she asked, "What did the Magus mean when she said every time Iliryans use Dark Magic it causes problems for the Southlands? And how could they possibly know about Dark Magic anyway?"

Marandir's face drew together, pained. Asher guessed he was remembering the devastation Dark Magic had caused so recently in Ilirya. How well had he known the three Regiment members who had collaborated with the Dark mages? How did he feel about his own captain being part of the coup against the king?

"I don't know. We know so precious little about Dark Magic. It seems there is much that we Iliryans don't know but the Southerners do."

He sighed. "I hope they see fit to tell us. I don't like feeling as though we're searching for answers they already know."

"Is the Magus right that we caused a dragon to come here? How?"

"I don't know how it could have happened."

Unexpectedly, Lan pulled his horse up short and raised his hand. The knights behind him stopped, looking around. Had he seen something? From the trees, the wolves started to howl. The eerie wailing gave Asher goosebumps. It was a testament to Cloud's temperament and training that he remained calm.

Commander Bronwen trotted to join Lan at the front of the line, her eyes scanning the horizon. "What is it?"

"The wolves sense the dragon is near."

Asher scanned the blue sky above them but saw nothing. A moment later, the timbre of the wolves' voices changed. They began to bark and whine, darting between the trees and running in circles with their gray tails tucked between their legs. Asher realized they were afraid. Her heart beat faster with anticipation. A shadow passed over her, momentarily shading the world black, then raced across the ground in front of her. Its shape—clearly described in Iliryan lore—was unmistakable. It was a dragon.

Asher's blood ran cold. It was unquestionably the biggest creature she'd ever seen. It was so large that when it was directly overhead, its body eclipsed the sun. Asher estimated that its long, leathery wings spanned at least seven horse lengths and its body, including the long tail that trailed behind it like a banner, was half again as long. It was identical to the dragons of legend, down to its small, triangular head. But the legends—which Asher had always assumed were nothing more than imaginative fables—hadn't said how to kill one. Was it even possible?

"Ooooooh," Jazmen said. Her voice was too full of awe and wonder to leave room for fear.

"You've got to be joking!" Henrek's eyes were wide. "We're supposed to kill *that*?"

"It's bigger than a house!" squeaked Taz.

"How are we to get to the dragon?" Commander Bronwen asked Lan, ignoring them. Her voice was full of purpose. "Will it land?"

"Oh yes, lady knight. It will most certainly land. We have found dragons to be very vicious, territorial creatures. Having sighted us, it will attack us until it has killed at least some of us. Or until you kill it."

Commander Bronwen spun Ever in a tight circle. Her eyes glinted with grim determination as she looked over her companions. "Now you have seen it, the dragon. It is a fearsome creature indeed. Right now, this dragon stands between us and our goal. You know the cost of failure. If we cannot achieve peace, all of Ilirya will fall. You are brave knights all, and I have faith you will prevail. Good hunting."

Asher fought down the horror that was climbing the walls of her stomach. How could they be expected to face the dragon? What hope did they have to defeat it? How could they possibly approach it without being burned to ashes or clawed to ribbons or swallowed in one bite? It was madness to even try. She wanted nothing more than to turn Cloud and gallop away in the other direction, and yet the Commander was right: what choice did they have? Besides, the Magus had made it clear that they must fight the dragon or die at the hands of the Isenii.

Jazmen sighed. "It's been a good life for me. Got no one at home waiting for me, do I? Right then, let's see if we can't get a few good pokes in before we're all dragon fodder." She untied the long white lance from her saddle and propped it crosswise across the saddle, ready for use, then dropped the visor of her helmet. Asher thought she heard Jazmen mumble in a muffled voice, "Tenner's still on Henrek."

Asher shifted in Cloud's saddle, unable to look away from the dragon as it continued winging away from them, a living storm cloud. She could barely breathe. They couldn't possibly prevail. Was this how their peace mission would end? With all the delegation's members killed by a dragon on their second day in the Southlands? She would gladly charge into an enemy line. She would even fight General Zadan, but this…this terrified her more than anything she'd faced yet as a knight. She looked at Taz. His face was white.

But then, to her surprise, he nodded slowly. "Strength and honor," he said, readying his lance. His visor made a loud clink as it slammed shut.

Asher could barely stop herself from gaping at him. Was this the Taz she had grown up with? His words humbled her. Although obviously just as terrified by the dragon as she was, he was nevertheless standing by his duty. Asher was ashamed of her own moment of weakness. If Taz could find a way to be brave, she could, too.

She straightened in her saddle, smiling thinly at him. "Duty and queen," she replied with a nod, untying her lance. Her trembling hands made the task harder.

Marandir, however, dismounted without saying a word. Asher stared at him. What was he doing? Was he refusing to fight? He handed Crow's reins to Henrek. Bowing to Commander Bronwen, he said, "I will do everything in my power to assist, Commander."

Right then, the dragon, which had been circling high above the group, swooped low over them and let out a piercing scream. It was so loud Asher ground her teeth together. The sound was like two swords scraping together. Cloud whinnied in fear and tried to rear, but Asher kept control of his head and forced his front feet back to the ground. All around her, the horses were panicking, trying to run from the danger. They may have been trained to charge humans and other horses in battle, but that training didn't extend to a deadly predator that could pick them up off the ground and carry them away.

Lan, whose horse hadn't so much as twitched in response to the dragon, held his hand out toward the other horses. Although Asher couldn't see his magic, she knew he must have done something because Cloud mellowed beneath her. The other horses calmed in response to the Therion mage's magic too. With a shock of clarity, Asher realized that was why the Magus had sent him: without him, the knights would have been unable to urge their horses close enough to the dragon to use their lances. The entire expedition would have been useless.

Ulu rode forward, joining Lan. He said to the knights, "If you're hurt, come to me immediately. I can heal some injuries, but I can't put your head back on after a dragon's bitten it off, so be careful. Mind the ichor and fire, and you'll have a chance. It's been done before. It can be done."

The dragon lined up for another overflight. Asher realized if they stayed where they were any longer, it might char them all with a single burst of flame as it flew past. The time for fear and doubt had passed. It was time for action. She kicked Cloud in the flanks, sending him galloping forward. First and foremost, she needed to lure the dragon away from the knight commander.

Taz drew level to her on her left while Jazmen took up a position slightly behind to her right.

"What are we going to do?" Taz yelled, his voice muffled by his helmet and the wind carrying his words away.

"I don't know yet," Asher shouted back.

She turned in the saddle to look over her shoulder. As she'd hoped, the dragon had decided to follow the galloping riders, ignoring the knight commander for now. With massive flaps of its black wings, it was quickly gaining on them. It shrieked and let out a blaze of fire. Asher shuddered. She needed to think of a solution. As Ulu said, the Isenii had killed a dragon once. She just had to figure out how.

The dragon overshot the riders, then banked to the right, making a wide arc in front of them. When it reached the halfway point of its circle, it turned to face them head-on. Asher jerked Cloud to a halt, preparing to wheel him to the side if the dragon launched a head-on attack. Visions of burning fire danced in her mind. The last thing she wanted was to charge headfirst into the dragon's flames. Instead of flying at them, however, the dragon fanned out its wings and braked in mid-air, dropping to the ground to land on wickedly taloned back legs. Spreading its inky black wings to their fullest extent and stretching its neck forward, the dragon opened its mouth and unleashed a primal, ear-piercing scream.

The force of the cry was enough to make Asher's heart skip a beat. Even at a distance, she could see the double row of white, dagger-like teeth in the dragon's mouth. The dragon could easily bite Cloud in half. She would be gone in a single swallow. All three destriers reared. Even Lan's magic was insufficient to curb the animals' overriding instinct to get away from danger. Asher's breath came sharp and fast. What to do, what to do?

As she struggled to think of a solution, a massive eagle appeared as a dark dot in the sky above them, flying at top speed toward the dragon. Asher stared at it. Where had it come from? Was the foolish thing really going to attack a dragon? Did it have a nest nearby that it was trying to protect?

The eagle plummeted toward the dragon in a steep dive, streaking through the sky as a brown blur. It pulled up at the last minute to land on the dragon's head above its left eye. Immediately, it clawed and pecked at the eye. The dragon tossed its head, trying to shake the raptor off, but the eagle was persistent, and its long, sharp talons found sufficient purchase on the dragon's bony, ridged head to avoid being cast off straightaway. The dragon took to the air, throwing its head over and over again, mad with pain and desperate to dislodge the bird.

Jazmen cheered. "Get him, Marandir!"

Asher stared at her. "Marandir?"

"He's a shapeshifter, remember? That's the stuff, Marandir!"

Asher blinked. The bird was Marandir? She'd never seen a mage in animal form before. She'd never have known he wasn't a real eagle.

The fight between the dragon and the eagle was short. The dragon was too heavy and too fast—when in a full dive—for Marandir to keep his hold. After a particularly violent toss of its head, Marandir went tumbling end over end behind the dragon's back. The dragon tried to pivot to pursue him but was too slow to turn its bulk. Marandir was long gone by the time it finally turned to look for him. By then, the damage was done. Judging by how the dragon lashed its head and screamed, Marandir had injured—possibly even blinded—it.

An injured dragon was even more dangerous than an undamaged dragon, however. Unable to avenge itself on the bird that had attacked it, it circled back to the knights.

"Scatter!" Jazmen yelled.

At once, the three knights wheeled away from each other, separating just as the dragon's flame scorched the earth where they'd been standing. It was so close Cloud bucked and cow-kicked with his hind leg as though to ward off the heat of the fire. The smell of brimstone burned Asher's nostrils and made her cough.

The dragon swept past them, unable to brake or adjust in time to the unexpected movement of the knights. Asher knew they couldn't evade the dragon forever, but how could they get close enough to it to use their lances when it could carbonize them with one breath? Marandir landed beside her and immediately reverted to his human form. His red hair was damp with sweat. His face was pale.

"We need to find a way to neutralize its fire. Taz, Jazmen, and I can't get close to it otherwise," Asher said.

Marandir's lips pressed into a tight line. "We need to control its head. That's the only way."

"How?"

The dragon swept low and headed toward Jazmen. Seeing it coming, Jazmen kicked her chestnut gelding Songcatcher into a gallop in the opposite direction. Song's flaxen tail flew behind him like a pennant as his body stretched into a single brown line.

Asher's heart leapt into her throat. *No!* With awful realization, she understood they'd been lucky. The dragon was faster than all their horses. That it hadn't scorched them or mauled them on its first few passes had only been chance. But their luck was running out. The dragon easily closed the distance to Song with each beat of its leathery wings.

"No," Asher breathed in horror. "Nononono." She gripped the pommel of her saddle. *Run, Jazmen! Run!*

Jazmen looked back over her shoulder, saw the dragon hot on their heels, and tried to pull Song to the right. But Song couldn't turn on a dime when running full out and so the turn arced wide. The dragon easily tracked the movement. Opening its mouth, it unleashed a massive jet of flame. For a moment, both horse and rider were enveloped by the bright orange and yellow fire.

Asher screamed, closing her eyes. *NO.* Seconds passed and she hoped that if she didn't open her eyes, it wouldn't be real. She couldn't bear for it to be real. But she also couldn't stay frozen or she might be next. She had to open her eyes again.

Marandir's voice next to her was strained. "If we don't find a solution soon…" he trailed off. They would all share Jazmen's fate.

Asher couldn't think about Jazmen. If she thought about Jazmen, she would shut down completely. She wouldn't survive if she thought about what she'd just seen and what it meant. Panic was building in the pit of her stomach, burning like a hot coal. What if there was no way to stop the dragon?

She was breathing so fast it was making her lightheaded. She forced herself to breathe more slowly. What would Tayanna do? What would Commander Bronwen do?

An idea struck her. It was a wild, remote possibility, but it was an idea. And it was likely their only hope. "Marandir, could you become a dragon?"

The mage's face registered surprise. "I…I think so. It's an animal…" And Great Mage Marandir could become any animal.

"If you can gain control of the dragon's head, Taz and I can attack with our lances."

Marandir nodded slowly. "I can try. But I won't be able to stay in such a large form for more than a few minutes. It will exhaust my magic too quickly."

Asher refused to look at the place where she had last seen Jazmen. She didn't want to see, didn't want to know. She would absorb the loss later. Now was not the time. She had to focus. She nodded at Marandir. "Do it."

A haze of dark yellow mist swirled up from the ground around Marandir and grew until it looked like a massive cloud resting on the ground. Cloud snorted and stepped away from it. When the magic dissipated, it revealed a new dragon identical to the one flying overhead. Asher marveled at the similarity. Marandir was indistinguishable from the real dragon. If he was equal in strength, too, could her idea work?

Marandir extended his new wings, testing them. His long black tail swept against the grass as he learned his new body, and he flexed his sharp claws open and closed. This close to him, Asher could see the individual dragon scales, impenetrable as armor. The dragon's leathery belly, however, was smooth and without scales, as the Magus had promised. This was where Asher knew she had to aim her lance. Like any other animal, its heart would surely be in its chest between its forelegs.

Marandir's exploration of his new body was cut short by a scream of challenge from the real dragon, who had noticed the intruder. Lan had warned that dragons were territorial, and this new dragon was a clear rival. The dragon banked into a turn, intent on confronting its unexpected doppelganger. Marandir looked at Asher through yellow eyes and flicked his head to the side. *Go.*

Asher wheeled Cloud to what she hoped was far enough away to be safe from dragon fire but close enough she could engage the dragon with her lance when the time was right. She might only have one opportunity and she didn't want to waste it. She wished she could communicate her plan to Taz, but he was too far away to hear her. She hoped he would figure it out on his own.

The dragon streaked toward Marandir, still screaming. Marandir jumped into the air and beat his wings, trying to gain altitude. He was ungainly and awkward in his new body. When the real dragon got close enough, it opened its mouth and released a stream of blistering fire.

Marandir managed to evade the brunt of it by plunging into a dive. The fire raced harmlessly across his black scales, which Asher guessed were specifically adapted to withstand fire, turning them a sooty gray. Flaring his wings out, he turned and presented his claws to the dragon that, unable to stop, plowed into them. The two locked claws like fighting eagles. The dragon furiously tried to bite Marandir's neck while Marandir used his back legs to slice at its belly. Together they tumbled toward the ground.

Asher sucked in a breath, terrified for Marandir. At the final moment, when it seemed they couldn't avoid crashing into the earth, the two dragons separated. Marandir kicked free with his back legs and arced away from the ground, racing back skyward using the momentum from their fall. Asher could see bright red ichor dripping down his neck from the wound the dragon had made. She hoped he wasn't hurt badly.

"Can Marandir kill the dragon?"

Asher had been so engrossed by the fight that she'd momentarily forgotten Taz. He sat next to her now, his helmet visor tipped up as he watched the drama above.

"Marandir's going to try and restrain the dragon on the ground, then it's up to us to attack it. He doesn't have long in that form. We have to be ready."

Marandir gained just enough distance from the pursuing dragon that when he stopped and inverted, his head down and his tail up, his plunge carried him like an irresistible missile toward the dragon. The dragon didn't have time to evade him. The two collided, tumbling back down toward the earth in an even more dramatic repeat of their previous fall. Only this time, Marandir didn't let go at the last minute. He clutched the dragon tight, digging his claws into the dragon's shoulder and riding it down as he positioned the dragon's body to take the brunt of their impact.

The two crashed into the earth, crumpling into a pile of wings and limbs. For a fraction of an instant, both were still. Asher held her breath without realizing it. Was Marandir okay? Then one of the dragons began to move. It wrapped its neck around that of the other and threw its body back, pulling the second dragon's head backward with him and exposing its chest. But which dragon was which?

Her heart leapt when she saw blood on the neck of the first dragon and the damaged eye of the second. Marandir had done it! This was their chance.

"Now, Taz!"

Asher sank into the saddle and kicked Cloud into action. The dragon bone lance she carried was surprisingly light. She guessed it was hollow, like the bones of a bird. It would have to be, for the dragon to be able to fly. She set the lance home in her armpit and leaned forward. She would only have one chance. She couldn't afford to miss.

The dragon struggled against Marandir, trying to flap its wings and digging its feet into the ground as it wriggled its body. Although Marandir's weight kept it pinned to the ground for now, Asher knew the window to attack was closing. Cloud lowered his head, preparing to charge as he'd been trained to do. Asher shoved her heels down in the stirrups and braced her body for the impact. There was a good chance she'd be swept clear out of her saddle by the force of the hit. She took deep breaths, clearing all thoughts from her mind. There was no room for fear or doubt.

The dragon's body loomed closer. She could see the veins that ran through its thin wings, the sharp claws on the middle joint and at the ends. Her vision scoped down to the spot on its chest between its short arms where she wanted the point of her lance to hit. Too high or too low and the dragon might survive. She had to be precise.

The dragon's arms windmilled as it tried to fight Marandir off. Although it couldn't see her coming—Marandir cranked its head backward so it couldn't roast her with fire—a poorly timed thrash would sweep her lance out of position and dash both her and Cloud to the ground. It would come down to luck.

Three, two, one. Cloud closed the distance in the blink of an eye. The lance point hit the dragon and the blow traveled back up the lance's body and into Asher's own. She was airborne, her body weightless. Cloud was out from under her in an instant, oblivious to the loss of his rider.

Asher hit the ground with a heavy crash, her helmet slamming backward against the grass. Shards of the lance rained down on her, hard white snowflakes. They could only mean only one thing. She had failed.

Chapter 5

"Your petition to be sent to the front is denied. My decision is final."

The knight commander stands and turns her back.

"No! You can't! Please, Commander—"

"The king would never allow the daughter of his favorite chancellor to be sent to the front and put in danger." Commander Bronwen sighs, bows her head for a moment, then turns back around. Her eyes are softer now. "I am sorry for your loss, Asher, but there's nothing I can do."

Asher was momentarily dazed. Stars danced in front of her eyes. She tried to focus, shaking her head to chase the bright white pinpricks of light away. The dragon looming above her bellowed with rage, unleashing a scorching pillar of fire. Because Marandir still had its head and neck twisted backward, the flames raced harmlessly into the sky, but the smell of sulfur filled the air. It signaled clear and imminent danger.

Asher knew she was too close. She had to move. If she didn't, the dragon would soon stomp her—accidentally or not—or break free of Marandir and roast her or bite her in half. Instinct and years of training screamed at her to run. She rolled to her hands and knees, her head still ringing. Everything around her was moving in slow motion. She was sluggish. Her only thought was how she and Taz were running out of time. If they couldn't kill the dragon while Marandir was in dragon form, there was no hope. They would likely all die. And with them, Ilirya's hope for peace.

The memory of what had just happened to Jazmen nudged into her mind, but she pushed it aside. Later. Now was not the time. The pale, jagged pieces of her lance lay around her, shattered and useless. She was too disoriented to worry about how she would fight the dragon without it. She needed to get to safety first, then she could consider what to do.

She ordered herself to move, to get to her feet and run. Then she felt rather than heard the pounding of hooves. Was Cloud returning to her? But Cloud had been trained to run straight after a charge and not to deviate, even if his rider had been unseated in the charge. It couldn't be him.

She looked up and realized with amazement that Fleet was charging the dragon. Taz's lance was lowered and his body braced. Seconds later, his lance struck the dragon square in the chest. It was a perfect, beautiful hit, the kind they'd practiced over and over again as squires against a quintain. As Asher had been, Taz was lifted out of the saddle and thrown violently backward by the force of the blow. But had he been successful? Had he accomplished what Asher had failed to do? For a moment, she couldn't tell.

Fleet raced away as Taz toppled to the ground. *Yes*, Asher realized with growing hope. Whereas her lance had shattered on contact, Taz's had sunk deep, a white pin in a large black pincushion. She didn't know whether it had struck the heart or another vital organ, but there was no doubt that it had struck. Taz landed on the ground, a disorganized pile of metal, as the dragon roared in shock and pain.

Asher scrambled to her feet and ran to him. She grabbed his glove and yanked him to his feet, then began to drag him behind her, away from the dragon. "Run!"

The dragon twisted and thrashed with renewed violence, pawing at the lance and unleashing shrill cries of agony. Red ichor oozed from the wound and down its chest. When it hit the ground, it sizzled, scorching the grass. As the two knights rushed to get away, the dragon lurched forward on unsteady feet. Behind it, Marandir faded behind a wall of yellow mist, his dragon form dissolving as his magic was exhausted. Had Taz attacked seconds later, it would have been too late.

The dragon took several more steps, too preoccupied with the lance to look for its attackers. It snapped its jaws and lashed its head and tail, mad with pain. Then it tilted precariously to one side as its right leg buckled. Unable to right itself and spurting blood, it slowly toppled over, landing heavily on its side and half-crushing its wing. It tried to roar, to defy death with its fearsome voice, but the sound came out choked.

The dragon made no move to rise as its whole body twitched. Its bright yellow eyes turned glassy. Thick red ichor began to bubble from its mouth and nostrils as it gasped with loud, labored breaths. After a brief minute, it was completely still.

Asher and Taz stared at its body, unwilling to move closer.

"I…I think it's dead," Taz whispered.

Asher nodded, taking a deep breath to settle the pounding in her heart. Her hands were shaking, and her mouth was dry. She could still taste and smell the brimstone around her. She had trained for years to ride fearlessly into battle against other knights, to fight and possibly die by the sword. Nothing had prepared her to face a flying lizard the size of a house that could stomp, roast, melt, or eat her. Now that the danger had passed, the fear she'd had to suppress in order to charge it came rushing in to fill the void its death left. It left her weak and trembling.

Marandir staggered toward them, his face bloodless. Asher rushed to him and put her arm under his shoulder, holding him up while Taz took up Marandir's other side. There were deep cuts on Marandir's neck from where the dragon had bitten him while he was in dragon form. They needed to get to Ulu. Who knew how much blood Marandir had lost or how much more he would if the mage healer didn't arrive soon.

"You did it," Marandir croaked, looking back over his shoulder at the dragon's corpse. His lips were almost white as he tried to smile.

"*We* did it," Asher said. "We couldn't have done it without you."

Marandir's face was turning an alarming shade of gray under his beard. Asher had trouble holding him up as he stumbled drunkenly, and his feet began to drag. She stopped and, catching Taz's eye, gently lowered him to the ground. To Asher's relief, Commander Bronwen, Henrek, Ulu, and Lan appeared in the distance, riding hard toward them. Crow was in tow behind Morningstar.

Asher squeezed Marandir's hand. "Hold on. Help is on the way."

When the riders reached them, Ulu yanked his roan to a halt and sprang to the ground. Asher made way for him as he crouched next to the injured mage to heal him. Orange-red magic flowed from his hands and covered Marandir from his shoulders to his head. Marandir's closed eyes fluttered, and his body relaxed as the magic revived him.

Seeing Asher's concerned expression, Ulu said, "He'll recover with no permanent injury."

Nodding, Asher stood and joined Taz beside the knight commander and Henrek. One matter remained. "Jazmen..." She couldn't finish the sentence. The lump in her throat blocked the words.

"I know." Commander Bronwen's voice was soft, her eyes sad.

Taz asked, "What would you like us to do for her, Commander?"

The knight commander's cheek twitched, and Asher recognized the pain of loss crossing her face. But what could they do for Jazmen? She had died in battle and deserved an honorable burial, but they had no shovels, no way to bury her. Could they bring her back to the Isenii village? How? Without looking, Asher knew that what remained of Jazmen was a melted jumble of armor, like a handful of coins half-melted.

Unexpectedly, Lan said, "We will bury her here."

Asher cocked her head, frowning. "But how?"

"Wolves dig, lady knight. My companions will dig a grave for your comrade."

It seemed incredible, the idea of Southerner wolves digging a grave for a fallen Iliryan knight, but what choice did they have? Commander Bronwen nodded. "Thank you."

"I'll get the horses." Henrek's voice was gruff. He wheeled Morningstar around and cantered away, having untied Crow from Morningstar's saddle. Asher noticed the tears in his eyes as he left.

With Jazmen's loss weighing heavily on them, the group was somber. No one spoke, each absorbed by their own thoughts. They rode slowly to where Jazmen and Song had fallen, leaving behind them the dragon with the lance still lodged in its chest. Ulu said the Isenii would come later for its bones. Asher hoped they would never have to use them again. She still didn't understand how the evil of Dark mages in King's City had caused the dragon to be unleashed in the Southlands.

Asher was astounded at how deep and how quickly the wolves dug using only their front paws. She watched them work intently, unable to look at Jazmen's crumpled, melted armor or think about what had happened. It was too awful. And but for chance, it could have been her own grave they were digging. Or Taz's.

"How do we reach Nyara from here?" Commander Bronwen asked Ulu.

"If you ride southeast, you'll reach the road. It runs north-south from the border to Nyara. So long as you travel east, you can't miss it. That will bring you to the capital."

"Are there any more dragons?" Asher didn't miss the sharpness in the knight commander's tone.

Ulu shook his shaggy head. "No, just the one."

"Are there any other dangers we should know about?"

He pursed his lips, eyes troubled. "Perhaps. Dark calls other Darkness to it."

Commander Bronwen looked at him sharply. "What do you mean, Ulu?"

He gazed out over the horizon. "It means Dark things are drawn to Sarsenia like moths to light. The dragon may not be the only Dark thing you encounter on the road to Nyara. You should be careful."

Before he could say anything more, Lan announced, "It is done."

The rough hole was approximately seven feet long by six feet wide and five feet deep. It was an adequate grave, if primitive. No scavenging animal would be able to reach Jazmen's remains. She would lie in peace for eternity. Commander Bronwen nodded to her knights, her face pinched. It was time to give their companion a proper send-off to the Eternal Realms.

Asher, Marandir, Henrek, and Taz dismounted, and the two Isenii retreated on horseback to a respectful distance, the wolves beside them. At the knight commander's signal, Henrek and Taz picked Jazmen up from where she'd fallen free of Song and, as gently as possible, lowered her into the grave. Asher dug her nails into her palms as she fought down bile in her throat. Hot tears burned in her eyes, but she blinked and refused to let them fall.

Jazmen's was the first death she'd ever witnessed. She'd known plenty of knights and soldiers who had died, like Tayanna, far away on campaign at the southern front, but this was the first passing that had occurred right before her eyes. She told herself that as a knight, she shouldn't be rattled by death, but she couldn't help it. During the long days of their journey to the Southlands, Jazmen had become a familiar presence. She'd been mercurial but funny, never taking herself too seriously. Asher couldn't bear to think that this was how she died. Ribald, quick-witted Jazmen had deserved better.

Commander Bronwen maneuvered Ever to stand beside Jazmen's grave. Her face was stoic as she gazed at her companions one by one. "Jazmen would have eschewed sentimentality at her death. She was not a sentimental person. But her sacrifice will not go unrecognized. She will live on in our memory and be remembered among Ilirya's heroes. We shall all meet again in the Eternal Realms one day. Strength and honor."

"Strength and honor," Asher, Taz, and Henrek echoed, heads bowed.

Asher knelt and picked up a handful of loose brown dirt that had been cast beside the grave by the digging wolves. The earth was soft and light in her hand as her fingers closed around it. She stepped forward to the grave and opened her fist, dropping the dirt into it. It made a soft pattering sound as it hit Jazmen's armor, gentle as rain. The other Iliryans followed Asher's lead.

"Lay down your arms now, Jazmen. You're home," Henrek murmured, so softly that Asher barely heard him. He pulled a tenner from somewhere Asher couldn't see and gently tossed the coin into the grave. It landed with a clink. "You were always a lousy bettor. Take that with you to the other side."

Asher put her trembling hand into Taz's and squeezed it, needing to be close to him in this moment of grief. He squeezed back. They both understood what it was to lose someone.

The four re-mounted and returned to their Isenii hosts. As they did, the wolves dashed forward to kick the piles of dirt back over Jazmen's grave. One day, grass would grow back over it, and no one would ever know that in the field there lay an Iliryan knight, buried far from home. Asher whispered a blessing for her.

Ulu said, "Please accept our condolences." His voice was sincere.

Commander Bronwen's face was closed, her jaw clenched. She snapped, "We have held up our end of the bargain. Now it is time for you to hold up yours."

Ulu nodded. "As the Magus has promised, you have Isenii support for peace. May the winds blow in your favor on your trip to Nyara and you return home successful."

In the flickering firelight, the knight commander's face was dark and brooding. Her hair, which Asher had let down for her when they made camp, cascaded over her shoulders, catching and reflecting the reds and oranges of the fire like a torch. Asher thought that although Commander Bronwen might not be considered conventionally beautiful, she was captivating in her own way. She was like the big mountain cats of Rath that Asher had seen in the zoo at King's City: strong, graceful, and intense. Even when cloaked in sorrow, she brimmed with strength. An inextinguishable flame burned within her that could never be dimmed.

After a long day of riding in grim silence, the group, now a mere five strong to carry Ilirya's heavy hopes for peace, had made camp. Henrek had disappeared immediately—Asher couldn't guess to where—while Taz and Marandir had wrapped themselves in their cloaks and promptly gone to sleep, leaving Asher and the knight commander alone at the fire. Commander Bronwen was propped against her saddle to keep her upright. She was so motionless that if not for her open eyes, Asher might have assumed that she, too, had fallen asleep. Asher wondered what she was thinking. Did she wish she'd pushed back harder against the Magus?

Without looking at her, Commander Bronwen said, "Asher, I intend to see this expedition through until the end. That includes the return of myself and everyone else who is here now to King's City. But if neither Henrek nor I make it, it will fall to you to tell Jazmen's daughter of her mother's passing. The Majordomo will know how to reach her."

Asher's eyes widened. "Her daughter? But Jazmen said—"

Commander Bronwen closed her eyes briefly. "We all make choices. Sacrifices for the knighthood. Jazmen was a knight first and foremost. She did not see her daughter often. As a result, I do not know if her daughter will care that her mother has passed. Forgiveness can be a hard thing. But she should know, in any case. Someone must tell her."

A wave of sorrow swept over Asher. In the blink of an eye, she relived all the loss she'd experienced over the years, all the people in her life who had died. How would she ever bear more losses? If they couldn't stop the wars threatening to engulf Ilirya, how could she say goodbye to knight after knight, year after year? And what if it had been Taz and not Jazmen who had been killed?

"How do you do it, Commander? She was your friend, wasn't she?" The knight commander hadn't shed a single tear for their fallen comrade. How did she beat back the emotions that she was surely feeling? Or did she feel nothing after so many years of war? Could a person become numb to death?

Commander Bronwen stared long and hard at the fire. "Yes, Jazmen was a friend, and I do not have many left after a lifetime of war. But she died exactly as she would have wanted—fighting. Jazmen loved being a knight. Riding into battle was her greatest pleasure in life, and she was willing to give up everything else for it. Even her daughter. She knew all of us will be called by Death eventually. She answered on horseback, lance in hand."

Commander Bronwen paused, then smiled fondly. "She always said the knighthood would be the death of her. I think she would have been disappointed if she'd lived to retire." Her large, round blue eyes met Asher's. They were sad. "We spent many campaigns together, she and I, when we were younger. Her loss creates a gap that can never be filled. I will miss her dearly."

Her eyebrows twitched, and the corner of her mouth twitched to suppress a chuckle. "She's a handful, you know. Death may send her back to us after all. Henrek always told her she was just the type to get stuck in your craw, like a chicken bone. Maybe Death won't be able to swallow her and will spit her back out."

Then her face fell again, the weight of the kingdom on her shoulders. "How do I do it? By honoring the sacrifice she has made and her decision to make it. I wish Jazmen were here with us now, recounting with much cursing and hyperbole how she almost died today, but her sacrifice, her death, keeps the hope of peace alive. We will continue on to Nyara, now with the support of one of the Southerner tribes. If we succeed in winning peace, her death will save thousands of Iliryans. It will save Ilirya itself."

Asher nodded. "The greater good."

The precept of always acting for the greater good was a key tenet of the knighthood, taught from the time knights were pages. The greater good placed the well-being of society above any individual's need. Dedication to the greater good is what separated knights from civilians. The former acted selflessly while the latter acted selfishly. To that end, a good knight would gladly sacrifice their life to benefit the greater good. A single life was a small price to pay to save that of thousands.

Commander Bronwen nodded. "Jazmen believed in peace. That's why she joined this expedition when few others would. Like all of us, she lost many friends in the war. She was willing to die so that her grandchildren wouldn't be fighting the Southerners too."

The knight commander fell silent and stared into the fire for a long time, her eyes sparkling with unshed tears. She smoothed her deep-blue tunic over her thigh as well as she could with her left hand, pushing back against whatever thoughts were troubling her. "A leader must learn to compartmentalize sorrow, or it will become overwhelming. I have known every knight who has died in the last thirty or so years. And now, as knight commander, I am responsible for every death that occurs as a result of my direction. It is a heavy grief to bear."

Asher hadn't thought about it that way before. She'd always blamed the Southerners for the deaths of the knights who fought them, not the commander. But it was true she had ordered them to fight. If not for their orders to deploy to the southern front, they would still be alive. Even Tayanna. But she couldn't blame the commander for that. She was only doing what was necessary to keep Ilirya safe.

Commander Bronwen continued, "The knight commander may mourn the deaths of her knights, but she must be strong enough to send them into battle even knowing the cost. Ultimately, she must accept responsibility for both the lives of her knights and their deaths. It is a very great responsibility indeed. There are few people who are strong enough to bear the burden of it."

Asher bowed her head. The fierce passion in the knight commander's voice reminded her so much of Tayanna.

"A real knight understands the meaning of sacrifice," Tayanna had declared.

Still a squire, Asher hadn't understood her at the time. She thought Tayanna was being melodramatic. Now she was learning. Sacrifice took many forms. Jazmen's relationship with her daughter. Tayanna's life.

Tayanna had always understood all its facets. She would have made a good knight commander one day. Asher could picture her standing beside the queen, her back straight and her eyes fixed ahead. Tayanna had been born to lead. But Tayanna was dead and all her potential lost with her. How many other bright futures had been snuffed out during the forty years of war?

Commander Bronwen sighed. "Leaders are not leaders by virtue of being the best fighters. They are leaders because they see the entirety of the battlefield, from each individual soldier to the whole of the army. Every person counts. A bad leader does not hesitate to send knights to their deaths. A bad leader sleeps soundly at night. A good leader, however, knows that each death takes with it a part of her soul and still she sends her knights anyway because that is the price that must be paid."

She leaned her head back, gazing at the thousands of stars twinkling above them. "I remember every one of them, Asher. And I honor their sacrifices. They did not die in vain."

True to Ulu's word, they encountered the road to Nyara the next morning. Asher was glad to be on it once more. Everyone was dealing with the shock of unexpectedly losing Jazmen in their own way. Taz was chattering away to her as though he needed to use all the words he knew before sundown, Henrek was acting belligerent and short-tempered—when he wasn't being sullen and brooding—Commander Bronwen was silent, and Marandir was scouting far ahead in the form of a raven. Asher hoped that the rest of the journey would be uneventful. Already a small delegation, they couldn't afford to lose anyone else.

The group traveled on the road for three days without seeing anything but trees and prairie around them. Asher was continually amazed by how empty the land was around them. Unlike in Ilirya, there were no rest houses along the route, no villages to pass through. There were no merchant caravans journeying from one town to another with wagons stacked full of wares, no travelers with heavy packs voyaging to parts unknown. There weren't even farms or pasturelands on which grazed half-dozing cows, sheep, or goats. It was, as Henrek announced loudly on the second day after their battle with the dragon, spookily uninhabited.

"Where are all the Southerners?" he demanded. "There are plenty enough of them at the front. Where do they all *live*?"

None of them knew, and there was no one to ask. Were the Southlands so vast there were large, unoccupied spaces between Southerner habitations?

Parts of Ilirya were sparsely inhabited; perhaps the same was true of the Southlands. Or could it be that whatever its size, much of its population was squeezed into only a few key areas? Asher wished they'd been able to ask more questions of the Isenii. In retrospect, it seemed imprudent to have pushed ahead alone after Jazmen's death and not returned to the Isenii village to query them about the Southlands and the other tribes.

Lady Avrill, for whom she had squired, would have been displeased. "Only a fool runs into battle without a plan," she used to tell Asher.

Their desire to flee the scene of their tragedy and be free of the cause of their sorrow had overcome their good sense. They were paying for it now. They didn't even know how long it would take to reach Nyara.

By the morning of the fourth day, the grass around them had begun to thin out, revealing reddish, clay-like dirt beneath. The trees gave way to a thin, pale green scrub brush that speckled the ground in uneven clusters. At last, what looked like miniaturized mountains appeared on the horizon, tall and dramatic and red. Asher was amazed. This new land was like nothing she'd ever seen before.

"Reminds me a bit of Rath," Marandir said.

"It's beautiful," Taz marveled.

Asher agreed, craning her neck to take it all in. She'd been raised in the northeast quarter of King's City, surrounded by the city's tightly packed houses and buildings. She was used to the bustle of city life, the sound of wagon wheels on cobblestones, the booming cry of vendors hawking their wares to passersby, and the smell of food cooking on the street. Compared to what she knew, the soaring red and brown rock all around them could have come from the fantastical stories her father told her growing up.

The group arrived at the edge of a cliff right as the sun was setting. From their high vantage point, they could see across a seemingly endless valley, from which rose rocky outcroppings like crumbled towers. The dying rays of the sun painted the sky exotic blues, purples, and pinks unlike any Asher had ever seen in Ilirya. The splendor of it took her breath away. If she were a painter, she doubted she'd ever find the colors to reproduce what was before her eyes.

Marandir returned to the group from his reconnaissance flight and landed at the horses' feet, transforming in the blink of an eye from a black crow into a tall man. Unfolding himself, he reported, "The valley ahead continues as far as I could see. I found a small stream some ways off the road, but otherwise it's a deserted land where little life flourishes. We'll be hard pressed to find food and water here."

"At least there are no dragons, even if we'll be hungry," Taz said.

"We'll make camp here for the night. With no wood to burn, we'll have to go without a fire. Asher, you take first watch," Commander Bronwen ordered.

Asher was about to agree when Henrek made a strangled sound and convulsed in his saddle. As the others turned to watch, he went still. His body slumped over his saddle, his chin sinking onto his chest.

"Henrek?" Commander Bronwen's voice was full of concern.

He jerked to attention, his body straightening, and turned in his saddle to look at her. His face, which had been stormy all day, now looked severe, his eyes unusually hawkish. The hairs on Asher's arms stood on end beneath her armor. Something wasn't right.

Henrek stared at each of the members of the expedition in turn as if seeing them for the first time. He appeared to be assessing them. "Who are you and why do you seek to enter the Hollow Lands?" His imperious voice both was and was not Henrek's.

"He's been warged!" Marandir cried, drawing his sword. His narrowed eyes were locked on Henrek as he took a step toward him.

A thrill of surprise coursed through Asher's body. Wargs were mages able to take control of the body of another person, effectively turning them into puppets. In war, they could use these human puppets to spy on or attack the enemy. It was impossible to dislodge a warg once they had taken over. They would only relinquish the body if they no longer needed it or if the body was killed. Many Iliryan fighters—knights and soldiers alike—had been forced to execute their friends and comrades after Southern mages had warged them to attack their own side. It was an Iliryan's worst nightmare. If anyone could recognize a warg, it was Marandir, who had spent several campaigns at the front.

Asher and Taz exchanged horrified glances. Neither wanted to have to kill Henrek. It was bad enough to have lost Jazmen to a dragon. Having to kill a member of their party might be even worse. But how could they get the warg to relinquish him?

Commander Bronwen glared at Henrek-who-was-not-Henrek. "Who are *you*?"

"I am the Guardian," Henrek—or rather, the Guardian—said. "I am the protector of the Maji."

"I suppose that is one of the five Sarsen tribes?"

"It is."

Asher looked around but saw no one for as far as the eye could see. Where was the Guardian? She vaguely remembered from her lessons as a squire that a warg had to be within eyesight to warg someone. Where could the Guardian be hiding?

Commander Bronwen said, "In that case, I am Lady Bronwen, Knight Commander of Ilirya. My companions and I are traveling to Nyara on behalf of Queen Alea of Ilirya. We request safe passage through your lands on our way to the capital."

The Guardian shook their head—Henrek's head. "You must not enter the Hollow Lands." The words were laced with deep foreboding.

"The Hollow Lands?" Marandir asked.

"This valley." The Guardian indicated with Henrek's hand the land that lay before them. "It is not safe for travelers to pass through."

"In that case, how are we to reach Nyara? Is there another way?" Commander Bronwen asked.

"No. The only way to Nyara is through the Hollow Lands."

The commander's eyes glinted with determination. "Then we have no choice but to cross the valley. Our mission is of the utmost importance. We cannot turn back. My companions are skilled. They will defend against whatever danger lies on the road."

"If you set foot in the valley, you will all die. Since the return of Dark Magic to the world, the Hollow Lands have been infested with wights. They will destroy you."

What, Asher wondered, *is a wight?*

Chapter 6

"It's best to stay out of politics," Lady Avrill says. "Trying to chart the course of the kingdom is like holding the wrong end of a torch. You'll only be burned."

"It didn't burn my father," Asher retorts, feeling rebellious. She has just turned fifteen and her father is dying.

"An exception. Not the rule."

"What are wights, Guardian?" Commander Bronwen's red brows were knitted together.

Asher guessed she was calculating. How much danger was an acceptable risk to her delegation? With only five members remaining, they had to be careful. They couldn't afford to act rashly. At the same time, they had little choice. They *had* to cross the valley. They had to reach Nyara, and soon.

The Guardian gazed out across the valley through Henrek's eyes, surveying it. Looking for wights, perhaps, whatever they were. Nothing moved as far as the eye could see, however. The land was still and lifeless, just as Marandir had reported it was. The sun had dipped below the horizon, leaving a midnight blue night sky in its wake. Even this color was exotic and beautiful.

The Guardian—Asher caught herself assuming it was a man just because the warg was using Henrek's body and stopped herself—looked back to Commander Bronwen. "Wights are evil creatures. They are corpses whose spirits long ago left for the Eternal Realms. They are decaying, twisted reflections of the people they used to be. Skin and eyes rotted away, they are ghoulish, unrecognizable approximations of humans."

"Wights exist only to destroy life. They are drawn to living things and attack them mercilessly. If they had minds left, I would say they are jealous of that spark of vitality that burns inside the chest of every living thing and desire nothing more than to tear it out and extinguish it. But they are mindless monsters. There are no thoughts or feelings in them."

The description made Asher's skin prickle.

"If they are spiritless corpses, what compels them?" Commander Bronwen asked.

"They are animated by Dark Magic." Henrek's eyes closed for a moment. When they opened, they were heavy with sadness and regret. "Ever since a gash was torn in the fabric of the world, wights have been converging on the Hollow Lands. There are hundreds if not thousands of them here now, and more come by the day. It is unsafe for the Maji to go near the valley, and I fear that in time, the wights will spill out of the Hollow Lands and into our camps."

Asher shivered, unwillingly remembering the sight of the rebellious One God, his tumescent, headless white body motionless on the dais next to King Hap's throne in the Great Hall. The swirling black vortex of Dark Magic that had pierced the veil between the two worlds—and then became the instrument of his destruction—closed above him and disappeared. The bodies of the king and all his court were strewn around the Great Hall like flowers uprooted and scattered by a storm, the bodies of the god's acolytes cut down during the battle to stop his entry seeded among them. The god's attempt to enter the mortal plane and rule there may have been stopped, but the shockwaves of the event still resonated even months later.

It was *her* people, the Iliryans, who had torn the hole in the world. *They* were responsible for the dragon and now the wights ravaging the Southlands. But how? How had that brief breach between the mortal and divine realms far away in King's City resulted in the plague of monsters here? It didn't make sense.

The Guardian motioned to the valley. "This is why if you try to cross the Hollow Lands, the wights will destroy you. There are too many to fight, and you are few in number. They will swallow you up. No trace will be left of you."

"There must be a way." Commander Bronwen said. "How does one kill a wight?"

"The only way to stop a wight is to decapitate it. No heart pumps blood in the wights' veins, nor do they draw breath in their lungs, so dismemberment or puncture will not deter them. Nor do they feel pain."

Commander Bronwen squinted into the distance. "How wide is the valley?"

"It would be a day and a half's ride if you risk breaking your horses' wind and gallop the whole way. But the wights come out at night, and you'll have to go slowly then, or you'll risk breaking your horses' legs too. The Hollow Lands have plenty of holes and rocks that will trip or lame a horse."

"I think we can beat back a few corpses," Taz scoffed.

"You underestimate the peril." The Guardian shook a finger. "In the blackness of desert night, you won't see the wights until they're already upon you. Like a pack of wild dogs, they'll descend on you and tear you to shreds. The last thing you'll see is their grinning skulls coming out of the dark at you, and then it will be too late."

Asher swallowed. She didn't like that image at all.

"Where did the wights come from?" Marandir's head was cocked, his face curious.

"Throughout all the Southlands, we believe. Some come here wearing the armor and trappings of centuries past, only a few strands of hair still clinging to their eyeless, skinless skulls. Others are from a much more recent time. From the graves they once occupied, they have walked, crawled and dragged themselves across our lands to reach this place, attacking anything human or animal they encountered on their way."

"Why here?"

"We do not know. The Hollow Lands are too barren to sustain most life. Perhaps there is something present here—invisible to our eyes—that calls to them."

"We must cross." Commander Bronwen's tone was abrupt and decisive. "If this is the only way to Nyara, then there is no alternative, no matter the danger. We will make camp here tonight and set off with the sunrise."

The Guardian appraised her hawkishly. "If you are determined to continue, I wish you luck. But be warned: do not look to the Maji for help if you fall into difficulty, for no help will come to you. You are on your own."

In an instant, the Guardian was gone. The tension that had filled Henrek's face turned to slack and the knight, disoriented and confused, looked half-dazed at his companions out of his own eyes once more. His hands found his face and his fingers rubbed his eyes as though he could wipe away the memory of the Guardian's presence in his mind. Asher imagined it hadn't been pleasant to be warged. He grunted. "Augh. That was terrible. I'm glad he's gone."

"Are you sure you want to continue, knowing what awaits us, Commander?" Marandir asked.

Commander Bronwen's face as she looked over her diminished delegation was fierce with resolve. "We have no choice. We will continue making camp here. In the morning, we will enter the valley. Sleep well tonight. You will need it."

Tayanna is buckling Asher's spurs over her sabatons, the plated armor that fits snugly over her boots. They're short spurs, intended more for decoration than real use, but they're one of the symbols of knighthood, and on this day, the day of her knighting, Asher is proud to don them. It's the first of several traditions she will experience today, and a swell of pride washes over her looking at them. They're a gift from Tayanna. Inscribed on the outside of the arms are Asher's initials. On the inside, Tayanna had her own initials carved. It's a secret only the two of them will know, a frivolity that Avrill would have rebuked, but it means that wherever they are, they will always be together. It's exactly the sort of thing Tayanna would think to do.

Tayanna runs her hands with practiced experience up the back of Asher's legs, feeling to make sure the greaves, poleyns, and cuisses are all buckled neatly in place. Asher relishes the feeling of Tayanna's agile fingers brushing over her, the rushing in her chest that catches at her breath and steals it away. She will never tire of Tayanna's touch, even when Tayanna doesn't mean it to be anything but business-like. Her heart is overflowing with pride that Tayanna is the one preparing her to be knighted. Now they will be knights together—true equals. They can go on campaign together in the south or ride the circuit around the kingdom, but no matter what, it will be the two of them together. Always and forever.

Asher knows she's dreaming again. The knighting ceremony was a year and a half ago. Although she recognizes this is a memory and nothing more, she doesn't care. If she can see Tayanna again in her dreams, she never wants to wake. She'll stay forever dreaming. The day of her knighting was the proudest, happiest day of her life. If she could live in a memory, this is the memory she would choose. It was the day when everything was perfect.

The tasset—a sort of metal skirt that will protect the top of her thighs when mounted—squeaks quietly as Asher leans forward, catching Tayanna's attention. Understanding what Asher wants, Tayanna stands and kisses her lightly, but then returns immediately to her work checking the straps on Asher's cuirass, drawing a childish pout from Asher.

"If you're late, I'll never hear the end of it," Tayanna says.

She turns to retrieve Asher's sword from where it lies on Asher's bed. It's a beautiful piece of metalwork, a gift from her father, Lord Chancellor Ivar. When Asher became a squire, he commissioned its fabrication from the most reputed swordsmith in King's City. It had taken months to make and cost more than many of the city's citizens would earn in a lifetime, but he had been determined that his daughter would have the best protection that his money could buy once she became a knight.

It would end up being the last gift he gave her. He died only a few weeks after commissioning it and never saw the finished product. Asher treasures it as a posthumous reminder of his love for her. Although he, like her mother, worried about her becoming a knight, he wanted her to follow her passion. He was proud of her.

Her family's crest, a black boar on a field of red, is set in ruby in the pommel. Unique in the kingdom, her sword will be instantly recognizable as hers to anyone who knows her family. Should she fall in battle, it will help identify her. Even though the sword was finished years ago, today is the first time she'll be able to belt it to her side, another tradition.

Asher sighs petulantly, trying to cross her arms over her cuirass, but her armor makes the action awkward and uncomfortable. She lets her arms fall as Tayanna wraps her sword belt around her. The belt is flat and plain, but the scabbard that hangs from it is extremely detailed, befitting the sword sheathed within. It has a royal blue, hand-stitched leather exterior embossed to look like vines twining from one end to the other. Her family crest is prominently displayed on the scabbard's gold throat.

Although both sword and scabbard are a reminder of Asher's roots, as a knight, she serves her kingdom first and foremost, not her family, and she must never forget it. She has forsaken the life of a noble in return for becoming a protector of the realm. Strength and honor, duty and king. She believes in the creed wholeheartedly.

Tayanna straightens and looks at Asher, pride glimmering in her dark eyes. Her white, heart-shaped face is slightly flushed with happiness. Her armor has been polished to a brilliant shine for the knighting ceremony. She wears it naturally, like a second skin. As though she was born wearing it. She is strong and fearless, and Asher hopes one day she will be half as good a knight. Tayanna takes Asher's face in her hands and tilts Asher's head down so that she can kiss her forehead. Her lips are soft. She whispers, "My brave knight. I couldn't be more proud of you."

It should sound funny coming from Tayanna, who Asher believes is the bravest knight in all Ilirya, but it doesn't. Instead, a glow of warmth fills her from the top of her head to the tips of her toes. To be a knight is all she's ever wanted, from the time she was a young girl barely able to walk, and today she'll see her dream realized. She might as well be floating on air. She only wishes her father could be there to see it.

Tayanna gives her a quick peck on the lips. "I'll see you soon. You look…ravishing."

She slips out of the room, leaving Asher alone. Ten minutes later, there's a knock at her door and a dour-faced servant in Iliryan blue livery announces the time has come for the knighting ceremony. Asher is so overcome with emotion her hands are shaking, so she hooks her thumbs into her sword belt to steady them. She hopes she doesn't look as flushed as she feels.

She and the servant exit the garrison and walk across the green toward the palace. It's a beautiful summer day. The sun is shining, and the world is overflowing with hope and happiness. Asher feels as if she could stop and breathe in with one giant breath all the beauty and wonder in Ilirya, but they can't be late. The servant leads them through a side door and up a set of narrow stone stairs that spits them out into the antechamber of the Great Hall, where petitioners to the king usually wait to be heard. The antechamber's walls are lined with huge tapestries depicting the history of the Lamid monarchs. Everything is meant to awe and impress the king's visitors, but Asher, who has seen them many times before, is too distracted to pay them attention.

She knows what lies through the massive double doors to the Great Hall: the king and his court, all waiting. For her. Asher is the daughter of the king's favorite chancellor. Many of the kingdom's notables will be in attendance to see her knighted out of deference to his memory. The thought that so many people respected her father gives her comfort. Although he's gone, his memory lives on through the court…and through her. She raises her chin. She will make him proud.

The servant cracks one of the doors open, whispers something to whomever is on the other side, and a moment later both doors sweep open, revealing Asher on one side, the full royal court on the other. Asher takes a deep breath, then steps into the Great Hall. Her heart is beating wildly. There's no reason to be nervous, and yet she is. With so many eyes upon her, she is terrified of making a mistake.

As she walks down the aisle to the dais where King Hap sits on his throne, her eyes dart around the room, identifying attendees. Iowin, the wiry, lithe captain of the King's Guard, stands flanking the king on his right side, while Knight Commander Bronwen stands to his left. Lady Marshal Heika leans casually against a balustrade, her green-clothed form tall and muscular. The solid, sleepy-eyed head of the Mages' Council, Garreth, stands near to the dais conversing with two mages in heavy maroon robes. Asher recognizes a handful of barons and baronesses from the baronies around King's City mixed among the dozens of nameless courtiers, as is the king's spymaster, Zaphrys, whom Asher has only seen once.

Asher knows that in the present time, only Commander Bronwen and Zaphrys remain of all the people in the room on that day. All the others were cut down during the Night of the Long Swords and the assault against the palace that followed. The people before her on this day are, although they don't know it yet, ghosts. A shiver of sadness and regret runs down her spine at the sight of them so full of life in her dream, but her sorrow for them doesn't belong in this memory so she lets it dissolve away from her. This is a happy memory, and she is determined for it to remain that way.

She catches sight of an unfamiliar face in the crowd and frowns. She doesn't remember him at her knighting. Who is he? His face is long, too rugged to be handsome, and he has deep set hazel eyes. He looks foreign, not Iliryan. When he notices Asher looking at him, he slips between two courtiers and disappears.

Asher doesn't have time to dwell on the stranger. She sees Tayanna standing at the front of the room, next to where she'll kneel to be knighted, and has to stifle the smile of pure joy trying to break out across her face. Tayanna looks so noble and dashing in her armor that Asher doesn't know if she's more proud to be standing in the Great Hall about to be knighted by the king or that of anyone in the kingdom, Tayanna chose *her*. Tayanna winks at her, and Asher forces herself to look away or she will be lost in Tayanna's dancing smile.

Standing next to Tayanna are Avrill and Sir Idras, the two knights for whom she squired. Avrill has a small smile on her face. Asher knows she's pleased with herself. Asher is her third squire, and all of them have advanced to become knights. She is trusted by the knight commander to develop and nurture fine warriors, and Asher will be the latest example of her reliability.

Avrill is dwarfed by Idras, whose hulking body is made even larger by his armor. His gray beard, wild and unkempt as always, spills halfway down his chest. Asher only spent a year with him as his squire before she was reassigned to Avrill, but she has a fondness for the giant. His ebullient energy is infectious to anyone who spends more than a few minutes with him. A gambler and a braggart, he is almost the opposite of everything she would expect of a knight, and yet somehow he has carved out a place for himself in the knighthood. Moreover, it is he who has claimed the right to give Asher her first destrier, which she will receive from him later today in private.

Catching her eye, he grins and mouths, "Good on you, lassie."

A herald announces Asher to the king, but she barely registers her voice. She's focused on the two people on the dais who alone matter of everyone in the room: King Hap and Commander Bronwen. The knight commander stands erect and proud at the king's side, her bright red hair braided back behind her shoulders and her right hand on the pommel of her sword. At six feet tall, she is imposing in her dress armor, which twinkles in the yellow light that falls into the Great Hall from the tall windows on both sides.

Through everything that happens later, this is how Asher will always remember her: the resplendent embodiment of knighthood at the pinnacle of its vigor. There is no question how she rose to become the knight commander. She is noble and strong and dynamic. Ilirya's knights would follow her anywhere. As head of the knighthood, it is she who will lead the knighting, with the king stepping in only at the final moment. Although the knights of Ilirya obey the king, their oath is technically not to him but to the land and its people. There is a beauty to being a servant not of a single person, but of an entire kingdom.

Asher is mere feet away from the king when she stops walking. Up close, she can see the gray hairs that have begun to grow in the black dreadlocks on his head. Yet although his close-cropped beard is almost completely gray, his dark face seems ageless. He could be forty years old or he could be eighty. If she didn't know, she wouldn't be able to guess. He wears thick gold chains that hang over his fitted leather jerkin, which is dyed deep Iliryan blue, and a cloak is draped behind him with the splendor of a peacock despite the summer heat. On his head rests the royal crown of Ilirya, dramatic and shining.

Asher kneels before him, dropping her head in obeisance as she's been trained to do. When she looks up at him, he's smiling at her benevolently, and she knows he sees in her face the memory of her father. Commander Bronwen steps forward so she is closer to Asher but not directly in front of the king. Her face is impassive as it looks out across the Great Hall and then back again to Asher. It is unusual to have so many spectators for a knighting, and certainly so many of the city's notables. She draws herself up, preparing for what is to come next.

"Asher of King's City, daughter of Ivar, also of King's City," she omits the honorific titles that Asher and her father would normally be accorded because as a knight, Asher is an equal to all her peers, "you stand before the king and his court today in supplication. You seek to become a knight in the service of Ilirya. To fight and perhaps die for your country. Do you come willingly, of sound mind and without coercion?"

"I do."

"Being a knight requires sacrifice and hardship. It requires selflessness. Do you vow to defend this kingdom and protect her citizens, putting the good of Ilirya above all else from now on? To always place concern for the welfare of others over concern for yourself?"

"I do."

"Do you vow to abandon all claim to luxury and title in favor of a life of austerity and humility? To act with honor and justice at all times?"

"I do."

"Do you vow to defend your fellows and never flee the field of battle? To go where commanded and fight until victory is achieved no matter the cost?"

"I do."

The knight commander nods, her mouth set in a thin line. "Then with these vows made, I hereby accept you into the knighthood. May you bring honor to yourself and the order and always walk the path of righteousness."

She draws her sword, which sings as it clears its plain black scabbard. The sound is as loud as a clap of thunder to Asher, whose entire body is tingling with anticipation and eagerness. This is the moment she's waited for all her life. Commander Bronwen turns a quarter turn and at the same time pivots her sword so the flat of the blade rests in her hands. This is so the king can easily take it from her, which he does after he rises from the throne. He walks forward and descends the dais so that he is on the same level as Asher. Asher bows her head respectfully, still kneeling.

"Your father would be proud," King Hap says in a voice that only she and the knights around her can hear. "He was a good man. I'm sure that you, too, will serve the kingdom well."

He raises the sword and taps Asher once on each shoulder. "Arise, Lady Asher."

The dream slipped away like a fish through water and was gone. Its end was so abrupt Asher couldn't even grasp for it to try and keep it. It was gone in the blink of an eye.

Her sleep was shattered by a soft moaning that pulled her fully back to consciousness. Instantly on alert, she looked around for danger while reaching for the scabbard that lay on the ground by her side. But the sound was only the knight commander, whose head thrashed violently from side to side in her sleep.

Asher crawled on her knees to the commander and held her shoulder down. "Shhh. It's a dream, Commander, that's all."

Commander Bronwen whimpered, still asleep, but seemed to settle. Asher sat down next to her, drawing her knees to her chest and watching where the sun would rise. At the edges of the horizon, the sky was starting to turn from black to gray. The stars, too, thousands of white pinpricks of light, were fading. There was no use trying to fall back asleep. It would be daylight soon enough and then it would be time to go.

She looked around at her companions. Taz was sprawled on his stomach, his hair sticking out from his head like dry straw as he wrapped his arms around the bundle of clothing he was using as a pillow. Marandir had rolled himself so totally in his blanket that all Asher could see was a shapeless lump of dark fabric, with no sign of his distinctive flame red hair. Henrek, however, was awake and watching her. He'd drawn the last watch of the night.

"You were dreaming too, weren't you?" he asked when their eyes met. He gestured at the sleeping figures. "They all are. I can tell. Your friend Taz has been laughing his head off. Whatever he's dreaming, it must be a real laugh."

He shook his head, his expression pensive. "You know, I never dreamed before coming here to the Southlands. Now every night I dream. It's odd, isn't it, how a new place can unlock old memories? Even some I thought I'd forgotten long years ago."

Were his happy or sad memories? His face was unreadable. Asher didn't know what to say, so she asked instead, "What was it like to be warged?"

Henrek spat on the ground. "Like a kitten whose mother has picked it up by the scruff of the neck and is dragging it around. That Guardian fellow was gentle, I suppose, but imagine suddenly being locked out of your own body and all you can do is feel it acting without you."

Asher could easily imagine it. She hoped she would never be warged. It sounded immensely unpleasant, even if the Guardian had only done it to communicate with them. She wondered once more how far away he was. Could he really have warged Henrek from miles away? How many?

Henrek looked at Commander Bronwen, who, although she was still now, had a grimace on her face. His own face became troubled. "I hope we reach Nyara soon. The commander hasn't got much time left."

Asher started. "What do you mean?"

He waved in the knight commander's direction. "She hides it well, but the Dark Magic is eating her up inside. The mind can only drive the body for so long before there's nothing left. Her body is crumbling beneath her. She should have stayed in King's City, but that's the commander for you. No one can tell her what to do."

Asher's mouth was dry. "But—but she's..."

Asher didn't know what to say. She remembered what Lyse had told her: "The longer your journey, the worse her pain will get." Although she had given Lyse's brown leather pouch of painkilling herbs to the commander, looking at Commander Bronwen's face, she realized Henrek was right. The pain was starting to become a relentless constant for their leader, even if she hadn't uttered so much as a single word about it. Her face was pale and drawn even in sleep. Asher didn't know what would happen if...she couldn't finish the thought. There simply was no way the knight commander wouldn't lead them all the way to Nyara. She had to.

Henrek shrugged. "She won't leave the Southlands and she knows it. But then, it's what she chose. She could have sent anyone in her place, but she didn't. She wanted to go out on her own terms. That's the commander through and through."

Asher bit the inside of her lip, pushing back against the tears pooling in her eyes. She wanted him to be wrong, but she knew he was right. Commander Bronwen was fading fast. They were running out of time.

She thought of Jazmen, who would never come home from the Southlands either. There would be two Iliryans buried in the Southlands. Asher realized that although he didn't talk about it, Henrek was still mourning her loss. She knew from their conversations that they had known each other for decades and had each other's backs at the southern front more than once. "I'm sorry about Jazmen."

Henrek's shoulders slumped. "We all die eventually." His voice was rough. He didn't meet her eyes.

Asher opened her mouth to offer him consolation when she saw movement out of the corner of her eye. She didn't have time to turn her head before something barreled into her, knocking her over. Air rushed out of her lungs as she landed heavily. She rolled, grappling with her attacker as they tried to pin her to the ground. Long, skeletal fingers with nails like claws raked at her face. She batted them away at the last minute and pushed against the ground with her legs, trying to unseat whatever was lying on top of her by bucking her hips, but the attacker clung desperately to her, and she couldn't dislodge them.

A moment later, the weight was lifted as Henrek kicked the attacker off of her.

She rolled in the other direction and scrambled to her feet. "What is *that*?"

"If I had to guess, I'd say that's a wight."

Henrek assumed a fighter's crouch next to her, his sword drawn and held at the ready. Asher wished she had her sword, too, but she'd left it next to her bedroll when she'd crawled to Commander Bronwen. In fact, she was completely unarmored, since she slept in only trousers and a shirt. Blood pounded in her veins, making her ears ring.

The wight floundered to its knees and slowly stood, swaying slightly during the transition. Asher stifled a gasp of horror and revulsion. It was more than a skeleton, less than a corpse. Where its face should have been, there were gaping eye sockets and a nose hole. Its yellow teeth were broken and jagged. Here and there, patches of desiccated white skin hung half-peeled from its skull. Long, thin black hair fell sparsely from the top of its head. The creature wore the remains of a black jacket, moldered and tattered, and long black trousers that half hid the wight's partially mummified feet. Although it had once been human, it was human no longer.

Asher realized why they hadn't seen it coming. In the darkness of the pre-dawn, the wight blended in seamlessly with its surroundings. Nor did it wear any metal whose clanking might give it away. It moved with the quiet rustle of fallen leaves. Even so, Asher cursed herself for letting it get so close to them. This was the second time the Southlands had caught them unawares, and she didn't like it.

Henrek waved her back. "I can handle this."

The wight lifted its bony white arms as if it intended to either grab or strangle the two knights, but before it could get within arm's length, Henrek had already sprung into action. His sword moving so quickly Asher couldn't see it in the dim light, he severed the wight's head from its body. It dropped to the ground, landing with a dull thwack. The body stood a moment longer, appearing almost indecisive, then collapsed silently into a lifeless pile. The engagement had lasted only a few seconds, barely long enough for

Asher to blink. Henrek kept his sword at the ready for a moment longer, then cautiously sheathed it, still watching the headless corpse as though it might come back to life.

Content at last it was slain for good, he walked over to the head and nudged it with the toe of his boot. It rolled away easily, like a ball. Where the neck had been severed, there was no blood. Asher couldn't help but stare. How could something that clearly had been dead for years come back to life? Or in any case, become semi-alive? It made her skin crawl. Dead bodies attacking the living seemed a perversion of the natural order, like a goat with two heads. She didn't like it at all.

Henrek grunted and shook his head. "Fighting a dead man. Who'd have ever thought?"

Asher stepped around the wight's body to pick up her sword, buckling it to her waist and feeling immediately better once she had. If there were any more wights lurking in the dark around them, she was prepared now. She tried to peer through the veil of twilight but could make out nothing more than a few yards in any direction. *Were* there more? If so, how many? The hair on her arm stood up. Suddenly the night seemed much more menacing.

Commander Bronwen, who had been awakened by the fight, caught her eye. "Dress me. We must leave here at once. The longer we stay here, the more will be attracted to us."

"There's no need to hurry, Commander," Henrek argued. "It was just one wight."

Then the second one appeared.

Chapter 7

"No one is truly fearless, lassie. Deep down, everyone is trying not to soil their britches. Everyone is afraid," Sir Idras says.

"That's not true," Asher snorts. "The knight commander, for one, is totally fearless."

"Oh no, the commander is the most scared of all. You know why? Because all the wee sprouts like you are her children, and she can't bear to lose a one of you."

"I've got it." Asher drew her sword. Stepping toward the wight, she barked, "Taz! Marandir! Protect the commander!"

Both men, who were still blinking and drowsy with sleep, fought to throw their blankets off of them. Taz's face registered shock and confusion when he got a good look at the headless wight on the ground near him. Then the second wight staggered into the middle of their camp and all eyes were drawn to it. This one had been a soldier. It wore a dented, pitted bronze helmet and a brown leather breastplate half dissolved with age. In its right hand it carried a falchion—a slightly curved blade popular in Ilirya two centuries before—that glimmered dully in the pre-dawn light.

Asher took a half step back in surprise when she saw the blade. She hadn't considered that the wights might be able to use weapons. Little more than a skeleton as it was, how well could it really fight? "Henrek, look for others," Asher called over her shoulder.

She advanced cautiously toward the wight. It made a hissing sound like a snake as she came close and readied its falchion, dropping into a fighter's crouch. Asher was unsettled. The creature's jaw was mostly unhinged, cracks radiated from what had likely been a blow to its left cheekbone, and its arms were completely without flesh or muscle. White hipbones poked up from a tattered brown leather sword belt that now hung limply around its pelvis. This wight had likely been dead for centuries.

She began stepping to the left, trying to lure it away from Commander Bronwen. The wight's head tracked her as she moved, watching her even though it didn't have eyes. "That's right," she encouraged it, "follow me. Come on."

The wight took a step forward, then another, committed to her. When Asher judged she'd enticed it far enough away from her companions, she leapt, bringing her blade down as hard as she could on top of its head, trying to shatter its brittle skull through the helmet. She envisioned the old bone exploding into a hundred pieces, putting a quick end to the creature. The wight parried in time, however, and the vibration caused by the two swords clashing together ran up her arm and into her chest. Asher was surprised. She hadn't expected the wight to move that fast, much less be able to resist the force of her weapon. Just because it had no muscles didn't mean it wasn't fast and strong, apparently.

Since the motion of her blade had been stopped, she was forced to withdraw her sword and reconsider her line of attack. As she did so, however, the wight lunged unexpectedly and made a quick draw cut across her chest. Asher immediately realized her mistake. She was too used to having her armor to protect her from glancing blows like that. Had she been wearing her cuirass, the falchion's edge would have scraped harmlessly against it. But she wasn't wearing any armor at all. The blade didn't score deep, but it scored nonetheless.

Where the rusty blade touched her, her skin burned like it had been scalded by a hot poker. She groaned, the muscles in her chest flexing involuntarily against the searing pain. She gritted her teeth and stepped back to buy time and distance. She was lucky the wight hadn't scored a deeper hit, or else she would have been in trouble. She glanced down to assess the damage. Her tunic gapped where the fabric had been cut, revealing a line of bright red blood. Although it was more than a scratch, she guessed it wouldn't need stitching.

The need to end the engagement quickly became more urgent. Asher couldn't afford to fight for long without her armor. She was a competent swordswoman, but she was primarily trained to fight on horseback in armor, not barefoot and in only her tunic and leggings. Without a healer nearby, she couldn't afford to be hurt badly.

She decided to switch to fighting defensively, waiting for the wight to attack first. She didn't have to wait long.

With a soundless scream, it charged, swinging its falchion in a wide arc toward her head.

She stepped back to evade it, but the wight used the weapon's momentum to sweep the blade back toward her. She was ready for it. Before the blade could hit her, she stepped forward and blocked the wight's arm, shoving it back toward the wight's chest and neck so that it was trapped with the blade safely outside the line of Asher's body.

She raised her sword to decapitate the wight, but it stepped backward too quickly for her to compensate. Instead, her falling blade cut off its arm just above the elbow. The lower half, still holding the falchion, fell to the ground. Although the wight was now weaponless, nevertheless it charged a second time, its jaw shaking in a silent roar of anger. Instinctively, Asher raised the tip of her sword, skewering the wight through its paper-thin chest. The impalement had no effect. The wight continued to rush her.

Asher braced her body, too close to do anything but absorb the impact. The wight crashed into her and they began grappling. The wight clawed at her, grabbing anything it could reach with its remaining hand, its broken arm waving uselessly and its jaw flapping. Years of training, of scrapes with Taz as a page and long afternoons in the training ring as a squire, kicked in. Without thinking, Asher used the ball of her foot to kick out the wight's right knee at the same time that she used her left elbow to smash the creature's chin. The bones of the wight's leg gave way like dry kindling and the wight collapsed to the ground, Asher's sword still protruding from its chest.

The wight was fast, but Asher was faster. Before it could roll away, she stomped on its face as hard as she could, crushing the fragile bones so completely that her foot only stopped because it had reached the ground below. The skull was dust and fragments. The wight immediately went still.

Asher waited for a moment to see if it would rise again, her breath heaving, then pulled her sword from its chest. She sheathed it, then rushed to grab her armor, strapping it on without stopping to tend to her cut.

Although it burned, she would check it more fully later. The priority now was to break camp and get away from this place.

She looked to Henrek, who was finishing strapping on his cuirass. "Are there any others?" Her heart was still pounding from the fight.

"No. I'll get the horses. That is, if these abominable skeletons didn't get to them first."

Asher's eyes widened and she took a sharp breath. The Guardian had said wights were attracted to *any* living creature, not just humans. Since their destriers had been picketed, if wights had come for them, they wouldn't have been able to run to save themselves. She shook her head to dispel the image of a wight's sharp, bony claws raking across Cloud's flank. The image was too terrible to consider.

From a practical perspective, they could get by with just one horse to carry the knight commander, but they would be slow and easy prey for however many wights haunted the valley the Guardian had called the Hollow Lands. If wights had gotten to their horses, they would have to abandon their mission. The endless walk back to Ilirya would be devastating. Asher took a series of deep breaths to quell the panic in her chest. All wasn't lost yet. She shouldn't imagine scenarios that hadn't necessarily occurred.

Now armored, she stood guard as Taz and Marandir dressed the knight commander. Even Commander Bronwen seemed unsettled by the bodies of the two wights, her gaze flickering to them time and again. After a moment, she gently pushed Marandir away. "Go, Marandir. Scout ahead. We need to know what we'll be riding into. We need to know how many wights may await us in the valley."

Marandir stopped buckling on her greaves. "Yes, Commander."

He bowed, then in an instant transformed into a brown eagle with bright yellow eyes and a wickedly sharp beak. He stood almost to Asher's waist, the largest bird she had ever seen. Beating his massive wings, he launched himself into the air and was gone, the silhouette of his large body hidden against the retreating night sky. Asher watched him go, hoping any news he brought back was good. How many wights were just out of view, watching and waiting? What if the Iliryans were totally encircled?

"Where did they come from?" Taz asked Asher, breaking into her thoughts. His blue eyes were wide with concern.

"I don't know. It was too dark to see. They're quiet as ghosts. They were on us before we even saw them." She knelt to help with a leather shoulder strap on the knight commander's cuirass, then moved the spaulder over to cover it.

"We're not even in the valley yet," Taz protested. "The Guardian said all the wights were in the valley."

"A knight is ready at all times." Commander Bronwen's voice was sharp. "At least now we have seen them and know what to expect."

Asher eyed the two twice-dead creatures in their camp, one almost totally a skeleton, the other more than halfway to becoming one. *The dead should stay dead,* she thought, shuddering.

Henrek walked back into camp leading Ever, Cloud, and Fleet. Morningstar and Crow followed untethered behind them. He dropped the leads for Cloud and Fleet and led Ever forward. Breathing a sigh of relief that the horses were safe, Asher grabbed Commander Bronwen's saddle and swung it over Ever's white and yellow back while Taz took the bridle and fitted the bit into his mouth. When Henrek tapped Ever's left knee, the horse stretched out his front legs so that his withers dropped, enabling Taz and Asher to lift the knight commander into the saddle.

They tightened the straps around her legs as she took up the reins. When Henrek tapped again, Ever stood up. The two male knights dispersed to mount their own horses, but Commander Bronwen laid her hand on Asher's shoulder. Her face in the thin morning light was bone white. "Should we be attacked again, defend yourselves first, not me."

Asher blinked, confused. "Commander?"

"If there comes a time that we're overwhelmed by these creatures, I am not your priority. *Peace* is your priority. The petition for peace is written on a scroll in my pack. If it comes to it, any of you can carry the petition. Do you understand me?"

"Commander—" Asher's voice was full of protest. She would never abandon the knight commander. No matter how besieged they might become, she would always defend the commander first and foremost. It was unthinkable not to.

"Protect Ilirya first, not me. That is an order, Lady Asher." The commander's voice was hard as rock and brooked no compromise.

"Yes, Commander. But you'll deliver the petition yourself in Nyara."

"Where do you think the wights come from?" Taz asked. He held his hand on his forehead, trying to shade his eyes from the bright sun. It didn't help. The reddish, sandy soil on which they walked seemed to reflect the sun back at them from all directions. There was no escaping it.

"The Guardian said from all over the Southlands, remember?" Asher wrinkled her nose as she thought about the skeletal wights crawling and staggering mile after mile toward the Hollow Lands. Had the Isenii seen them? If not and the Magus found out about them, would she expect the Iliryans to stop all the wights, too? How many were there?

The cut on her chest under her cuirass ached. There was nothing she could do about it, however. They hadn't stopped to rest since breaking camp hours ago and she wasn't about to take her cuirass off while they were riding. At least they didn't have to worry about another ambush by wights. Not only was the sun high in the sky now, but the land was so flat they'd be able to see any coming miles away. Marandir, who had reported no wights as far as he could see, had given up scouting and was riding at the head of the group, confident they were safe for now.

Taz huffed. "I mean where do the bodies come from? Did they crawl out of graves?"

Asher shrugged. "They must. The Guardian said they were Southerners, after all. But where did the dragon came from?" It was a question that had been bothering her. The Magus said the dragon was a consequence of the use of Dark Magic in Ilirya, but *where* had it come from? Were there dragons in other parts of the Southlands? What if they began to appear in Ilirya? Ilirya had enough problems to deal with without having a dragon infestation too.

Taz shuddered, and as if reading her mind said, "I hope wights and dragons never come to Ilirya. Do you think they will?"

"What was it Ulu said? Dark calls other Darkness to it? And the Guardian said the wights were drawn to the Hollow Lands. But I don't know what any of it means."

They rode silently for a few minutes, then he said in a low voice, "I'm glad you're here."

She cocked her head. "What do you mean?"

He looked at his hands. "I know it's been hard for you the last year. I was worried you might not want to still be a knight. But I'm glad you stayed. You're a good knight and we need good knights, now more than ever." He looked up and gave her a small, crooked smile.

Asher thought for a moment. The last year had been beyond hard. It had been harder than she thought anything could possibly be. She had been crushed, empty, devastated. She had spent weeks at a time refusing to leave her bed beyond the absolute minimum. But even in the darkest times, when she lay on the floor and hoped never to wake up again, it had never crossed her mind to leave the knighthood. There was no question that she would remain a knight.

Tayanna's lilting voice echoed through her mind. "Knights are born, not made. You never stop being a knight. Never."

Asher waited for the usual crippling pang of pain that accompanied memories of Tayanna, but for the first time, it didn't come. Instead, she felt a glimmer of pride. Tayanna had believed in her. She had known that no matter what happened, Asher could be counted on to fulfill her duty. And no matter how hard it was some days, Asher had. She had done more than that, even. She had done things of which even Tayanna would have been jealous.

A smile danced upon her lips as she thought of the adventures she'd had. "We slayed a dragon, Taz. And I fought a wight! I even met Kjelborn, the Sword of Ilirya. How could I have given that up?"

Taz laughed. The sound was light and carefree. In hindsight, it was easy to forget how scary those things had been in the moment and only remember instead the positives. "Strength and honor," he said.

"Duty and queen."

Before they could say anything else, Commander Bronwen called out, "Riders, halt!"

Asher and Taz reined their horses in immediately, looking at each other with eyebrows raised. Had the knight commander seen something? Asher put her hand on the hilt of her sword as they circled their horses around her.

Commander Bronwen announced, "We'll rest here for a few hours. Get some sleep as best you can. We won't stop at all during the night and you need to be alert and watchful for wights."

Asher took stock of their surroundings. They were stopped next to a tall outcropping of pale brown rocks. The shadow it provided would protect them from the bright sun, as well as cut off the possibility of attack at their backs. It was the best shelter they could hope for in the deserted valley.

"I'll keep watch," Marandir said.

The commander shook her head. "Not the whole time. You need sleep, too."

"I'll spell him," Asher offered.

"Good. We'll resume our journey when the sun is just above the horizon."

The knights dismounted and helped the commander down, laying her on her bedroll without removing her armor. Henrek didn't bother unrolling his bedroll at all and instead collapsed in a pile on his cloak, sending up a puff of sandy dust. Asher lay her bedroll near to where Marandir had sat down to look out over the valley. He appeared tranquil, and Asher wondered if the sight reminded him of home, wherever that was for him.

She realized she didn't know much at all about him. He had kept mostly to himself on the trip. Perhaps he had sensed the knights' initial suspicion, their concern he shared the revolutionary, iconoclastic views of the coup plotters, and kept himself apart from them as a result. They were well beyond that now. He had proven himself while fighting the dragon. She ventured, "Are you missing home?"

He rubbed his red beard, which was becoming shaggy. All of them had become a bit shaggy over the course of the journey. "I can't say I have a home anymore. Being the Regiment's messenger means I never stay in any one place too long."

His voice sounded melancholy. Asher experienced a twinge of pity for him. What would it be like not to have a home? "Where would you like to stay?"

He smiled dreamily. "I wish I could stay in bird form forever. Then I could live high in the mountains, riding the thermals every day. You know, there's nothing like the feeling of giving up control to a fast air current. It's exhilarating."

"Why don't you?" Asher knew members of the King's Regiment took vows to serve "for life," but she'd always assumed that was hyperbole. After all, she'd never seen any seventy-year-old soldiers wearing the Regiment's distinctive black armor. Surely they weren't really expected to never retire?

Marandir's eyes dropped to the ground before his feet. They were sad. He plucked at a clump of grass at his fingertips. "I can retire from the Regiment when Ilirya is safe."

Asher frowned. "But Ilirya is never safe!"

Forty years of war had taught her that. And even if the King of Cats agreed to peace, Ilirya was still threatened by the Northmen. Who knew they wouldn't have forty more years of war, this time in the north? He nodded. He saw the same problem.

Asher winced, but she understood his predicament. She was duty bound to serve too. But her heart cried out that she wanted so much more for Ilirya. She wanted peace for the first time in her lifetime. She wanted children born in the coming months to reach adulthood without ever having seen war. She wanted Marandir to be able to live out his dream.

But to have even a hope of achieving peace, first they'd have to cross the Hollow Lands and make it out alive. She thought of what awaited them on the other side if they succeeded. "How far away do you think the Guardian is?"

Marandir perked up, his body coming back to life. "There's no telling! The Guardian must be dozens and dozens of miles away, judging by the size of this valley. It's incredible that he can warg at such a great distance. The fact that he could sense us entering Maji land and then control Henrek, well, the few wargs in Ilirya don't even *dream* of such power. It's completely unheard of. They can only warg people immediately around them. The Guardian must be extremely powerful."

The only Iliryan warg Asher knew of was Raelan Bloodmoon, and it was for the best he hadn't been able to warg like the Guardian. He had been one of the conspirators against King Hap, and it had been he who had warged Lyse and tried to kill her partner Aeryn. "What else can the Southerner mages do that Iliryans can't?"

Marandir shivered, looking away. "Golem crafting."

"What's that?"

"Golems are non-living, vaguely human-shaped creatures that mages can animate to do their bidding. They can be made of water, fire, metal… almost anything. They are nearly impossible to stop. There was a war mage in Ilirya who could make a stone klant, which is very like a golem. He died on the night the king was killed." He stopped abruptly. Another of the conspirators.

Asher cocked her head. "So golems are a bit like wights?"

"I suppose you could think of it that way. But golems are controlled by a golem mage and were never human, while according to the Guardian, wights aren't controlled by anything. Which is for the best. I wouldn't want to encounter a mage so powerful they could manipulate a handful of wights, much less thousands. Rest now. I'll wake you in a few hours."

Asher didn't feel tired, but she knew he was right. She'd need to be alert and ready tonight. She unbuckled her cuirass and slipped it off. Peeling her sliced shirt back, she looked at the wound from the wight's falchion. It was approximately four inches long and a bright, puckered red. It might scar, but at least it had scabbed over and could begin to heal. She rebuckled her cuirass and lay back uncomfortably on her bedroll. The sky above her was endlessly blue, no cloud in sight.

Asher couldn't help but feel a little homesick. The sky was beautiful, but it wasn't *her* sky. She missed the familiarity of the garrison. The sounds of the city echoing up around her. She missed the smell of horses in the stables and the clatter of hooves on cobblestones. She wondered if she would ever see any of it again.

When Marandir shook her awake with a gentle hand, the light was fading in the sky. She rubbed her eyes, squinting at him accusingly. "You didn't wake me!"

He shrugged. "You looked like you could use sleep more than me. I don't sleep much. Now let's wake the others and be off. The scrub brush here is too dry to use for torches when it gets dark. It will burn to ash in under a minute. Since we'll be stuck with only the moonlight to illuminate what's around us, we should get as far as we can before twilight. We're lucky it won't be a moonless night."

Asher hoped the white sliver of the waxing moon would be enough to see by. The less light there was, the closer wights could get before they would be seen, as had happened in their camp that morning. "Did you see anything?" Just because the wights came out at night didn't mean there weren't other dangers in the valley.

"No. I understand why they call it the Hollow Lands. I didn't see so much as a mouse. We're the only living things for miles."

And that meant the only thing the wights would be drawn to. Asher rolled up her bedroll and attached it to Cloud's saddle, then nudged Taz with her foot to wake him. Once he was awake, they worked to put the commander on Ever while Marandir woke Henrek. When all the knights were mounted, Marandir tied Crow to the back of Asher's saddle. Stepping away from the horses, he transformed into a brown and white owl with a triangular face and small black eyes. He was no taller than the length of Asher's forearm. He jumped into the air, beat his white wings a few times, and landed on the cantle of his saddle, looking at the valley around him with new eyes.

Henrek nodded. "Clever. That'll give us a heads up if any wights come."

Asher experienced a brief wave of misgiving. What if they were riding to their deaths? How would the queen learn the peace expedition had been lost? Perhaps they should send Marandir forward with the petition. At least then they would be sure someone made it. But without Marandir, they would be blindly walking into unknown danger.

Through the interminable night, the delegation had been forced to ride slowly, as the Guardian had warned them they would. In the darkness, it was impossible for anyone but Marandir to see more than twenty feet in any direction. The horses stumbled over small divots in the road and knocked their hooves against half-buried rocks, all but blind to anything other than the edges of the road to Nyara. Asher, who rode in front of Henrek but behind Commander Bronwen, couldn't even see Taz at the front of their line, swallowed up as he was by the night. If not for Marandir's excellent owl night vision, a horde of wights could have fallen on them and they wouldn't have known until bony fingers grabbed at them from the dark and it was too late.

During the first few hours, the Iliryans had ridden with all their senses attuned to every sound or movement, worried it might signal the presence of wights. But after hours of travel without a single sign of danger, their attention lapsed. They slowly lowered their guard. Perhaps the wights in their camp that morning had been an anomaly and the Guardian's dire warnings little more than hyperbole. Where were the terrible monsters they'd been promised?

The monotony of Cloud's easy amble made it hard to stay awake as the night dragged on. Asher had started to nod off to sleep when Marandir flew screeching back to the group from a scouting flight. As she startled to attention, he landed on his saddle and reverted to his human form. "Wights ahead!" He yelled loud enough the entire group could hear. The riders halted immediately, collapsing into a tight group to hear his report.

"How many?" Taz asked.

"How far?" Henrek said at the same time. Their voices cancelled each other out, making a jumble of their words.

The hair on the back of Asher's neck stood up. She ran a hand along Cloud's smooth red-brown neck, more to soothe herself than him. She didn't like not being able to see the danger around them. Even though she knew the wights must not be close, it still felt like they could be lurking just on the edge of their field of vision. She wasn't the only one. The darkness made everyone jumpy. The riders unconsciously communicated their anxiety to their horses, who snorted and pawed unhappily.

"A few miles away." In his black armor, sitting on a black horse, Marandir was difficult to see. His voice seemed to drift out of a void in the night.

"How many?" Commander Bronwen demanded.

"Dozens at least. It could be a hundred. Standing all together as they are, it's hard to tell."

"Can we go around them?"

"No. They've gathered in a narrow pass through which the road travels ahead. There's no way to avoid it. To get to Nyara, we'll have to go through them."

Commander Bronwen frowned deeply. "I do not like it." Her eyes were troubled. She said no more, and Asher knew she was calculating the risk. Could they ride through? If not, what could they do?

Henrek cleared his throat. "You saw the wights this morning—they're nothing but a bunch of hoary skeletons. They won't be able to stand against a cavalry charge. With enough momentum, we can break through their line and run straight to the other side of the pass. We can do it."

Could they? Asher considered. It was true the two wights had been little more than skeletons. A hundred of them would be a large horde, but they were light and fragile. As Henrek had pointed out, the horses might be able to drive through them the way a boat prow parts the water. Asher thought he might be right. Perhaps this wasn't an insurmountable obstacle after all.

Commander Bronwen nodded, although she was still frowning. "It would be better if we had lances and the horses were armored, but you may be right. We will decide what to do once we have seen for ourselves what awaits us."

As they approached the pass, massive rock walls rose up in front of them, hulking black shadows against the slightly lighter colored night sky. These were what had created the natural choke point where a wight army awaited them. Asher understood why Marandir thought there was no way around. Who knew how far the walls went in either direction through the Hollow Lands? They seemed to go forever.

Commander Bronwen halted the group just close enough that they could see the gap between the walls illuminated by the light of the moon, but not in range of the wights Marandir reported were inside the canyon. Then she and Marandir rode forward for a closer look. When they came back, both looked grim.

"It can be done," Commander Bronwen said carefully, "but it will take skill. The charge must not be stopped. And no matter what, you *must not* be pulled from your horse. A mob—even one made of skeletons like this one—will tear you to pieces in seconds. Your armor will not save you once you are at their mercy. Ride as hard as you can and don't stop for anything. For *anything*."

Asher hadn't known how to fight a dragon, but she knew how to charge infantry. And the wights were no army. They were a hodgepodge of skeletons and bodies drawn from their graves equipped only with their burial accouterments. On foot, she'd been repelled by the corpses assailing her, horrified by their rotten skin and shattered bones, but sitting astride Cloud's back, she felt much more confident. If they were lucky, they could cut through the moldering skeletons like a hot knife through butter, scattering them in every direction.

"Commander, you ride between me and Taz," she said. "Henrek can take point and together we can charge through the wights with a wedge."

"*I* will serve as point," Marandir announced.

Ignoring the knights' confused objections, he dismounted and walked a few paces away from the group. In an instant, he became a massive brown bear. He stood almost as tall at the shoulder as Crow, who whinnied in fear and tried to shy away from him. Since the gelding was still tied to the back of Asher's saddle, however, he was trapped, and stood trembling, his nostrils flaring as he eyed the predator standing beside him. Asher noticed proudly that Cloud didn't so much as flinch.

Marandir rose onto his back legs—Asher estimated that standing, he was almost nine feet tall—and waved his paw, motioning to the knights to follow, then took off loping in the direction of the pass. Henrek kicked Morningstar into a fast trot behind him and Taz, Asher, and Commander Bronwen followed. Asher began to breathe heavily, anticipating the fight to come. Her body tingled. Everything around her seemed sharper, clearer. This was both the thrill and fear of battle.

The night was so dark it wasn't until the final moment that the swaying throng of wights finally came into view, dark as ink poured into a black ocean. Marandir switched from a lope to a full-out charge, roaring a terrifying battle cry, and crashed into them. Bodies went flying all around him like tossed rag dolls. Henrek was hot on his heels, swinging his sword left and right over Morningstar's brown shoulder. Wights crumbled beside him, felled by the heavy blows raining down on them and by Morningstar's body bowling through them.

Hope blossomed in Asher's chest. They were doing it! They were slicing through the wights like a scythe through wheat. She whooped and brandished her sword as she, Taz, and the knight commander entered the fray, Marandir's horse still tied behind Cloud.

Asher gave Cloud his head and he barreled into the wights in front of him, mowing them down under his churning hooves. Meanwhile, she used her sword to knock away any bony hands close enough to reach for her legs. On the other side of Commander Bronwen, Taz did the same. Asher couldn't hear anything over the blood pounding in her head and the occasional clang of her sword hitting centuries old metal armor. A smile stretched across her face. They could do this. They could drive through the wights to the other side of the pass.

Dark and crowded as it was in the narrow pass, she soon lost sight of anything ahead of them. Marandir and Henrek had pulled away, leaving the bodies of wights—battered but mostly with their heads intact—in their wake. The wights tried to rise to fight anew, but before they could, they were trampled under the heavy hooves of the oncoming destriers. The cut on Asher's chest from the morning burned, perhaps as sweat irritated it, but she ignored it.

Then in an instant, everything went wrong.

Asher pulled back on her reins so hard Cloud's front hooves came off the ground in an unhappy levade. In front of them, Morningstar lay fallen on the ground. Still alive, he was swarmed by wights that ripped the flesh from his bones with long, sharp nails even as he squirmed and tried to kick them. A black puddle of blood pooled around him, growing larger each second. Asher's body reacted as though it had been hit square in the chest by an axe. All the air rushed out of her chest. Shock exploded down her arms and down her legs.

"Henrek!" The cry was ripped from her mouth.

Where was he? She looked for him but couldn't see him. The wights were too densely packed and the night too dark. He could have been anywhere among them, fighting for his life or pinned down and in trouble. She started to pant as fear rose in her chest, choking her. They couldn't afford to lose anyone. Not after Jazmen. They were too few as it was. Where *was* he?

"Nononono." Her voice was shrill, hysterical. She stood in her stirrups to get a better view, but there was none to be had. The night swallowed everything. Including Henrek. "Henrek! Where are you? Henrek!"

"Asher!" The knight commander's voice sliced through the air like a sword. It was the sternest Asher had ever heard it. "Asher, listen to me. We have to keep going. Do you hear me? We have to keep going."

The three knights were totally stationary now, and while many of the wights had been distracted by the fallen horse, others were crowding far too close to them. Crow squealed loudly and kicked at them, trying to keep them away, but still they came. Asher hacked at the ones closest to her, trying to buy time to look for Henrek, but there were too many. She gasped, "But he needs us! He's out there somewhere."

The knight commander growled. "Do you want to die, too? What did I say? *Don't stop for anything.*"

"He could be alive! We can't leave him!" She kept trying to look, to see if she could find Henrek, but all she saw were the tops of dozens and dozens of heads. It was a nightmare.

Commander Bronwen's voice was tight. "If we stop any longer, we'll *all* be dead. *Keep going.*" Before Asher could argue again, Commander Bronwen took the loose end of her reins and slapped them across Cloud's neck as hard as she could.

Weak as she was, Cloud reacted as though whipped. Lunging ahead so forcefully he pulled the reins out of Asher's hands, he took off into the mob of wights ahead of them. Asher was thrown back helplessly against the high cantle of her saddle, which was the only thing that kept her from falling off as Cloud's powerful haunches drove him forward. When she recovered her seat, it was too late. When she looked backward, she couldn't see where she'd just been. Taz, Commander Bronwen, and Morningstar had been swallowed by the wights and the darkness.

Chapter 8

"Asher—" Taz doesn't have to say the words. His face carries the news he was sent to deliver. The words Asher never, ever wanted to hear.

Her scream reverberates through the entire garrison as she collapses. Part of her has just died forever.

Cloud did what he'd been trained to do: he ran until there were no more enemies before him. Until he and his rider were safe. There was little Asher could do to stop him. He ignored the bit yanking against his mouth, pulling his lips down as Asher hauled desperately at the reins. It was only when he burst through the final ranks of the wights that she was at last able to wrench his head around and bring him back to face the pass, Crow still tied behind.

She saw nothing, only the swaying, lurching, grasping skeletons. They were an endless, impenetrable sea and her companions were lost somewhere within it. Her heart slammed against her chest. Her breath came in sharp gasps. Where were Taz and the knight commander? Where was Henrek? And Marandir? She was all alone. Utterly, completely alone.

Panic formed a lump in her throat, choking her. Her stomach twisted in knots. *No. No. No. No.* This couldn't be happening. "Taz!" Her voice was high and terrified.

She couldn't bear to lose him. He was the one constant in her life, the person who knew her best in all the world. He was her best friend, her family. She had promised they would always have each other, but she had abandoned him. How could she have abandoned him?

There was no response to her screams. The air was so still it could have shattered like a pane of glass. Asher was equally fragile, teetering on the brink of hysteria. Everything felt like a surreal nightmare. Taz and

Commander Bronwen couldn't have been swallowed whole by the valley and the wights. This wasn't how their journey ended.

"Taz! Commander!"

How could everything have gone so wrong so fast? One moment they were plowing easily through the wights, the next...she blocked out the image of Morningstar swarmed by the revolting, monstrous wights. She was more scared than she'd ever been. Facing the dragon had been nothing compared to this. She couldn't be the only one left. She couldn't ride to Nyara alone. It had to be the commander. The commander knew what to do, not her.

She untied Crow with trembling, clumsy fingers, fumbling to cast his reins free of Cloud's saddle. She would ride back into the horde of wights. It wasn't too late. There was still time. She could find them. She could bring them back. Just as she was about to spur Cloud back into the fray, however, a hand reached out and grabbed Cloud's rein near the bit.

"Marandir!" Relief washed over her. He had made it through the pass. She wasn't the only one still alive. Together, they could go back and find the commander and Taz. Even if Commander Bronwen was right and it was too late for Henrek, they could still save the others.

The mage, no longer in his bear form, looked up at her, his face pale and bleak in the moonlight. There was a new cut that dribbled a single drop of dark red blood halfway down his cheek, and his hair was matted with sweat. When he spoke, his voice was low and urgent. "You can't go back. We have to keep going and get away from here."

"But they're still in there! We have to go back. We have to save them!"

He grabbed Asher's calf with his other hand and shook it, drawing her attention. "It's too late. They're gone. We have to continue without them."

Asher refused to accept that. She couldn't. As long as there was hope, she had to go back. Maybe even if there wasn't hope. "No. Let go. I'm going back."

When he didn't let go, she fought him with reckless abandon, trying to pull the opposite rein so Cloud would shake free and they could run back. Cloud bunched his haunches and danced in place, squealing unhappily at being caught between two opposing forces. Marandir kept a tenacious grip, moving with him so that Asher couldn't break free. The struggle lasted mere seconds but felt like minutes. Minutes Asher didn't have.

Marandir gritted his teeth. "Think about it. That canyon is full of hundreds of wights. You'll never find them even if they are still alive. Separated as we are, *none* of us will have a chance of survival if we go back. All we can do now is follow the commander's orders and push on to Nyara. Remember the stakes. If we can't win peace, thousands of Iliryans will die. We have to deliver the petition for peace."

"Then you go on. But I have to go back."

She was about to spur Cloud forward when she heard an echoing sound like the call of a war horn in the distance. It was enough to momentarily distract her. She stopped fighting and looked behind them, seeing nothing in the impenetrable darkness. "What's that?"

Marandir, who had also gone still at the sound, had no answer. The two of them stared in the direction from which it had come, trying to divine its meaning but without any context with which to understand it. Who would be blowing a horn in the middle of endless desert? A moment later, they heard the pounding of hooves against the ground, distinctive as a roll of thunder. Just above the horizon, a cloud of dust rose that veiled the moon like a lady's silk scarf.

In the dim light that remained, Asher could make out a line of cavalry careering toward them. She gaped, her lips parting into a small "o" of surprise. Who were they and where were they coming from? She didn't have time to consider the question. The galloping horses quickly erased the distance between them. The riders—a good two dozen in number, short lances set and armor gleaming in the moonlight—poured past the two Iliryans, charging into the wights with all the fury of a wave crashing against the shore.

Asher was transfixed. What was happening? She was so distracted that for a moment, she completely forgot about Taz, the knight commander and Marandir. All she could think of was the fairy tale-like riders that had materialized out of the darkness and swept past to fight the wights. Was she imagining it all? But Marandir had seen them too, so they must be real.

The wights crumbled before the cavalry, helpless to resist the momentum of their onslaught. Shattered and broken into pieces, many were unable to rise again. They raised skeletal hands to the sky, the magic in them still compelling them to attack. Asher didn't know what to do. Should she follow the strange warriors? Although she'd planned to go back before the riders' arrival, now they were here she was immobilized by bewilderment. Were they friends? Enemies? Mystical beings that would evanesce with the rising of the sun?

Marandir swung into Crow's saddle. "Stay now. If any of the others can be saved, it may be that these soldiers can save them."

Asher wasn't sure. After all, how would they know that Taz, Henrek, and the knight commander were still lost in the fray? And who knew what their goals were in charging the wights? Surely they had a purpose of their own. Nevertheless, Marandir was right. If there was any hope for the other Iliryans, it was from these unexpected warriors, not from her. But was it too late?

After what seemed like half an eternity, during which time Asher barely dared to breathe, the familiar rumble of hooves signaled the return of the riders. The cavalry once more swept past the two Iliryans, this time going the opposite direction. Cocooned among them were two riders. Asher's heart leapt when she saw them. It was Commander Bronwen and Taz. She was overwhelmed with relief and happiness. A weight lifted off her chest and she took her first deep breath since entering the pass.

Her elation, however, was instantly blown away by a blast of shock. The commander was slumped forward in her saddle, body slack, chin on her chest. Was she dead? Icy fear settled in Asher's chest and wrapped its freezing fingers around her lungs, squeezing until not even a hairsbreadth remained. She couldn't move. "Commander!" The word should have come out as an anguished scream, but instead it was a whisper so soft not even Marandir beside her heard it. Her mouth had gone dry.

No! The commander couldn't be dead. She just couldn't be. What would they do without her? How could they go on? Asher's thoughts crashed together like the clash of cymbals, filling her head with ringing. She couldn't think properly. She maneuvered Cloud through the strangers' horses to get closer. She needed to know the commander's condition.

She reached Taz first. Deep gouges had been made in Fleet's dapple-gray haunch. Dark red blood flowed from them and dripped down his legs and into his white tail. In the darkness of early morning, it looked like black paint. The poor horse was trembling, his head down and his legs braced.

At least Taz looked unhurt. He had no obvious wounds, no signs of injury. Nevertheless, his eyes were fearful and haunted when they met Asher's. What had happened to the two of them? What had he seen?

"The commander?" Asher asked.

"Unconscious but alive."

"Is she hurt?"

"No."

Asher's heart fluttered with relief.

"Henrek?"

He shook his head, not meeting her eyes. A wave of nausea swept over her. Their party was down yet another member. Only four remained now to carry Ilirya's hopes.

One of the strangers, Asher guessed their captain from the way the other soldiers parted to allow her to pass, approached on a short buckskin horse. "We must go now before the wights recover." Before Asher could say anything, she pulled a horn from her belt and blew it, a long, clear sound. It was the same horn that had announced the arrival of the strangers. Half the riders dashed away, disappearing as abruptly as they'd come.

"Who are you?" Asher asked.

"We were sent by the Guardian. Come away now. You are safe."

So their mysterious rescuers were the Maji! But the Guardian had said he wouldn't help. So why had he? The captain whistled, and the remaining Maji started to move. They circled their horses around the four Iliryans, and when they began to canter away, the Iliryan horses were carried along with them. Asher didn't have the will to question where they were going or why.

As they rode, the blackness of night turned to the dim purple of morning. None of the Maji spoke, and the Iliryans—at least the conscious ones—were too demoralized to utter a single syllable. Asher kept replaying what had happened over and over again in her mind. There were too many unanswered questions that pulled at her attention, too many "what ifs." How had it all gone wrong? Could Henrek have been saved if they'd just ridden closer to him? Why was the knight commander still unconscious and slack in the saddle hours later? Taz knew the answer to the latter, but he was lost in himself, his eyes unfocused and his face drawn.

Finally, Asher couldn't take it anymore. "What happened?" she asked, riding Cloud so close to Fleet that her leg bumped against Taz's. What had happened after Cloud carried her away? How had the Maji found them?

He shook his head, refusing to meet her eyes. His chin quivered, and he reached up to rub the back of his hand over his mouth.

The burning sting of guilt pricked her chest. She should have been there with them, fighting beside them. He shouldn't have had to fight alone. She pressed, "What happened to Commander Bronwen?"

Taz looked at the unresponsive figure beside them. The only things keeping the commander in the saddle were the straps around her legs and waist. "She collapsed. I don't know why. It was right after you…" He swallowed hard. "She slumped over. I didn't know what to do. I—I—"

"It is the Dark Magic." Asher was surprised to hear the cavalry captain speak. Her voice was low and rich.

"What?" Asher said.

"You should not have brought her to the Hollow Lands." The woman's tone was disapproving. "The poison inside her spreads faster here because of the presence of the wights. So much Dark Magic in one place speeds the poison's progress. It was too much for her and she collapsed."

Asher couldn't stop herself from staring. "How did you know about the Dark Magic in her?"

The captain waved her hand in the direction of Commander Bronwen's body. "I can see it. It looks like black lichen." She dropped her hand. "And she is overrun by it. She will not last another week."

No. Asher's heart skipped a beat. *That's not enough time. Can we reach Nyara in a week?* Her armor felt unbearably heavy. Everything was going so terribly, terribly wrong. The expedition was crumbling. Jazmen and Henrek were gone, they had no idea how far away Nyara was, and she didn't know if Commander Bronwen would ever wake again.

Asher was filled with black, miserable despair. Even if they reached Nyara and delivered Queen Alea's petition for peace, there was no guarantee the King of Cats would agree. Their journey—and the sacrifices made during it—could be for nothing. Ilirya would still fall. She would return to a city of bone and ash. Did anything matter anymore?

After a few hours of riding east from the road to Nyara, during which time the land only became bleaker and more barren, the Maji brought them to a camp that sat high on a cliff overlooking the Hollow Lands. To reach it, they had to climb a narrow trail just wide enough for one horse at a time. Asher noted with relief it would be impossible for wights to reach the camp from the valley below. If they tried, they could easily be picked off one by one.

She shuddered as she remembered the yellowed, rotting faces of the wights. Their cracked teeth and their tattered clothes. She started to imagine them converging on Henrek, dragging him down with their claw-like hands, but quickly shut down those thoughts. She could mourn Henrek later. As her father had taught her, it was only after her duty was fulfilled that she would have the luxury to feel emotions about it. Until they were safe, she had to remain focused. Just because they had escaped the wights for now didn't mean they were safe.

The sun peeked over the horizon, providing just enough light to illuminate the Maji camp. Asher blinked in surprise when she saw it. It looked like a trader's camp. Was this how the Maji lived? Long, brown, rectangular tents formed a horseshoe around a central campfire. Men, women and children moved between the tents, carrying blankets, cauldrons, and pillows. Were they preparing to strike the camp?

The first riders were already busy untacking their horses in front of the tents. A tall man, so gaunt he looked emaciated, stood watching them. He was completely hairless, lacking even eyebrows, and on each cheek was tattooed three horizontal red lines. All he wore was a white sarong tied around his waist, leaving his thin chest exposed. His skin was cinnamon, and when the sun caught it just right, it seemed to almost shimmer like bronze. Asher was both amazed and intrigued by it. Then she realized he wasn't the only one. When they removed their helmets, many of the Maji looked like him.

Flanking the man were what looked like two gray lions with thin, tawny manes. They were no ordinary lions, however. Folded against their backs were feathered wings and from their fierce, narrow heads sprang long, slightly curved black horns. Asher had never seen anything like them before. She didn't know whether to fear them or be fascinated.

"Welcome," the man said in a deep, gravelly voice. Asher guessed he must be around seventy years old, but it was hard to tell. He gave a shallow bow. "I am the Guardian of the Maji."

Asher raised her eyebrows. So this was the Guardian! The Maji who had accompanied them dispersed and then began to dismount, leaving the Iliryans alone with their leader. Asher looked to Taz, her eyes questioning. What should they do now? Without Commander Bronwen to direct them, they were leaderless, adrift. What did the Guardian want from them? And what would he ask in repayment for saving them from the wights?

A young girl of no more than eight appeared beneath Cloud's nose, her eyes a brown so dark they were almost black. She paid no mind to the fearsome lion-like creatures behind her. She held out her hand.

The Guardian nodded to her. "Your horses will be taken care of. Please, join me in my tent."

Short of spurring their horses and hoping to outrun the dozens of Maji cavalry, the Iliryans didn't have a choice but to obey. But what to do about Commander Bronwen? She was still unconscious, with no sign she would ever wake again. Still, they couldn't leave her strapped to Ever's saddle. With Taz's help, Asher pulled the knight commander from Ever, grunting as her armored body landed awkwardly in her arms.

The Guardian watched. "Bring your leader. Our healer will see to her." He turned and walked to the farthest tent. The two lion creatures accompanied him, their unnaturally long tails waving in the air behind them as they walked.

Asher looked once to her two companions to ensure that all were in agreement, then followed, Commander Bronwen limp between her and Taz. Her mind raced. With Commander Bronwen incapacitated, at least for now, she needed to think, to plan. Why had the Guardian saved them after warning he wouldn't? Would he demand they destroy the wights just as the Magus had demanded they kill the dragon? She looked around the camp. Flight wasn't an option. The Maji horses were much lighter and faster than their destriers. If necessary, they would have to try to negotiate their way out.

The inside of the Guardian's tent was bright and colorful. Pillows of every size and shade covered the floor. Intricately wrought iron lamps hung from poles set up around the tent, illuminating every corner and crevice.

The Guardian himself sat at the center of it all, while the two winged lions lay on either side of the tent. One rested its head on its paws, its eyes heavy with sleep, the other gnawed a bone almost as long as Asher's arm.

Asher gently lay the knight commander down on the cushions near the tent's opening. Commander Bronwen's face was bone white, her breathing shallow. If the commander never woke, she, Taz, and Marandir would have to carry Queen Alea's petition for peace to Nyara without her. Asher refused to think about it. The commander would be fine.

The Guardian motioned for the three Iliryans to join him. As they sat on pillows near him, their armor sinking into the cushions like quicksand, he poured them each a glass of amber-colored tea. When Asher held it to her lips, it smelled like mint. After one sip, she put it down. It tasted like syrup, too sweet for her liking.

The Guardian leaned back on an elbow and appraised them with light gray eyes. "You dared cross the Hollow Lands even knowing they were overrun by wights. Why? What was so important that you risked the death of every member of your party for it?"

Marandir set his tea down. "We have a petition for peace from Queen Alea. Ilirya wants an end to the war."

The Guardian tented his fingers thoughtfully but said nothing.

Asher asked, "Why did you rescue us? You said you wouldn't help."

A ghost of a self-deprecating smile snaked across his face. "I realized that no Rann has entered Sarsenia for time immemorial. To have come this far, against all odds, you must have an important task. If you died in the Hollow Lands, all your efforts would be for nothing, and that would be a great misfortune. I see now I was right to help." His face became serious. "The Maji have no love for war. If the Rann want peace, we should work together for this goal. May the King of Cats see it this way as well."

Asher leaned forward. Something in the Guardian's voice suggested reservation. Perhaps even doubt. "Why wouldn't he?"

The Guardian took a sip of his tea, then swirled it in the glass in his hand. "I cannot guess what is in his mind. The reasoning of the King of Cats is his own."

Asher frowned. That hadn't sounded positive at all. Was the King of Cats unreasonable? Mad? If it came to it, was there a way around him? Her mind raced, considering possibilities. "If the King of Cats rejects peace, could you refuse to send soldiers to the border?"

According to their leaders, both the Maji and the Isenii supported peace. How many soldiers did the two tribes supply? If they refused to fight, how badly would it hurt the Southerner army? If nothing else, a weakened opponent would buy General Oran time. The Iliryan line wouldn't be in immediate danger of falling, although it wouldn't free up many troops to stop the Northmen.

The Guardian tilted his head and stared at her, his face neutral. "What the King of Cats commands, all five tribes are bound to obey."

Her shoulders fell. So it was all or nothing. Peace or war. They were at the king's mercy.

Taz set down his empty glass. Asher was glad to see some color had come back into his cheeks. "Why is he called the King of Cats?"

"It is the name he chose for himself. He says the five tribes are like cats. As the saying goes, it is impossible to herd cats."

"What *are* the tribes?" Marandir asked.

"You have passed through the land of the Isenii, who are the forest dwellers. Now you are in the land of the Maji, who live in the desert. Next you will come to the land of the Walakai, the people of the hills and plains. Nyara lies within the land of the Avicini. To the south can be found the coastal cities and harbors of the Llini."

"What do the others think of peace?" Asher was still searching for a solution. If all the tribes supported peace, could they pressure the King of Cats? But how could they contact the other tribes?

The Guardian shook his head. "I do not know. There is little communication between the tribes, and never about the war." He smiled. "Perhaps the king is right, we are indeed cats."

The tent flap opened behind them, and a hooded figure entered. Asher watched him, concerned until he knelt next to the knight commander. His hands glowed turquoise as he passed them over her body. Could the Maji's mage healer help her? Asher held her breath. What if he couldn't?

After a long minute, the healer looked up and nodded at the Guardian. "She will recover. At least, as much as is possible for her. She sleeps now."

Their host nodded with satisfaction. "Tell Saraya to double the watch tonight in case any of the wights followed."

The healer bowed and left.

"Have they come here before?" Asher asked.

"We have not yet observed wights leaving the Hollow Lands. But there may come a time when they do. We must be prepared."

Asher thought about the wights that had attacked them the day before. That hadn't been part of the Hollow Lands, had it? Were they already spilling out of the valley? She crossed her arms reflexively, or at least, as well as she could with her armor on. "There's nothing you can do to stop them?"

The Guardian's eyes were troubled. "No. We have tried to destroy them, but every time their numbers are simply replenished. And so we move our camp often, hoping they stay in the Hollow Lands and do not try to leave."

Asher had nothing to say to that, so she asked, "How far is it to Nyara?"

"Four days' hard riding. The intersection of our land with that of the Walakai and the Avicini is on the third day. To reach Nyara is one day more heading southwest."

Asher looked to Taz. "We should leave immediately." She was thinking of the knight commander. Did Commander Bronwen have four days? She began calculating what they would need to reprovision from the Maji and how they could divvy up the night watch. The knight commander wouldn't be made to take a shift. She needed to rest.

The Guardian rose, unfolding his long brown legs like a spider. Instantly alert, the lion creatures stood too, padding over on giant paws to join him. He placed his hands on the top of their heads and ran his long, thin fingers through their manes. For a moment, Asher wondered if he was a Therion mage, but Marandir had said that like the Iliryans, most Southerners seemed to only have one affinity each. Since the Guardian was a warg, he was unlikely to also be a Therion mage. "You have traveled all night and are weary. Sleep, eat, and then my fighters will happily escort you in the direction of Nyara."

Asher glanced at her companions. Taz was half-asleep, his eyelids heavy and his face slack. Marandir was little better. His face was streaked by dust and sweat, and the cut on his cheek needed tending to lest it become infected. The need to press on as quickly as possible for Commander Bronwen's sake was outweighed by the Iliryans' need to rest. So, too, did their horses.

Asher rose to her feet, feeling for the first time just how exhausted she herself was too. "Fine. We'll stay a few hours. But no more."

The Guardian led them to an empty tent—Asher didn't have the energy to wonder where its regular inhabitants had been sent—where Taz and Asher tried to arrange Commander Bronwen as comfortably as possible. As she laid the commander's limp arms beside her body, Asher realized with a deep, biting sadness that it fell to them alone to care for her now. Jazmen and Henrek were gone. And no matter what happened in Nyara, if the Maji were right, they would return to King's City without her. She looked at Taz, who was too spent even to remove his boots and had collapsed fully clothed onto the blankets the Maji had laid on the ground, and made a vow: whatever happened, she wouldn't leave the Southlands without him. They would make it home together.

In the cavernous ballroom of the palace, men and women whirl across the floor on light feet. They move like ghosts, untethered from gravity, spinning and swirling, animated by the music of a small orchestra playing discreetly in a corner. The room is lit by a dozen chandeliers, whose candlelights are reflected a thousandfold by the mirrors that ring the room on three sides. To an outsider looking in, the room must look like magic.

Dances like these are for King's City's nobility, an opportunity for the kingdom's rich and powerful to preen and strut like peacocks around each other. For politicians to celebrate and be celebrated. For young nobles to woo and be wooed. Asher isn't impressed. Although this flaunting of privilege is part of her birthright, she forsook that life when she began training to be a knight. It means nothing to her now. She yawns and scratches her nose. In an hour or less, she'll be back in her bed sleeping.

She is standing beside Avrill, who is dressed, like the other knights in the room, in Iliryan blue silk breeches tucked into knee-high black boots, a fitted white silk vest, and a blue waistcoat richly embroidered with golden thread. At her side hangs her sword, a reminder of her station. Asher wears a similar costume, but since she is only a squire, she wears neither Iliryan blue nor a sword. Asher pulls at the collar. She's not used to being stuffed into formal clothing. For years she's only worn her rough squire's tunic, just like all the other squires in the kingdom. She's forgotten the feeling of silk on her skin, and now it itches when it should feel luxurious.

Since Avrill doesn't dance, they stand to the side of the room, Avrill conversing with acquaintances about the state of the war and of the kingdom while Asher waits a respectful distance away. This is the first time Asher has accompanied Avrill to a court dance. When she was Idras's squire, he was never invited. Even if he hadn't been a lumbering giant whose outsized boots threatened to crush any lady's delicate feet that came too close, he was raised to be a fisherman in Gent, making him forever an outsider to this exclusive scene. These were Avrill's people, and she blended seamlessly into them.

Although Asher is not prohibited from dancing, none of the dancers catch her fancy. To be honest, she would rather be polishing Avrill's armor. Motion catches her eye, and she turns her head to watch a new knight enter the hall. Asher isn't the only one. There's something about this knight that draws all eyes to her. The entire room seems to have gone quiet.

The knight stands proudly erect at the door, her hand resting lightly on the pommel of her sword. Even though she's still young, she's poised, polished. If she notices the way people are staring, she gives no sign of it. Her narrow eyes flicker around the room, assessing it. There's a calm quietness to her, a deep confidence. She steps forward into the crowd.

Asher steps forward and touches Avrill's elbow. "Who is that?"

Asher has never seen her before. It disconcerts her because she prides herself on knowing all of Ilirya's knights. How does she not know this stranger?

"That's Lady Tayanna. She rarely comes to King's City. She must be back from the southern front, where she spent the last year. They say she's the next coming of Commander Bronwen. She's made quite a name for herself. A war hero, they say." Asher hears the admiration in Avrill's voice. Normally, Avrill is miserly about compliments. This knight must be particularly impressive if she's won Avrill's respect.

Asher tries to watch the knight, but she catches only glimpses of Lady Tayanna as she makes her way across the ballroom floor, flashes of blue satin among gowns of yellow, blue, and white. There is strength in the knight's body. Her waistcoat stretches tight across her shoulders, suggesting shoulders and arms well muscled from years of fighting. Asher finds she can't look away. She wants to know more. Who is this knight who can make an entire room of courtiers go silent?

Lady Tayanna stops to speak to a group of knights, and when she glances around the room, her face is both serious and intelligent. Unexpectedly, her eyes meet Asher's. A thrill races up Asher's chest. The feeling is electric. Her breath catches for a fraction of a second. Simultaneously, an emotion flickers across Lady Tayanna's face almost too quickly for Asher to see. She thinks it's...interest. Curiosity.

One of the knights says something to Lady Tayanna, and she turns back to listen to him, cocking her head as she absorbs his words. The moment has passed. Asher's heart is beating embarrassingly fast. She forces herself to turn away, to watch the dancers before her even though she really wants to be continuing to study Lady Tayanna. When she looks back, a minute later, the knight is gone. Although Asher scans the crowd for her, looking for her tailored blue outfit, she has disappeared.

Asher experiences a pang of disappointment. Where did she go? For the next several dances, Asher looks around impatiently for the knight, hoping to see her again, but she has vanished without a trace.

Asher is on the verge of asking Avrill permission to retire back to the garrison when the dancers before her part to reveal Lady Tayanna crossing the floor in her direction. Asher's eyes widen. She looks around, trying to see whom the knight is coming to talk to, but without her noticing, the crowd has ebbed away from her. She's alone. There is no mistaking it. Lady Tayanna is aiming toward *her*.

"I'm Tayanna," the knight says, extending her hand. Her dark, slanted eyes dance with life and she smiles with an open, honest expression.

Asher is momentarily transfixed. An unexpected lightness in her chest steals her breath away. "I'm...Asher."

"Hello, Asher. Nice to meet you."

Tayanna bows respectfully over Asher's hand. Asher doesn't breathe. Can't breathe. When Tayanna's eyes meet hers, they seem to see into and through her. There's a knowing cast to them, a certainty about herself and everything in her life. Asher is overwhelmed, unable to speak much less think. She's never met anyone like this before.

Tayanna tilts her head toward the dancers on the floor. "Would you care to join me?" Her voice is rich and mellow.

Yes, Asher would like to join her. She wants to know everything about her. What has she done on the southern front? How has she gained Avrill's respect?

Because Asher's mouth refuses to work properly, all she can do is nod. Still holding Asher's hand, Tayanna escorts her to the floor, blending in effortlessly with the other dancers. Tayanna's hand rests comfortably on Asher's waist as she sweeps her into a waltz. Asher realizes the word she's been looking for to describe Tayanna is *dashing*. Tayanna is unlike any of the other knights because she's *dashing*. It's something inherent in her, an innate quality that cannot be taught.

"We haven't had the pleasure of meeting yet. For whom do you squire?" Tayanna asks.

"Av—Lady Avrill." Asher's tongue is thick and catches on her teeth.

"She is an excellent knight. Have you squired for her long?" Tayanna's eyes don't leave Asher's even as the waltz requires them to step side by side. Asher notices they're the same height. Tayanna is older than her. Asher guesses by seven years or so.

"Two years." Her face flushes. She feels acutely every place where Tayanna is touching her. Her palm tingles, pressed to the knight's.

"Avrill has a reputation for producing fine knights."

They spin together.

"She's very good. I'm lucky to have her. I was with Sir Idras before."

Tayanna chuckles. "I imagine that didn't last long?"

"No." Asher fights against a smile, fondly remembering her time with the gargantuan knight.

"You look lovely this evening. Blue suits you."

Asher hopes her face hasn't turned a bright scarlet. If it has, Tayanna shows no sign that she's seen it. Asher murmurs, "Thank you." She wants to stare at Tayanna but drops her gaze instead.

"Where is your family?"

"Here in King's City." Asher doesn't mention her father is Lord Ivar. Being the daughter of a former Lord Chancellor has its benefits and its downfalls. Tonight, she'd like to be just Asher. "Yours?"

"Qarys, although I haven't been home in years. My family was none too happy when I announced my intention to become a knight." She grins, spins Asher out, then back again into her arms.

Asher frowns, concerned on Tayanna's behalf. "But surely they've forgiven you?"

The outline of a smile plays across Tayanna's lips. "This many years later, I hope so. But my family is stubborn." The way she says it is filled with humor. She forgives them their opinions.

Asher looks for something more to say. She wants to know everything about Tayanna's life. It must be fascinating and thrilling. "You've been in the south?"

Tayanna's eyes glitter. "Mmhm. The war can't last forever. I intend to see its end." Her expression is so passionate and earnest that Asher believes her. In that moment, Asher would believe anything Tayanna told her. She's still breathless, her heart pounding.

"They say you're a war hero." The words slip out without thinking and Asher immediately regrets them. They sound silly and childish. And yet she can somehow imagine Tayanna in battle, her sword flashing as she slices through the enemy. She can imagine Tayanna as a war hero.

Tayanna's expression turns fierce. "It's my duty—like that of all knights—to protect those who cannot protect themselves. No more, no less. I'm no more a war hero than anyone else who fights."

Asher worries she's offended the knight. Trying to redirect the conversation, she asks, "Will you stay in King's City for long?"

They spin again, and Tayanna lifts her slightly off the floor. Asher is dizzy, but not from the dance. She never wants the dance to end.

"Perhaps. If there's a reason to stay." Asher thinks she sees a light sparkle in Tayanna's eyes. Or is she imagining it?

For the next several minutes, the dance is too fast for them to speak. Asher, who was trained almost from the time she could walk to dance, is surprised to find that Tayanna has no trouble keeping up with her. She moves smoothly across the floor with the ease of a courtier. Was she raised in a noble House, or did she learn it during her time as a page and squire? There's no opportunity to ask.

When the music winds down, Asher is desperate for their time together to continue. There's so much more she wants to learn about Tayanna. She looks to the musicians, hoping they'll quickly move to the next song, but they've lowered their instruments and are allowing the dancers to reposition themselves. A knight steps forward from among the spectators and taps

Tayanna on the shoulder. She drops her head to hear the shorter knight's words, and then her mouth pulls into a frown.

She turns back to Asher and bows politely. "Please excuse me a moment." Then she disappears back into the crowd, leaving Asher alone on the ballroom floor.

Her place is immediately filled by a stranger. Except, Asher realizes with a small jolt, he's not a stranger. Although she can't pinpoint where she's seen him before, his long brown face and hazel eyes are familiar. Who is he? She knows he shouldn't be here, but she can't figure out why not. Frozen by surprise, she puts up no resistance when he takes her hand as the music begins and follows his lead. Her mind is reeling, telling her that something is wrong, but what?

"What's your name?" His voice is slightly accented but otherwise unremarkable, and though he is marginally taller than her, he is neither fat nor thin, ugly nor handsome.

"Asher," she replies automatically.

"And who is she, this knight of yours?" He looks in the direction Tayanna left. His hand is light and insubstantial as air against Asher's, but she doesn't want to be touching him at all. She wants to be in Tayanna's arms again.

"Tayanna." She is staring at him, trying to put together pieces of a puzzle that don't fit. Who is he? Why is he here? She looks around the room, wanting Tayanna to come back.

The man cocks his head, peering at her. He seems to be examining her. "This memory is special to you. You must care for this Tayanna very much. Where is she now?"

Asher stops dancing. She blinks. A *memory*. The word causes the truth to come crashing down upon her. This room is not real. The people in it are not real. In real life...

"She died."

Once the words are out, they fly around her head like bats bursting free of a cave. There is no way to push them back in. They beat at her, screaming for attention. A lump lodges in her throat and swells, choking her. Tayanna is dead, and this memory is all that remains of her. Never again will Asher see her beautiful face or hear her melodic voice.

The world is spinning. Her knees are weak. The dancers, too, are spinning around her, creating a kaleidoscope of color. Impossibly, they avoid crashing into the two stationary dancers. In fact, they don't even seem to know Asher and the man are there. Asher stares at him, anguished. "Who are you?"

He doesn't answer. This cherished memory has turned into a nightmare. Asher starts to shake as her mind recoils from the juxtaposition of the terrible, devastating knowledge of Tayanna's death with the happiness of this memory. Asher fights to separate the two feelings. She wants this memory to remain pure, untainted by the dark clouds of Tayanna's eventual death. But it's too late. Overpowering grief and sadness are already battering at her, trying to force her to her knees. Tayanna is dead.

She presses the heels of her hands into her temples, trying to block out the memory of the agonizing days and weeks after Tayanna's death. The dancers are now whirling at breakneck speed around her, too fast to be human. The music is loud and manic, the strings screeching as the bows rub over them. The entire ballroom tilts under her feet. Then blessed darkness swallows everything.

When Asher woke, her heart was pounding. From the soreness of her jaw, she knew she'd been clenching her teeth in her sleep. Lingering feelings of sorrow and loss told her she must have had a nightmare. She rubbed her eyes, trying to remember what she'd dreamed. She had a vague memory of dancing and of a stranger, but the specifics were quickly dissolving. Where had she been dancing and why? She didn't know. She allowed the dream to dissipate without clinging to it. It didn't matter.

In a corner of the tent, Marandir and the knight commander were engaged in a quiet but intense conversation. Someone, she assumed Marandir, had pulled Commander Bronwen to a sitting position with Ever's saddle behind her back. Her face was wan, her red hair disheveled and halfway out of its braid. She was sicker than Asher had ever seen her. *We're running out of time*, Asher thought, her stomach roiling.

Commander Bronwen saw her sit up and motioned weakly with her left hand. "Come. You need to hear this too."

Asher immediately went to the knight commander's side and knelt next to her.

Commander Bronwen took a shallow, shuddering breath. "I have been foolish. It was shortsighted of me to ask you to rely on a single scroll to carry the hopes of our kingdom when paper is so easily destroyed. In case the petition for peace should be lost, as it almost was in the pass last night, you must all know the conditions that Queen Alea is prepared to accept so you can carry on without it."

She paused, and the moment settled heavily. Asher stretched toward her, eager to hear. What? What was the queen offering to end forty years of war? What card did Ilirya have to play that would tip the scales of peace?

"The terms are *peace at any cost.* Whatever the King of Cats demands, the queen is prepared to give it."

Asher gasped, her hand flying to her mouth. What? Unconditional surrender? Had they really traveled this far to deliver Ilirya into the Southerners' hands? How could they simply give up after all the sacrifices their soldiers had made? Surely there must be another solution. Marandir, too, was taken aback. He ran his hand through his short red hair, his eyes uneasy.

Commander Bronwen continued, "Within some semblance of reason, that is. But still, we must have peace, even at great cost to our dignity. We are caught in a vise. The Northmen could attack at any moment from the north, while our line at the southern front is crumbling by the day. We *must* be prepared to accept great loss if we are to have any hope of saving Ilirya. Like you, I wish there was an alternative, but there is not."

Asher understood, but she still didn't like it. No matter how badly Ilirya needed peace, the idea of what was tantamount to surrendering to the Southlands left a bitter taste in her mouth. Was this what Tayanna had died for? What so many knights, soldiers, and mages had died for? A groveling peace? It felt wrong. She didn't know what she had expected Queen Alea and Commander Bronwen to offer, but it hadn't been this.

"One more thing. If I am incapacitated, Asher, you are to take leadership of this expedition."

Asher's heart skipped a beat. Had she misheard? "Commander?"

"Yes, you."

Asher stared at her blankly. Her? In command of the delegation? No, she couldn't. It was too much responsibility. How could she be expected to carry the future of the entire kingdom on her shoulders? She wasn't anything like the knight commander. She was still a new knight, and this was her first major expedition.

Commander Bronwen rested her hand on Asher's. Her voice was soft. "I have faith in you. You can do it."

Asher stared at their hands, old on young. Did *she* have faith in herself to do what the commander asked? What if Commander Bronwen was mistaken? By taking command, she would be responsible not only for herself, but for the lives of Taz and Marandir as well. It was a heavy responsibility. What's more, how could the commander ask her to be the one to all but surrender Ilirya to the Southlands? It was a terrible thing to ask.

Commander Bronwen coughed. The sound was dry and weak. It was the cough of a dying woman. Asher caught Marandir's eyes over her head. They had to move fast if there was to be any hope of the knight commander presenting the petition for peace herself. Asher was determined to make that happen. Queen Alea might be willing to give the King of Cats whatever he asked, but Commander Bronwen wouldn't be so flexible. If there was any hope of an honorable peace, it rested on the commander herself negotiating for Ilirya.

"We'll ride out now," Asher said.

She sprang into action, rousing Taz from sleep and then stepping outside to find their horses already waiting. The healer had closed the gouges on Fleet's flanks, and the horses looked refreshed and ready to go. Additionally, while the Iliryans slept, the Maji had kindly refilled their traveling packs, enough that they would have at least a few days' worth of food. There was nothing left to do but mount and depart.

As Taz and Asher hoisted Commander Bronwen into the saddle, the Guardian approached, the lion-like creatures still at his side. "I wish you luck on your journey. Sarsenia can be treacherous and unpredictable even for the Sarsen, and even more so these last months." He paused. "Above all, beware your dreams lest they unwittingly betray you."

"What?" Taz frowned. "What do you mean?"

"The King of Cats is a dreamwalker. He is wont to come to you at night and steal your secrets when you're least prepared to stop him."

Chapter 9

"Although our House is one of the oldest in Ilirya, we have always served the people. We never shirk our duty. That is what it is to be a member of this family."

"Yes, Father," Asher says.

Taz was ten when his father died in a plague outbreak. Although he was a stern, cold man who never showed his only son the love and approval he desperately craved, Taz had nevertheless been devastated by his death. He had cried for days, his eyes red and his face tearstained. It had been an experience that had brought him and Asher closer together. In the place of his father, Asher, already his best friend, had become his family. It was she who held him when he cried and listened to his wild imaginings of how his relationship with his father might have been if only he'd lived. It was she who procured a sword for his knighting and who made sure he wrote his mother regularly.

Asher had never seen Taz as devastated as he'd been the day the terrible news arrived until they began the solemn ride from the Maji camp, accompanied by five Maji escorts. His face bore the same sunken expression of loss, his eyes the same unfocused desperation as on that day.

Asher reined Cloud over to Fleet's side, concerned. "What's wrong?"

Taz stared ahead vacantly, the spark of life snuffed out of his eyes. Asher was alarmed by this unexpected listlessness bordering on despair. She repeated, "What is it? What's the matter?"

"I—" He faltered and stopped. He looked down at Fleet's silky white mane. "I—I shouldn't be here." His agonized voice was so low it was almost a whisper. The words quivered with overwhelming emotion.

"What? What are you talking about?"

"Asher, I..." His lower lip quivered and for a moment she thought he would begin to cry. When had he last cried? Not since they were children. "I should be stripped of my knighthood. I don't belong on this expedition or in the knighthood at all. I should be cast out. I'm a disgrace."

Asher frowned. What was Taz talking about? Cast out of the knighthood? For what? She shook her head. "I don't understand. What happened?"

"I did a terrible thing." His eyes met her, and they were haunted. His body shriveled into itself, racked by misery. His quivering lips pulled his mouth into an unwilling grimace, a parody of a smile.

Concern and a feeling of misgiving made the hair on the back of her neck rise. "What did you do?"

Taz's answer was high-pitched and feverish. "I was so scared in the canyon. I was out of my mind! The wights, they were all around us. Their hands...grasping...white bone reaching out from the blackness trying to tear us off our horses..."

He shuddered. "I couldn't stand it. You were gone and Henrek was undoubtedly dead, and we were all alone. We were going to die too. We were going to die in that godsforsaken pass and never get back to Ilirya. All I could think about was getting out of there. I had to—I had to escape. Anything to escape. To live. I wanted to live."

He looked at Asher desperately, willing her to understand without having to say the words. His body stretched toward her, his eyes beseeching. But she didn't understand. What had he done? Her skin prickled with unease. Cloud, feeling her concern, shifted under her, sidling away from Fleet.

Taz didn't notice. In a hushed, horrified voice, he whispered, "I tried to leave her. I tried to leave the knight commander behind."

No. Asher stared at him blankly, not wanting to understand what she'd heard. It was too terrible. Leave Commander Bronwen?

Taz licked his lips. The next words tumbled from his mouth like an unstoppable torrent, all his guilt and fear and shame rushing out of him at once. "I kicked Fleet...I—I was so scared all I could think about was getting free of her. Henrek was dead and Morningstar was...and I had to get away to survive. I saw Cloud's tail disappearing, and I knew if I stayed with her, I would die. So I tried to get away. I tried to leave her."

A wave of nausea hit Asher and she had to fight not to retch. Her mouth watered and she swallowed once, twice, pushing down on the revulsion rising in her. The knight commander was helpless to defend herself. She would have been killed almost instantly on her own. She would have been torn to pieces. How could Taz have done such a thing?

Her face must have shown what she was thinking because Taz started to bawl, great, heaving sobs that shook his entire body. The Maji around them looked over curiously, then pretended not to see. Whatever was happening among their Iliryan guests, it was not a matter for them. The closest soldier rode his blue roan horse wide, giving the two Iliryan knights space.

"How *could* you?" Asher hissed. "Commander Bronwen is our *commander*. How could you leave her?"

"I was so scared! I'm not brave like you!" Taz's eyes were becoming red, his face puffy. He sniffled miserably, his cheeks damp with tears. "I did an awful thing, I know. I don't deserve to be a knight anymore. I'm a failure. I let everyone down. So strip me of my knighthood and turn me out. It's what I deserve."

Under chivalric law, Taz had technically deserted. He had abandoned the field of battle. *And* he had failed to protect the knight commander, which was so bad there wasn't even a rule about it. The punishment for desertion was to be cast out of the knighthood. Although the punishment was rarely invoked, it had happened several times since Asher had begun training as a knight.

Asher was so appalled and angry she could barely think. She would *never* have abandoned Commander Bronwen. No matter what, she would have fought to the last breath to protect her. How could Taz have put her in such mortal danger? How could he have been so selfish and cowardly? Where was his honor?

She took one breath and then another, trying to calm herself. Her body was numb with revulsion, her hands clenched so tightly that the reins bit into her left palm. Taz had betrayed every vow he'd made as a knight. She could barely stand to look at him. When she could finally speak, she asked, "If you fled, then how is it you and Commander Bronwen left the canyon together?"

Taz covered his mouth with his right hand, which was shaking. "I hadn't gotten very far when the Maji came. They saved both of us. If not for them…oh gods, if not for them…"

If not for them, Commander Bronwen would have died, torn from her horse and then ripped to shreds by the ravenous wights. And it would have been all Taz's fault.

But then, had he stayed with her and the Maji cavalry not come, he, too, might have died. Then only Asher and Marandir would have survived the awful ordeal. Grudgingly, Asher had to admit it was better he had lived, even under ignoble circumstances, than both died. And perhaps the commander had thought the same. Perhaps she would have done to Fleet what she'd done to Cloud, sending both her knights onward without her, trading her life for theirs.

Even so, it wasn't Taz's decision to make. As a knight, it was his duty to protect her no matter the danger to himself. "What did Commander Bronwen say?"

"Nothing." Taz's voice was so soft behind his hand Asher could barely hear it. He still couldn't meet her eyes. He stared at Fleet's mane through tear-drenched lashes. "She hasn't said anything about it even though she knows what I did. And it's—it's so awful!"

He looked up at Asher. "I can't look at her. *I* did it. *I* left her to die. You never would have left her. There's no excuse for what I did. I…failed. I'm no knight."

Asher let go of her reins and used both hands to rub her face. Part of her agreed with him. His cowardice made her skin crawl. He was right to be ashamed of himself. He had betrayed all of his oaths as a knight. It was only by luck and through the timely help of the Maji cavalry that the knight commander had survived. By all rights, he should be cast out of the knighthood and his name sullied by his dishonorable act.

But another part of her was more forgiving. In her mind, she saw Taz charging into the black dragon after she'd already tried and fallen. She'd always known he could be tentative and timid, but he could be brave, as well. Should one moment of overwhelming fear, one failure, be held against him so permanently? Perhaps, she realized, that was why Commander Bronwen had done nothing. She forgave him that moment of weakness.

Asher thought of Avrill, who had never fought at the southern front despite having been a knight for almost three decades, and of all the knights who had refused to come to the Southlands as part of the knight commander's expedition. They had all been afraid, too. Commander Bronwen had once said, "Bravery cannot be taught," and now Asher understood what she meant. Taz had done the best he could. He had been as brave as he could be, and when his bravery had finally run out, he had broken and run. It wasn't really his fault.

She softened as she looked at Taz's crumpled, morose face. This wasn't the face of a traitor. It was the face of a human, flaws and all. "You're not a bad person. You were scared. Your fear overwhelmed you in that moment, but you're not a bad knight."

Taz squeezed his eyes together. There was so much anguish and self-loathing in his face. "How can you say that? I'm an *awful* person. I don't deserve to wear this armor. The Commander must hate me."

Asher realized if she didn't get through to him soon, she might lose him forever. He would sink so far into a pit of self-blame he would never come out again. He would cast himself out of the knighthood and never see himself as anything more than a coward. He would forever be the knight who failed in the moment of greatest need.

She gave him a small, encouraging smile. "Everyone makes mistakes. Everyone does things they wish they hadn't. Commander Bronwen knows that. I'm sure she doesn't blame you. One moment of weakness doesn't erase all the good you've done. You're still a good knight. You can make up for it one day."

Taz sniffed and wiped his nose with the back of his hand. "Do you really think so?"

She nodded. "I know so. You know what Idras told me? He said, 'No one is truly fearless. Deep down, everyone is trying not to soil their britches.' So you see? You're just like everyone else. We're all trying to do our best. Besides, I almost wet myself when I saw the dragon! You saw how scared I was!"

The barest shadow of a smile appeared on Taz's blotchy red face. If they had been walking, Asher would have hugged him. Instead, she tried to give him as heartening a look as she could. She knew then that even if it took time, Taz would recover. And the next time, she didn't think he would run so easily.

Once Taz seemed calmer, she rode forward and caught the attention of the Maji captain, who she'd learned was named Saraya. Asher had a question that had been bothering her as they rode south on the road to Nyara. "Is it true the King of Cats can enter someone else's dreams?"

Saraya's black hair was cut short and slanted across her forehead toward her left ear like a shaft of light. When she nodded, it swept almost into her green eyes. "It is true, yes."

"How?"

"It is his mage gift, but I do not know anything more than that. They say he is the only oneiromancer in the entire kingdom."

"Has he walked in your dreams?"

"Perhaps. But I have no secrets worth stealing. If he came at all, I doubt he came a second time."

Asher cocked her head to the side. The Guardian had also mentioned secrets. "What do you mean he steals secrets from dreams?"

Saraya pressed her thin lips together. "People are much less guarded in sleep than waking. They say he teases secrets from dreamers without them knowing. It is how he keeps a close eye on Sarsenia."

"He doesn't hide what he does?"

"No. The Sarsen know not to keep secrets from their king."

Asher didn't like the sound of that. She wished she could remember what she'd been dreaming while she was in the Southlands. Could the King of Cats have visited *her* dreams? What would he have sought from her, a mere knight in the knight commander's retinue? What secrets did she know?

"Are the Sarsen afraid of him?"

Saraya's face was troubled. She chewed her lower lip for a moment. "The King of Cats is a clever man. He has to be, to have ruled the five tribes for as long as he has. And so long as he wields the Death Stone, he is more powerful than anyone in Sarsenia. Perhaps the people are not afraid but rather…wary. One would not want to cross the King of Cats."

Asher's ears pricked up. The Death Stone? Wasn't that what King Izmar had mentioned in his letter to the Iliryan King Savin right before the war began? "What's the Death Stone?"

Saraya immediately looked uncomfortable. She rubbed her right palm against her thigh. "It is best not to speak of it."

Asher wanted to ask more questions, but Saraya's closed face suggested she was not open to further discussion. A moment later, Saraya pointed at Asher's chest. "I am sorry you were injured by Dark Magic."

Unconsciously, Asher drew her right hand to her chest, where the wight's falchion had scratched her. Beneath her cuirass, she could feel a lingering ache that was ebbing by the hour. She shrugged. "A scrape and nothing more. The wight was lucky and found me when I'd just awoken."

Saraya's dark eyebrows came together. "More than a scrape, lady knight. The wights' weapons are edged with Dark Magic. You were not only injured, you are *infected*."

All the breath seemed to have been sucked out of Asher's body at once. Her stomach dropped and her skin instantly turned cold as ice. A shiver ran up her arms. Infected? No, she couldn't be. Her mind raced. What would happen to her now? Would she be crippled like Commander Bronwen? How much time did she have?

Asher tried to choke out a question, but no words would come. Saraya's green eyes softened. "It will not kill you tomorrow. It seems the blade just nicked you, so the poison will grow slowly. It will be many, many years before its effect will be seen. I can barely see the blackness now. It is a faint shadow, nothing more."

"Can it be cured?" Asher's voice was choked and small.

She knew the answer to her question, of course. Both Lyse and the Magus had said there was no way to stop Dark Magic's infection, and the Maji had done nothing to indicate they knew of a cure. But she had to ask anyway.

Saraya shook her head. "No. But take heart. You will be old and gray before the magic starts to affect you."

Asher was paralyzed. She was mortally wounded. She was dead. The world swirled around her, and she had to clutch Cloud's saddle to stay upright. She pulled at her cuirass, trying to find the air that wouldn't fill her lungs.

Through the tornado of emotions spinning through her mind, a memory flickered to life. It was of her father, lying on his deathbed. Sickness had ravaged his body, and he was no longer the strong, vigorous man he'd been months before. His face was pallid, his eyes sunken, and his lips cracked. When he reached out to Asher to hold her hand, his was little more than dry kindling covered with rice paper.

"It's all right, daughter," he rasped. "There's no need for tears. We all meet our end some day."

"But I don't want to lose you!" Asher fell onto his chest and buried her face in his purple robe, sobbing. "Not yet! It's too soon!"

"One day you'll see that death isn't as awful as it seems. It's like reaching the end of a good book. You might wish there were more to read, but you enjoyed what was there. Your story will write itself every day of your life. At the end, if your story has been full of love and happiness and honor, you'll have no regret about closing the cover. Or at least, not many regrets. *My* only regret, the *only* one," he tried to smile, "is missing your knighting. You will do us proud as a knight."

In the Southlands, tears pricked Asher's eyes. Her father had died only a few days later. She sat straighter in the saddle. She was Lord Ivar's daughter. Like him and the knight commander, she would face the spectre of her death head-on and without self-pity. She would continue on the same way she had before and forget the Dark Magic's poison seeping into her veins. There was no use worrying about it anyway; she could die from other causes long before the Dark Magic killed her.

She squeezed her legs, urging Cloud forward. She intended to ask Commander Bronwen how she planned to negotiate with the King of Cats once they reached the capital, but when she saw the knight commander's face, her heart sank. Commander Bronwen's face was gaunt, her eyes dull and half-open. They had trouble focusing as they found Asher's face. Asher tried to forget Saraya's words: "She will not last another week." The Knight Commander still had time. They could still reach the capital. She could still negotiate for peace. It wouldn't fall to Asher.

Commander Bronwen squinted at her. "Asher?"

"Yes, Commander?"

She tried not to think about the fact that one day she would be like the knight commander: crippled by Dark Magic and slowly losing control of her body. Disintegrating piece by piece.

"If negotiations fail—"

"They won't fail. You'll convince the King of Cats to agree to peace."

Commander Bronwen's voice was firm. "If they fail, you must send Marandir home immediately, without a second to lose. The queen and her council will need to be informed of the failure."

Asher shuddered. The consequences of failure were too great for her to consider. Devastation. Total defeat. She didn't notice the commander's other words: "If they fail, *you* must send Marandir home."

In a low, cautious voice Asher asked, "If *we* started the war, wouldn't the King of Cats be more likely to accept peace?"

"We may only hope." Commander Bronwen's voice was tired.

"Did we?" Finally, she might get an answer to a question that had nipped at her heels throughout their entire journey.

Commander Bronwen's tone was flat. "Officially, no."

Even though it wasn't a total surprise, the commander's tacit confirmation that it was the Iliryans and not the Southerners who had started the war still shocked Asher. Every hair on her body stood on end. Why had King Hap's father, King Savin, lied? And why had his council and his generals gone along with the lie? "Why? Why did King Savin do it? Why did he start the war?"

"I don't know."

Asher thought she heard sadness and frustration in Commander Bronwen's words. The commander had been only a child when the war began. When had she found out the truth about it? When she became knight commander? Who else knew?

"Does the queen know?"

Commander Bronwen looked at her sharply, the weariness in her face momentarily replaced by reproach. "Our duty is to end the war, not to ask questions."

Asher wanted to protest. It *was* their job to ask questions. What if the very key to ending the war lay in discovering its origins? What did Commander Bronwen know that she wasn't saying?

Commander Bronwen's face went slack. Her eyes lost their focus and she looked around. "Where is Henrek?"

Asher knit her brow. "Commander?"

"Where is he? Where is Henrek?"

Asher's heart skipped a beat. Commander Bronwen knew where Henrek was. She had seen what had become of Morningstar with her own eyes and knew before anyone else what it meant. Something was wrong.

Asher tried to keep her voice calm, but still it came out too high. "What do you mean?"

Commander Bronwen's chin sank to her chest. Half to herself, half to Asher, she muttered, "He shouldn't come with us to the Southlands. It's too dangerous. I've lost too many friends already. Tell him not to come. Tell him to stay in King's City, where he'll be safe."

Oh no, Commander, no. Please no, Asher thought, horrorstruck. She swallowed hard, her mouth dry. "Commander, do you...do you know where we are right now?"

Commander Bronwen's eyelids fluttered, but she didn't look up. "What do you mean? Of course I recognize Prabst. I should know my own home."

Asher couldn't breathe. The weight of the entire sky was bearing down on her, crushing her beneath it.

"Did you hear me?" Commander Bronwen's voice cracked the air like a whip. "I said to tell Henrek not to come! You have to find him and tell him that!"

Asher's spirit crumbled. She bit down so hard on the inside of her cheek she drew blood. Would the commander come back to herself? *Please come back*, she whispered in her mind. *Please. What will we do without you?* Commander Bronwen looked so lost. And sad. She deserved better.

Asher took a shaky breath. "No, Commander. I'll be sure that he doesn't come. He'll stay safe in King's City."

Commander Bronwen nodded, her head bobbing like a seabird on the water. "You're a good squire. You'll make a fine knight one day. I've always known you would. Your father will be so proud."

Tears made Asher's vision swim. She tried to swallow the lump that had formed in her throat and wiped the tears off her cheeks. The commander would recover. She was just tired. All she needed was rest. In the meantime, Asher would do what must be done. With Commander Bronwen's incapacitation, she was the commander of the expedition now.

Commander Bronwen did not recover, and every day the hope of the Iliryans succeeding in their mission seemed dimmer. The group traveled slowly in deference to her deteriorating condition, which weighed the Iliryans down mind and body. The knight commander was lost, drifting away into a world in which all the knights who had passed away were still alive. Strong as she was, no amount of willpower could force her mind and body to knit themselves back together enough to speak for Queen Alea before the King of Cats, and her periods of lucidity, few and far between, weren't enough. When the time came, it would be Asher who would have to negotiate for Ilirya's future.

Commander Bronwen's decline had a chilling effect on the remaining three members of the delegation. Jazmen and Henrek were gone, and the knight commander would join them soon. Everything about their expedition seemed doomed. How could two young knights and a shape-shifting mage carry out the delicate negotiations of statecraft? How could they carry the weight of Ilirya's future on their narrow shoulders? They had believed in the ability of Commander Bronwen's savvy and strength to save them. Without her, the prospects for peace seemed bleak.

Their anxiety over the success of their mission was compounded by sleep deprivation. Asher, Taz, and Marandir had all avoided sleeping as much as possible after the revelation that the King of Cats was a dreamwalker. None of them wanted to inadvertently reveal something in a dream that would cause the mission to fail. As a result, the Iliryans reached the border between the lands of the Maji, Walakai, and the Avicini demoralized, exhausted, and on the brink of one of the most significant moments in Ilirya's history with no plan for how to achieve peace.

Although the Guardian had told them it was possible to reach the end of the Maji's land in three days, it ended up taking them a full four, moving as slowly as they were. As they'd arrived in the evening, Asher decided they would sleep and then set off in the morning when it was light and they were better rested. As the Iliryans set about making camp, their Maji escort left them soundlessly, melting back into the trees like living shadows until only Saraya remained. When Marandir and Taz dispersed to collect firewood, she pulled Asher aside.

"If you wish, I will stay here with your commander and take care of her until she passes. It will only be a few days at most. I will see to it she is buried honorably, as is befitting a warrior of her rank. This will allow you to travel on to the capital unburdened."

Asher drew in a sharp breath. Abandon Commander Bronwen? Never! Iliryan knights would *never* forsake one of their own. Regardless of the commander's condition, she was still their responsibility. They would take care of her until… Asher pushed away a vision of Commander Bronwen's limp and lifeless body. She didn't want to imagine a world without the knight commander.

She stood straighter, raising her chin. "The commander will come with us."

Saraya frowned disapprovingly, long shadows from the setting sun falling across her face and deepening the line between her black brows. "A good leader knows when she has become a burden. I doubt your commander would want you to be encumbered by her. You need all your focus and energy for what is to come. The King of Cats is wily. It will not do for you to be distracted when meeting with him. If your commander understood the situation, I am certain she would agree."

Asher rested her hand on the pommel of her sword. The black boar beneath her palm gave her strength. It represented the line of service and duty that had been passed down for generations by her family. She raised her chin higher. "The knight commander is no burden. We will not abandon her."

Saraya sighed. "Well, you are no White Queen, that much is clear."

"Who?"

Saraya's eyes looked south, toward what Asher assumed were the Walakai's lands. "The new leader of the Walakai. She murdered their previous ruler, her own father, and took his throne several months ago. I imagine *she* would have cast your commander aside at the first sign of weakness." She shrugged. "But such are the Walakai. It is their way."

She gave a short bow, then swung onto her horse, taking up the reins in her hands. "I wish you well. I, for one, would be glad to see an end to the war."

She turned her horse and then was gone, leaving the Iliryans alone in the Southlands for the first time in days. Asher heard footsteps on the grass, and a moment later Taz joined her. His face seemed longer, more somber than it had when they'd started their journey. Some of the lightheartedness that had once filled his deep-blue eyes was gone. Had her face aged as well? Asher didn't know.

She nodded to him, and he nodded back. The air between them filled with the sounds of insects chirping. A firefly flew past, and Asher resisted the urge to reach out and catch it.

Taz said, "I can't believe we're almost to Nyara. It feels like we left Ilirya a lifetime ago."

Asher nodded. She could barely remember sitting in the Boar's Tusk Tavern, betting with Erborn and convincing Taz to come. It seemed like a dream. She had never imagined then what awaited them here. Had it been worth it? She wouldn't know until the last possible moment.

"How are we going to do it? How do we convince the King of Cats to agree to peace?" Taz's blue eyes were wide. "It should have been the commander meeting him tomorrow. *She's* the knight commander. *She's* prepared for this. How will you do it without her? What will you say to him?"

Asher rubbed the toe of her boot into the ground, watching as it dug a small divot. She'd asked herself the same questions for days, hour after hour as they rode from desert back to forested plains, lost in her own thoughts. Every time, she'd come up empty. She had no idea what she was going to do. What could she say to the mercurial King of Cats? How could she negotiate on behalf of an entire kingdom? She was a knight, not a diplomat. Her father had been the politician, not her.

None of her worrying mattered if she couldn't get close enough to him to say a single word. If he felt like it, he could have the Iliryans executed the moment they entered the city. After weeks on the road, their journey could end in the blink of an eye, and all of it would have been for nothing. Ilirya would still fall, and Henrek and Jazmen and the Knight Commander's deaths would have been in vain.

She rubbed her temples, helpless to stop the pressure building behind them. "I'll figure it out. We can't go back without peace."

The dying orange sun painted the thick clouds purple. Asher watched it with melancholy. The sight was lovely, but it wasn't *her* sunset. Her sunset was hundreds of miles away, in a land she might never see again. She faced Taz. "Why did she choose *me* to lead the expedition? Why not Marandir?

He's older and more experienced. It would have made sense for him to take over."

Taz shrugged. "He's not a knight. Peace is the domain of the knighthood, not the King's Regiment." He put his hand on Asher's shoulder. "And maybe she thought that of the three of us, you were the most likely to bring home peace. She believes in you."

Asher bit her lip. What if Commander Bronwen was wrong? What if she couldn't do it? It was so much pressure to put on her. If she failed, thousands of their people would die. All of Ilirya would likely fall.

He squeezed her shoulder. "I believe in you too. You can do it. I know you can."

Asher resisted the urge to hug him and hold him close for comfort. In situations like this, everyone sought solace. The future unknown was a scary thing. Instead, she clapped him roughly on the back. "Go get some sleep. I need both you and Marandir rested tomorrow. We can't ride into Nyara looking half-dead or the King of Cats won't take us seriously."

He snorted, then started to shuffle away.

"Hey, Taz!" she called. He turned to look at her. "Strength and honor."

He smiled. "Duty and queen."

Asher gathered a few final twigs for the fire. She'd assigned herself the first watch, but in reality, she didn't intend to wake Taz for the next shift. She wouldn't be able to sleep anyway, and he and Marandir needed rest more than she did, even if they were afraid to dream. She threw the twigs on the pile beside the fire, then sat down and settled her back against a tree, watching the orange flames crackle and dance in front of her.

She wished Tayanna was there with her. *What would Tayanna do? How would she convince the King of Cats to agree to peace?* Her heart convulsed as she remembered Tayanna's dark, sparkling eyes, but her mind found no answer to her questions. Whatever the answer, Tayanna's ghost was silent.

Asher only knew she'd fallen asleep because she was jerked into consciousness by the unmistakable sound of swords clashing and the scuffle of struggling bodies. In an instant, she was on her feet, her sword drawn. An attack? The fire had either died or been extinguished, leaving the camp almost pitch black. In the dim moonlight, she could barely make out shapes moving but she couldn't count their numbers. How many attackers were there?

Her thoughts immediately went to Commander Bronwen. Was the knight commander safe? She didn't have time to check. A black figure crossed her path and she instinctively attacked. The sound of her sword clanging against its helmet was like the muted ringing of a bell. The reverberations ran back up the blade and into her hand. The person—she couldn't tell if it was a man or woman—dropped instantly into a heap on the ground.

"Taz!" she screamed, trying to see his familiar shape in the darkness. Her heart was pounding. Why were they under attack? By whom? Had anyone been hurt? She cursed herself for falling asleep.

"Here!" Taz panted somewhere to her right. He wasn't where his bedroll had been. His voice was strained, and she could tell he was actively engaged in fighting.

"Marandir?" No answer. "Marandir!"

Asher swallowed a wave of nausea, fearing the worst. They were so close to Nyara. Why was everything falling apart at the last minute? Something slammed into her from behind, toppling her over. She landed on the body she'd just felled and rolled off it, springing to her feet and spinning to face whoever had attacked her.

But her attention was split. She wasn't fighting just to defend herself. She was still responsible for Marandir and the knight commander, wherever they were and whatever their condition. If they weren't safe, she had to find and protect them.

She called to Taz, "Is the commander safe?"

"I don't know." His voice was full of panic and fear.

The blood coursing through Asher's veins made her lightheaded. Taz couldn't be all that remained of the Iliryan delegation! There were too many questions. Where were Marandir and Commander Bronwen? Why weren't they answering? Who were their attackers?

A staff cracked her across her cheek, and she fell to her knees. In the black night, she hadn't seen it coming. Her face throbbed where the wood had struck her, and her head reeled. Her fingers dug into the ground as she tried to steady herself. She was dizzy.

Get up, she told herself. *Keep fighting. Protect Commander Bronwen.* She started to stand up, but it was too late. The staff slammed down against her head and everything went dark.

Chapter 10

"Promise you'll come back."

Asher says it every time. And every time, Tayanna promises. Tayanna reaches out and caresses Asher's cheek. "I never leave you. You are mine and I am yours."

Pain spread through Asher's head like cracks in ice, throbbing and piercing; sharp-edged shards digging into her brain. She groaned and curled into a ball, squeezing her eyes shut to keep any light out. For several minutes, she couldn't think about anything else. It was like knives thrust into the back of her head. She hadn't felt pain like that since she'd been knocked off Cloud's back in a joust and come to minutes later, laid out on the grass.

Eventually, however, the pain relented enough for her to evaluate her situation. Her last memory was of waking up to a fight. Someone had attacked their camp. But now she felt hard stone, not grass, beneath her, and that meant she wasn't in the camp anymore. Where was she?

She opened her eyes and immediately recoiled. A pretty young woman with bright blue eyes and wavy hair so light blonde it was almost white was staring at her. Asher scrambled backward, propelling herself on her hands and feet until her back smacked against a wall behind her. Her hand grasped automatically for her sword, but she found she was no longer wearing her sword belt. An amused smile pulled up one side of the young woman's mouth as she watched. It only unnerved Asher more.

"Who are you?" she demanded. "Where am I?" Looking around wildly, she saw she was in a small, empty room. Judging by the light that entered through the small window above, it was already day. Where were the others? Where were Taz, Marandir, and the commander?

The woman stepped forward and knelt down, putting her large blue eyes on the same level as Asher's. The fine, snow white dress she wore draped in folds around her ankles. "I'm Imari. Don't worry, you're safe now." Her voice was smooth and reassuring, but Asher didn't feel reassured.

"Where—what—what happened?" Asher's thoughts jumbled together, crowding each other out as they jostled for attention. Thinking made her head throb and her eyes cross.

"You were ambushed last night. We rescued you and brought you here."

Her answers only made Asher more confused. Who was *we*? Where was *here*? Panic was rising in her chest, causing her lungs to constrict. Why hadn't the others been brought as well? Were they still alive? The air was too thick to breathe. It filled her lungs like thick pine sap. The room started to spin, and she dug her fingernails into the stone blocks behind her to steady herself.

"What happened to the others? The ones who were with me? Where are they?"

Imari's thick, dark eyebrows rose. "You mean your three friends. I'm sorry to tell you we couldn't save them. Only you."

Asher's heart beat wildly. A trapped bird fighting to break free. *No! No no no no no!* It wasn't possible. It couldn't be. She imagined their crumpled bodies lying in the camp and then thrust the vision away.

Imari continued, "We couldn't stop them from being taken."

Asher unconsciously jumped forward, snatching at the glimmer of hope Imari's words offered. "What? Taken? By whom?"

Imari's eyes narrowed. "The King of Cats." She spat the words, as though they were bitter in her mouth.

"No!" Asher gasped. She wrapped her arms around her stomach. Why would he take them? How did he know where they'd made camp? Had the Guardian betrayed them? Had he found out from a dream? Her mind whirled, filled with questions for which she had no answer.

Her shock was quickly overtaken by despair. All hope for peace was destroyed. Surely the King of Cats didn't intend to negotiate in good faith after kidnapping his Iliryan interlocutors. All their efforts were for nothing.

She staggered to her feet, uncoordinated as a newborn foal and still dazed by the blow to her head. From the fog of her mind, one clear, overpowering thought emerged that drove her forward. "I have to go to them." She needed to protect the others. It was her duty.

Imari frowned at her, her full, pink lips puffing out into a pout. "You're in no condition to go anywhere right now! Look at you, you can barely stand!"

Asher looked around the room as though her sword would magically materialize before her, trying not to sway. She muttered to herself, "I need my sword. I need Cloud. I need to go."

Imari stood up, crossing her thin, bare arms over her chest. "And your plan is…?"

Asher squeezed her eyes closed, trying to will away the lingering pain in her head. It was distracting her when she needed to think clearly. "I'll figure it out when I get there."

Imari laughed. "I like you. One lone knight against the army of the King of Cats. Yes, I like you." Her eyes glittered with amusement. "Do you even know where *there* is? Where will you ride, brave knight? Where is the King of Cats keeping your companions?"

Asher's mouth twitched, then her shoulders slumped. Imari, whoever she was, was right. She had no idea where they were being held. She didn't even know where *she* was now. Was she still near Nyara? Was she on Maji land? She needed more information. Avrill would have admonished her for running heedlessly into danger without being prepared.

Imari cocked her head to the side, her lopsided smile inching higher and creasing the corners of her eyes. "I like your pluck."

Asher licked her lips. Her mouth was so dry it was sticky. "Why would he ambush us? We were coming to Nyara to negotiate for peace! We're no threat to him." Her voice was more plaintive than she'd intended. Desperate, even.

"Bargaining chips." Imari's eyes glinted when she said the words.

"Hostages, you mean." Asher's voice was full of despair. How had she been so naïve? Commander Bronwen would never have walked them into a trap like that. She racked her brain, trying to remember signs of an ambush that she'd missed, but she couldn't. How had she missed it?

Imari smirked. "Whatever it takes to gain an upper hand."

Asher rubbed her face. Her palms pulled at the skin of her cheeks. She didn't know what to do. What *could* she do? She felt sick when she thought of Commander Bronwen. Had she been thrown in a dungeon somewhere? Was she scared and in pain? Asher had to find them. She had promised Queen Alea she would protect the knight commander. Every second she spent away from the commander she was failing to fulfill her promise.

Imari stepped closer and laid a gentle hand on Asher's wrist. Her touch was soft and warm. "Don't worry about your friends. Everything will be all right. So long as the King of Cats thinks he can use them as leverage in negotiations, they'll be safe."

Asher nodded slowly. They were bargaining chips. They would be safe so long as the King of Cats had a use for them. She didn't have to rush away recklessly. She had time. She could afford to think and plan how to confront the King of Cats. Her body relaxed a little and she breathed more easily.

Imari smiled encouragingly, her cheeks dimpling.

Asher was momentarily struck by her beauty. Unconsciously, she played with the necklace she wore, Tayanna's necklace. "You're sure there's time?"

Imari nodded. "I promise." Then, her voice low and impassioned, she said, "The King of Cats is a tyrant. He's ruled the five tribes for far too long. No king is meant to rule forever. *I* intend to see his reign ended."

She stared at Asher with shining eyes. "You can help me stop him."

Asher took a step backward. "What? Me?"

Imari grimaced. "So long as he holds the Death Stone, the King of Cats can't be defeated. *I need that stone*. And you can help me get it."

Asher gaped at her, eyes wide. Once more, a mention of the mysterious Death Stone! What was it and what did it do? "What *is* the Death Stone?"

Imari recrossed her arms uncomfortably. Her eyes shifted away. "It's… complicated. Once you retrieve it, I'll tell you all about it. There will be more time then."

"But—"

"Don't be concerned. It won't hurt you."

Asher was bewildered. If the Death Stone was so important, how could she possibly get it? Where was it even located? And why was Imari asking her to help when she wasn't even a Southerner? Why couldn't she get it herself? Not to mention, who *was* she anyway? All Asher knew was her name.

As though she could read Asher's thoughts, Imari said, giving a small, triumphant smile, "Fate has brought you to me. You will be the key to the king's downfall, the chance I've been waiting for. When you go to Nyara, the King of Cats will invite you into the castle and allow you to get near him. He won't be able to resist himself. He enjoys nothing more than playing games with his enemies. He will want to see your face as he takes all hope from you."

She pantomimed the next part. "Because he carries the Death Stone with him on his scepter at all times, you will take it from him then, when he least expects it. After that, he will be easily defeated. Without the Stone, he is nothing."

Asher gaped at her. This was madness. Lunacy. Stealing the King of Cats's scepter? Why would she agree to such a scheme? Even if she did agree, how could the plan possibly work? *If* Imari was right that the King of Cats would want to see her and *if* she somehow managed to wrestle the scepter from him, how would she escape his castle with it? The plan seemed optimistic and incomplete at best, suicidal at worst.

She shook her head. Whether the King of Cats deserved to rule or not was an internal matter for the Southerners, not for her. She had to remain focused on her own mission, which right now was to save her friends. "I'm sorry. I can't help you. You'll have to find someone else."

Imari stepped closer. "You have no choice. The king is a despot. He relishes chaos and destruction. He kidnapped your friends. He will never give you true peace. If you want peace, this is the only way. Help me and *I* will give you peace."

She continued to move forward until her face was inches from Asher's. Asher could see she was barely older than Asher herself. "Help me," she whispered, taking Asher's hand. "The people of Sarsenia are slaves. Help me free them. The king does not grant audiences to his Sarsen subjects. Only you can get close enough to him to take back the Death Stone."

Asher was enthralled by the irresistible, intense light in her eyes. It made her want to agree to anything Imari asked. And why not? She was promising the very peace the Iliryans sought. If the King of Cats wasn't going to agree to an end to the war, perhaps it was time for the Iliryans to back one of his rivals. Whoever she was.

"If I help you, will you help me find my companions?"

Imari stepped back, a broad smile on her face. "Of course! When I'm queen, I'll have them released immediately. Not a hair on their Rann heads will be touched!"

Asher chewed her lower lip. Avrill had always warned her against becoming entangled in politics, but she didn't see an alternative. She needed help. Besides, what other choice did she have? She could hardly ride into Nyara and negotiate with the King of Cats while her friends were his hostages. She didn't even know in which direction Nyara lay. Imari was asking the impossible, but at least it carried with it the hope that it would lead to peace for Ilirya.

She nodded. "Okay."

Imari beamed. "Good! I knew destiny brought you to me for a reason. It's too late now to go to Nyara. You'll stay here tonight, and in the morning, we'll ride together to the capital."

"Where *are* we?"

"Come with me and I'll show you."

Imari turned and walked the few strides across the small room. As they exited into the hallway outside, two men who had been waiting on the other side of the door fell into line behind them. They were rough and muscular, with heavy swords and thick leather armor. At first glance, Asher assumed they had been guarding the room, but as she and Imari moved down one hallway after another and they continued to follow, she realized they must be bodyguards. Who *was* Imari?

As they made their way through richly furnished rooms that rivaled the residences of some of Ilirya's elites, Asher realized she was in a castle, and no small one either. She wanted to ask Imari the dozens of questions buzzing through her mind, but Imari seemed in no mood to make conversation. She walked quickly, determinedly, leading Asher to some destination unknown. At last, she pushed against a thick wooden door and they entered a modestly sized room with bookshelves that ran floor to ceiling on three of its four sides. The way the daylight entered through the enormous window on the fourth wall made the books' gilded bindings shine. Asher marveled. Even her own father, who had been fond of reading, hadn't owned so many books.

Imari walked to the large window that ran along the far wall and looked out, pride and satisfaction on her face. Asher joined her. The window, and therefore the castle itself, was situated on a hill high above the ground, overlooking a broad valley. Trees of all heights, colors, and kinds blanketed the hill, providing the castle cozy seclusion. In the valley, a patchwork of assiduously farmed brown and green fields blanketed the countryside, indicating that the area's inhabitants were primarily farmers.

"This," Imari announced, raising her palms with a flourish, "is Walakia."

"It's so beautiful!" Asher breathed. A thought struck her. She turned her eyes to Imari. "But if this is Walakia, then you're—"

Imari's cheeks dimpled with amusement. "The White Queen."

Her eyes sparkled as Asher's widened. So this was the leader of the Walakai, the third of the Sarsen tribes. Asher had never imagined she would be so young, given how old the Magus and the Guardian were. In fact, she was nothing like them at all.

Imari held out her hand, grinning. "Now that I've given my name, what's yours?"

Bemused, Asher shook her hand weakly. "Asher."

"Welcome to Walakia, Asher."

Casting an impish smile over her shoulder, Imari unlatched the window and pushed it open. Cool air gusted into the room. Stray strands of Asher's brown hair were momentarily batted around her forehead before they settled once more. Imari leaned out the open window and looked down.

Below them was a narrow, grassy terrace. On it, a man was engaging in what at first Asher assumed was falconry. She immediately realized, however, that those were no falcons sitting on block perches but rather two creatures the likes of which she'd never seen before. From a distance, they looked like bright red and pink birds, their wings tucked along their backs. But rather than having a bird's short neck and sleek tail feathers, they had long, snake-like necks and even longer tails that ended in spiked points. "Dragons!"

Her fingers tightened. She couldn't help the shiver that ran up her spine. She never wanted to see another dragon again.

Imari whistled, a high, shrill sound, and the red dragon looked up to identify the source of the sound. Immediately, it launched itself skyward, beating its leathery wings until it propelled itself not just level with the open window, but right through it! Asher jumped backward, shocked and concerned and fumbling for a weapon she no longer carried, but Imari—the White Queen—wasn't alarmed. Instead, she extended her forearm the way a falconer would to a falcon. Although the dragon, whose scaly red body was half as long as she was tall, seemed too large to fit, it nevertheless wrapped its sharp black talons around her arm and settled comfortably there just as a hawk would. Imari began to stroke the sharp ridge on its forehead with her index finger. The dragon closed its bright yellow eyes and made a soft whirring sound that Asher guessed was contentment.

Asher couldn't believe what she was seeing. Dragons were dangerous. Jazmen had been killed by one only days ago. Why was Imari keeping them as pets when they would grow to be larger than a house and destroy everything around them? They were vile, evil creatures. If only she had her sword, she would kill it herself.

Imari laughed. "Endorran isn't a dragon, he's a wyvern. They're related to dragons but they're smaller and don't breathe fire. And unlike dragons, they're not Dark, nasty creatures." She smiled lovingly at the creature. "I bred him myself. He would never hurt me. Wyverns are fiercely loyal. He would do anything for me."

She looked at Asher and something flickered in her eyes. "I wish people were more like wyverns."

"How big will he get?" Asher kept her distance, not chancing the wyvern's razor-sharp beak or claws. Every part of the creature was designed to gouge, slice, or mutilate, and without her sword she would be defenseless if it chose to attack. It certainly was not the type of pet she would have chosen for herself.

"He's a juvenile now, but full grown he won't be much bigger than a horse."

"What will you do with him?"

Imari looked the wyvern over. "He'll be part of my protection. Wyverns are ferocious fighters."

Asher remembered what Saraya had said. Imari killed her father to take his throne. If it was normal for rulers of the Walakai to be assassinated, she could understand why Imari would need all the help she could get.

Imari extended her arm and encouraged the creature to depart. It chirruped at her once, then took flight, soaring out of the room and into the bright, cloudless blue sky. Imari watched it go, then carefully closed and latched the window. When she turned back, her eyes traveled up and down Asher's body with the same appraising look she'd given the creature. "Perhaps you've heard of the customs of my people."

Before Asher might have spoken, she continued, "We're very quarrelsome, it's true, and for that reason loyalty is hard to come by. But you have no stake in this land, no ulterior motive. You have no reason to betray me. Once the King of Cats has been defeated, you could stay here as part of my retinue. I would reward you handsomely."

Asher knit her brow. Stay in the Southlands? It was unthinkable. Ilirya needed her. Not to mention King's City was her home. She knew nothing about the Southlands. What could possibly tempt her to stay?

She cleared her throat uncomfortably. "I couldn't. Ilirya is my home. All I want is to get back there."

Imari gave a half smile. "New homes can be made."

She crossed the room to where Asher was standing, her eyes holding Asher's. When she reached her, she ran her hand along Asher's jaw line. It was an unexpectedly intimate gesture, one that was so out of place given their recent introduction that it ordinarily would have shocked Asher. Without meaning to, however, she closed her eyes and leaned into Imari's touch ever so slightly.

"Promise me you'll at least consider it." Imari's voice was soft and soothing, and Asher could hear the smile in it. "Walakia has its attractions as well. You might come to prefer it here."

Asher did consider it. Maybe Ilirya didn't need her. If Imari delivered on her promise of peace, would Ilirya miss one knight? And what was waiting for her there anyway? Nothing and no one. Here in the Southlands, on the other hand, she could start over. It was a new and unexplored frontier unlike anything she'd ever find in Ilirya. And if Imari became queen, Asher would have a queen as her direct patron.

She nodded gravely. "Once the others are safe and we have peace, I'll think about it."

Imari's giddy smile stretched across her face. She dropped her hand away from Asher's cheek. "Good. Now, you must be starving. Come to the kitchen with me and we'll see if there's anything left to eat or if my hungry soldiers have eaten it all."

As if on cue, Asher's stomach growled. She realized she was starving. It had been almost a day since she'd last eaten. She hoped that wherever

Commander Bronwen, Marandir, and Taz were, they were being taken care of.

Asher lay on her bed, eyes open. To prevent the King of Cats from walking in her dreams and stealing the details of their plan, Imari had offered her a tonic that would put her so deeply to sleep she wouldn't dream, but Asher had refused. After having slept through the ambush that had resulted in the capture of the other Iliryans, she was leery of being so thoroughly unconscious. Instead, she tossed and turned on the soft bed Imari had provided for her, wishing the night would pass quickly and they could be on their way to Nyara.

When she was with Imari, the White Queen's confidence was infectious. She made it sound as though stealing the Death Stone, ending the rule of the King of Cats, and bringing peace to the warring kingdoms would be easy, but now that she was alone it seemed hopeless. Worse than hopeless. What if the king clapped her in a dungeon before she could even see him? Even if she made it to his throne room, he would be surrounded by guards. How could she possibly hope to wrestle the Death Stone from him?

Nor had Imari explained how they would spirit the stone out of the castle and back to Walakia even if she did somehow succeed in wresting it from the king. The closest Imari had come to detailing an escape plan was to intimate that she had spies everywhere. Asher assumed she meant within the palace itself, but what did that mean for how Asher was supposed to get away without being captured? The stakes were high. If she failed at any point, any hope for peace would be forever destroyed and Ilirya would fall.

Asher desperately wished she could ask Commander Bronwen what to do. What would the commander have done in her place? Would she have left immediately to rescue her kidnapped companions, ignoring the squabbling politics of the Southerner tribes, or would she have played and beaten the King of Cats at his own game? If Asher helped Imari, was she making a terrible gamble, or was she cleverly achieving peace without having to offer any of the concessions Queen Alea had been prepared to give? Asher felt like a mariner at sea on a cloud-filled night: lost with nothing to guide her home.

Suddenly, a flash of bright white light illuminated her dark room. It was so intense she had to shield her eyes with her arm, burying the bridge of her nose in the crook of her elbow. Even behind her eyelids, she could see the bright starburst of light. She waited a moment, then lowered her arm, checking to see if the light had faded. When her eyes adjusted, she was stunned to see Aeryn, the Iliryan war mage, standing in her room.

She gasped. "*Aeryn?*"

She couldn't believe it. How could Aeryn be here in the Southlands? Where had she come from? Asher sat bolt upright in her bed. Was it a dream? An illusion? What was happening?

Aeryn stepped forward and knelt beside her bed. In her black tunic and leggings, she might have been a shadow come to life. She put her finger to her lips, signaling for Asher to be quiet. She looked different from how Asher had last seen her. Normally pale as the snowy Ice Crown region from which she'd come, her skin was now so white it was almost translucent. Deep purple smudged the skin beneath her eyes. Asher had the curious thought that she looked like ice melting.

Most disconcertingly of all, Aeryn's eyes appeared to be frosting over. The irises and pupils of her eyes were almost lost behind a mist of white. Asher had only seen eyes like that among people going blind, but Aeryn was far too young for that. What had happened to her? Asher grabbed Aeryn's hand to assure herself she wasn't dreaming, but her hand was so cold she let it go immediately. It was like holding an icicle. She trapped her hand under her opposite arm, trying to warm it back up.

"Is it really you?" But for the brief feeling of Aeryn's hand in hers, Asher could have believed she was seeing an apparition. Even now, it seemed so impossible for Aeryn to be in her room that she had trouble believing it.

Aeryn nodded, her dark hair falling into her face. "Yes, it's me."

"How? How are you here?"

"I Gated."

"No, now I know I'm dreaming. That's impossible. Everyone knows it's impossible to Gate into the Southlands."

Asher scrunched her face together, trying to make sense of what was happening. She couldn't because it didn't make sense. Aeryn should have been in King's City, not here in Walakia. Another detail struck her. "And besides, you can't Gate…can you?"

She tried to remember what she knew about Gates and mages. Aeryn was a war mage who could create mage fire, a pyromancer. It was a relatively common magical affinity, and while it was useful in battle, it wasn't particularly noteworthy. Gate mages, on the other hand, were the most powerful of all mages. They were so rare they only occurred once or twice in a lifetime throughout all of Ilirya. If Aeryn was a Gate mage, Asher would have known. In fact, all of Ilirya would have known because she would have become the Queen's Shadow, a mage more valuable than all the jewels in the queen's treasury.

But Ilirya hadn't had a Shadow since the last one was murdered months ago. And even if Aeryn somehow could Gate, she couldn't have Gated into the Southlands. No Iliryan mage could Gate or eavesdrop into the Southlands. Aeryn's story didn't add up.

"I don't have much time to explain." Aeryn's voice was low and urgent. She sat down on Asher's bed, and Asher crossed her legs, making room. "I'm here for something called the Death Stone."

Asher couldn't believe what she was hearing. First King Savin, then Imari, now Aeryn! She leaned forward. "Why does everyone want this Death Stone? What does it do?"

Aeryn took a breath. "The Death Stone is a locus of Dark Magic. It's an object of immense power. More importantly, it doesn't belong in this world. It's throwing everything off balance. It needs to be removed before things get worse."

"A locus of Dark Magic?" Asher cocked her head, confused. She wasn't even sure she knew what a 'locus' was.

Asher slipped off the bed and began to pace. "Imagine all the magic in Ilirya concentrated into a single object no larger than your fist. Except rather than normal magic, it's Dark Magic. That's the Death Stone. It's so powerful that using it, Chancellor Vandys and Raelan could have torn a hole between the mortal and divine planes a mile wide during their spell to bring the One God into our world."

"If it's so dangerous, why does the King of Cats have it?"

"It's been used by the rulers of the Southlands for centuries. They were the ones who forged it."

"Why? What did they use it for?"

"Different purposes. King Izmar has used it for the last century and a half to avoid Death."

"King Izmar?" Asher frowned. The Southerner king to whom King Savin had written forty years ago?

Aeryn nodded. "King Izmar is the King of Cats. He's used the power of the Stone all these years to keep himself alive. That's why it's called the Death Stone now. Before him, it was called the Dark Stone. The Death Stone is so powerful that not even Death can take King Izmar so long as he wields it."

Asher was speechless. King Izmar, who ruled when the war between Ilirya and the Southlands began, was the dread and mercurial King of Cats? And he was using the same Death Stone that Imari wanted her to steal to keep himself alive? Was that possible? Could a person really stay alive indefinitely using magic? The thought was overwhelming.

Aeryn's voice vibrated with urgency. "The Death Stone doesn't belong in the mortal realm. Like all Dark Magic, it's an aberration of the natural order. So long as it's here, it will draw other Dark things to it like a beacon."

Like dragons and wights, Asher thought to herself with a flash of understanding. So *that* was why the Southlands suffered every time someone in Ilirya used Dark Magic. The Dark things were drawn to the Stone. But that still didn't answer where they came from.

Aeryn continued, "Ever since the One God's followers ripped a hole between the mortal and divine realms, loci of Dark Magic here in the mortal realm like the Death Stone have prevented that tear from closing completely. It *must* be closed. The Death Stone is the last locus. If it isn't removed from the mortal realm, everything will get much, much worse, and quickly. Many more Dark creatures will be drawn into our world."

Asher was too dazed to think clearly. There was too much new information for her to take in. An impossible Gate into the Southlands that brought an unexpected, familiar face. An immortal king who defied death using magic. A tear between the worlds of gods and humans that wouldn't heal. And a single stone made of Dark Magic that everyone seemed to want. How had she managed to get into the center of it all?

"Then go take it," she said.

Aeryn's mouth twitched unhappily. "I can't."

"Why not? It's in the king's palace, on his scepter. If you can Gate, can't you Gate into the palace and take it?"

Aeryn rubbed her forehead. Her face was creased with fatigue. Asher hadn't noticed how tired she looked, how worn out. "Like all the gods, Death isn't allowed to interfere on the mortal plane. I can't take it myself. You have to do it for me."

"What?" What did that mean and what did Aeryn have to do with it?

She stood and grabbed Aeryn's arm, ignoring the freezing cold she could feel even through Aeryn's thin black shirt. "How do you know all these things? How did you Gate into the Southlands? How is any of this possible?"

Aeryn looked away and shook off her hand. "It's not important right now. What matters is that the entire world is teetering on a precipice, and the Stone is the key to pulling it back. Do you understand? The only way to fix everything is to take it out of the mortal plane. I need you to bring it to me."

Frustration mixed with confusion boiled up in Asher's chest. She was exhausted from days without sleep and worrying about the safety of her companions. She heard Aeryn's riddles and prophecies of doom, but all she had the strength to think about was the mission she had been sent to fulfill. The one she had vowed to see completed no matter what.

"*Ilirya* is teetering on a precipice," she all but shouted, resisting the urge to seize Aeryn by the shoulders. "That Stone can buy us peace if I give it to Imari. If I give it to you, the King of Cats will still be king of the Southlands. We'll never have peace. You're asking me to betray our country."

Aeryn glared at Asher, gritting her teeth. "Have you heard what I said? Neither Ilirya nor the Southlands will matter if the Stone remains in the mortal plane. Everything will be in shambles. Think of the whole world, not only of Ilirya!"

Asher didn't know what to do and it made her stomach churn. Everything was so confusing. She trusted Aeryn…didn't she? But why wasn't Aeryn telling her everything? What was she hiding? And why?

All she knew was that if, after somehow managing to defy the odds and secure the Death Stone, she gave it to Aeryn, she was dooming Ilirya to fall. She was betraying everything she had vowed to protect as a knight.

She crossed her arms. "I'm a knight of Ilirya. My duty lies to Ilirya, not the world."

Aeryn balled her fists, which glowed a soft blue. "You don't understand—"

Asher shifted her hands on her hips as the two squared off. "What's happened to you, Aeryn? You're not yourself. You've changed."

Aeryn's thin, angular face twitched, then her shoulders slumped. As her fists relaxed, the magic went out of them. In a tired voice, she said, "I've been cleansing the world of Dark Magic. When this last locus is gone, the world will be safe again. I thought you would understand."

"How do you know where the Dark Magic is? How do you know about the Death Stone?"

"I'm sent to it."

"By whom?"

When Aeryn's whitewashed eyes stared at Asher, they seemed to stare into and through her. A shiver went through Asher. This was not the Aeryn she knew.

"By Death."

Asher shuddered. It seemed that death stalked her everywhere she went. She couldn't escape it. It had followed her from Ilirya, and now it was here in this room. But what did Aeryn mean? Her words didn't make any sense. How could Death have sent her? "I don't understand."

"The presence of Dark Magic in the mortal realm creates an imbalance in the Eternal Realms. Dark Magic draws power from Death and weakens the veil between the world of the living and the dead. When the Dark Magic Gate was opened between the mortal and divine realms, it made the imbalance much worse. Now, until all the Dark Magic is gone from the mortal plane, the Eternal Realms are unsettled."

Asher threw out her hands. "But why *you*? Why is Death sending *you*?"

Aeryn looked away. "It doesn't matter. What matters is getting the Stone and righting the balance."

The pieces of the puzzle were all the wrong shapes and sizes. They didn't go together. None of it made sense. Asher collapsed back onto her bed and rubbed the blanket, focusing on the feel of the fibers to ground herself. Maybe she *was* dreaming. It all seemed so fantastical.

She rubbed her temples. "Even if I were able to get the Death Stone, which will already be all but impossible, how would I give it to you? I can't bring it all the way back to Ilirya. I'd be stopped long before I reached the border."

"Nor could you cross the border with it even if you made it there. The Death Stone can't be removed from the Southlands. It's bound to the land here. Don't worry, I'll know when you have it. Then I'll come for it."

She paused. Then in a much softer voice she said, "Take care. The King of Cats isn't the only danger in the Southlands."

Asher was startled. "What?"

"Beware the White Queen. She's a mage, like all of the Southerner tribal leaders, and Lymon says she can influence your emotions."

"Lymon?" Asher blinked. "You don't mean Lymon who's Death's servant?"

A Gate opened behind Aeryn, so bright Asher was once again momentarily blinded. She squeezed her eyes shut, trying to block out the burning glare. No! Not yet! She still had so many unanswered questions. "Wait! How—"

"Get the Stone. Please. More lives than you know depend on it."

The Gate disappeared as suddenly as it had appeared, taking Aeryn with it. Asher was alone in her room once more. She lay back on the bed and curled into a ball, pulling her knees to her chest. Her head was spinning. What would Commander Bronwen do? Trust Aeryn and save the world but doom the kingdom? Or mistrust Aeryn and save the kingdom even if it risked dooming the world? It was all moot anyway if she couldn't get the Stone. The Stone was the key to everything.

Chapter 11

"You're too rash. You run heedlessly into things. You should have taught her better, Idras." Lady Avrill's voice carries a note of frustration in addition to admonishment.

Asher bows her head obediently. She hates to disappoint her new knight.

"She'll learn. All in good time. We were young once too." Idras winks at Asher.

Asher had never been so tired in her life. It felt as if her head was no longer attached to her body. As if fine grains of sand were trapped beneath her eyelids. Keeping her eyes open was an act of sheer willpower. She couldn't remember when she'd last slept for more than a few hours. Had it been the night the first wight had attacked? It seemed like a lifetime ago.

After Aeryn had left, she'd lain in bed, her eyes open, trying to make sense of what she'd been told, but it was impossible. If only she could sleep, she might be able to clear her head enough to understand, but it was too dangerous. What if the King of Cats—King Izmar—learned what she knew? She had to stay awake. Whatever decision she made, the future of Ilirya depended on it.

When morning finally came, there was a sharp rap on the door. Before Asher could answer, Imari swept in. Unlike the day before, when she wore an all-white dress that draped around the curves of her slim body, today she was dressed in a black riding cloak lined with purple silk, fine black breeches, and a purple tunic. Her dark clothing made the light color of her hair appear that much starker. She crouched next to Asher's bed and smoothed the hair away from her forehead tenderly. "You look so tired."

Asher flinched, remembering Aeryn's words. Could Imari really influence emotions? How? Would she try to influence Asher's? Would Asher even know if she did?

Imari immediately pulled her hand away. Her eyes widened. "What's wrong? Did you fall asleep? Did the King of Cats come to you? Does he know about our plan?" Her voice was worried.

"No. No, it's okay." Asher's words came out as a rasp. She licked her lips and swallowed, wishing she had water to drink. "I didn't sleep."

Imari let out a breath, her body relaxing. Her asymmetrical smile returned to her face. She ran a soft hand along Asher's cheek. "You poor thing. It will all be over soon. Then you can sleep as much as you like. You can even have my bed, if you want. It's soft and warm."

Her eyes danced. The offer she was suggesting was a bit more than for a pillow and a blanket. "Would you like that?"

Asher imagined herself lying on her bed at her family's home in King's City. It was wider than her arms could reach and covered in the finest, softest wool blankets. She envisaged closing her eyes and drifting into peaceful, dreamless sleep. No one was counting on her, no one was expecting things from her. She could just let go. The idea was indescribably luxurious.

She was just so tired. Of all of it. Tired of traveling. Tired of fighting. Tired of worrying. Tired of fearing she wouldn't be good enough to do what needed to be done. Tired of watching one member of her expedition after another fall, never to return to Ilirya. Tired of everyone around her knowing more than she did.

At least she could change the last problem. She sat up and pushed her long brown hair behind her shoulders. "Is the Death Stone made of Dark Magic?"

Imari cocked her head, her eyes narrowing suspiciously. "Yes, it is. But I told you before, it's no danger to you."

Asher nodded to herself. So Aeryn had been right about that. "And does it draw Dark things to it, like the dragon in the lands of the Isenii and the wights in the Hollow Lands?"

Imari peered at her blankly for a moment, then threw her head back and laughed. "Wherever did you get such an idea? Did the Magus tell you that? Of course it's not true! What a silly idea. No, those monsters—and the sea monsters in the south that are plaguing the Llini—have come as a result of something that happened in *your* lands, not ours. Soon we'll be rid of them and all will be well again."

She took Asher's hand. Her fingers were long and delicate. Unlike Asher's, they weren't calloused from holding a sword. She twined their fingers together. "If you want to know the truth, the Death Stone is the heart of Sarsenia itself. Its magic allows the Magus to bind together the magic of the Isenii into a shared affinity, the Guardian to warg anyone in his lands, and the Llini to power their flying ships.

"The Death Stone gives power to each of the five tribes. Think of it like fire taken from a great bonfire to light five candles. Its flame keeps us warm and lights our way." She smiled gently. "You see? It's a source of good for our people. It's been part of our kingdom for centuries. It's immensely powerful and utterly invaluable. That's why it's unfair for the King of Cats to keep it only for himself. He could do so much more good with its power."

Asher chewed her lower lip. Aeryn hadn't told her any of this. If Aeryn took the Death Stone from the mortal plane, it sounded like all of Sarsenia would be hurt. Maybe they would even lose their magic completely. Could Aeryn be wrong about the Death Stone? Like Asher, she was Iliryan. What could she really know about Southerner magic?

Asher's fingers tightened around Imari's without her realizing it. "You're sure it does no harm? The Dark Magic from the Stone doesn't leak out?"

Imari sighed, the way a parent would when patiently answering the questions of a small child. "We've lived with it for centuries with no ill effects. The Dark Magic is contained in the stone and can't escape. Even if the stone was broken and the Dark Magic released, it would simply dissolve away into the air. You see? There's nothing to worry about."

Ulu and Aeryn had both said the Dark Stone called other Dark things to it, but the things they meant, like the dragon and the wights, were only in the Southlands because of the Gate that had been opened in Ilirya. If not for that, it seemed to Asher that the Southlands wouldn't have these problems. Didn't that mean Imari was at least partially right? Her body relaxed a little. There was time to figure out what to do about the Dark Stone, if only she could wrest it from the King of Cats.

Imari stood and held out her hand to help Asher out of bed. "You'll feel better after some breakfast, I promise. Then we'll ride to Nyara and all of this will be over in a matter of hours."

Asher fought back the panic rising in her throat at the thought of facing the king. Everything might be over in a matter of hours, but that didn't mean it would end in her—or Ilirya's—favor. There was still so much that could go wrong.

Imari's eyes sparkled with excitement. "I have a surprise for you. You can see it after breakfast."

Asher looked at her warily. She was sick to death of surprises. She'd had more than enough in the last few weeks. "What is it?"

"You'll see."

Cloud whinnied when he saw Asher, tossing his head and pawing at the stall door in his eagerness to see her. Asher ran to him and wrapped her arms around his long face, stroking the thick muscles of his reddish-brown neck just behind his jaw. He bobbed his head up and down happily, trying to rub his bony face against her chest. Asher was so happy she could cry.

Imari gave them a moment alone, then joined them with a broad grin on her face. "Surprised?" Her expression suggested just how pleased she was with herself.

"How? I don't understand. How is he here?"

Asher couldn't believe it. She had assumed Cloud had been taken along with the other Iliryans. She never would have imagined encountering him here in Walakia.

"He wandered in last night after dark. When the King of Cats's soldiers took your companions, they must have freed him or else he got loose somehow. With that tack, I knew immediately he wasn't a Sarsen horse. I hoped he might be yours."

Asher wished she had a carrot or an apple to feed him. How had he found her? Imari said they were hours from the raid site. How had he known to come here? It strained credibility to think he'd coincidentally come to the exact place where his owner had been taken. But Asher didn't have the time or energy to worry about it. Cloud was here now, and his presence was the spark of hope she needed, a sign that maybe good things were on the horizon.

Imari's eyes danced. "I have something else for you too."

Asher boggled at her. She couldn't imagine what other surprises the White Queen had up her sleeve. Imari brandished something she'd been holding behind her back: Asher's sword. Asher had to stifle the urge to snatch it eagerly out of her fingers. When she woke up in Walakia without it, she'd assumed she'd somehow lost it in the ambush. She couldn't believe that in the blink of an eye, she now had both her destrier and her sword back. She could have pinched herself to make sure she wasn't dreaming.

Imari handed her the sword in its scabbard and watched as Asher buckled it to her waist. She said, "I'm sorry to say there's no mystery as to how I got it. I've had it the whole time. After we rescued you, we feared you would wake disoriented and try to fight, assuming you were still in your camp. For our own safety, we took it from you."

Asher ran her fingers along the leather belt, savoring the familiar feel. There was a nick on the left side where she'd missed the scabbard once.

Imari beamed. "It pleases me to see your happiness."

Asher blushed. She hadn't realized how incomplete she'd felt without her sword. It was as though she'd been missing a part of herself. Now, with it securely belted to her side once more, she felt whole. "Thank you." The words were sincere.

Imari stepped forward, gently placing her hand on Asher's, which was resting on the sword's pommel. Her proximity made Asher's skin prickle and her breath come faster. Asher tried to quell the reaction, to compel her breathing to subside, but Imari's bright blue eyes staring into hers seemed to catch and hold her like a snare. By any standard, Imari was beautiful, and coupled with her charisma, she was almost overwhelming.

She said, "I hope you've considered my request that you stay here in Walakia once we've defeated the King of Cats. I can see that you're a good, loyal soldier. I'll need such people in the coming months more than ever. And, well," she dropped her gaze for a moment, "a ruler's life can be lonely. It would be nice to have someone to talk to. I enjoy your company, as I hope you enjoy mine."

She looked up from beneath her long, dark eyelashes. "I would like to learn more about you."

Asher blushed harder. It was difficult not to want to know more about Imari too. Even when they'd been surrounded by cooks and servants in the kitchen the night before, Imari had a way of making Asher feel like they were the only two people in the room. Still, how could she even think about the future when it was still so uncertain?

Imari shook her head almost imperceptibly. "Don't answer now. Answer once we've retaken the Death Stone and put Sarsenia on its rightful path." She reached out and rubbed her palm against Cloud's broad forehead. "No one wants peace more than I do. Every day my brother Zadan leads the Sarsen army into battle is one more I worry he'll never return home. Once the war is over, Ilirya won't need you, but *I* will need you. You don't have to decide now, but I hope you'll consider it."

Asher couldn't help it. She gasped. "General Zadan is your brother?"

How could they be siblings? They looked nothing alike. She couldn't imagine the hulking, brutish fleshsmith sharing any similarities with the thin, pale White Queen. They might as well be two different species.

Imari nodded. "Half-brother. He's been my protector since we were children. Life wasn't always easy for us. My father was a violent man. That's why it's so important my brother return home safely. I need him beside me."

Her bright blue eyes stared into Asher's. When she reached up and ran her hand along Asher's cheek, Asher found it hard to think of any argument against at least considering staying in Walakia. Yes, she would consider it once there was peace between Ilirya and the Southlands. She could be named an emissary, perhaps. She had to admit it was easy to imagine living among Walakia's rolling green hills. After all, she had once intended to one day retire with Tayanna to Tayanna's family estate in Qarys, and Walakia's landscape was not so different. Maybe she could be happy here.

She shook her head slightly, trying to regain focus. First she had to do whatever it took to achieve peace. Her mission was nowhere near complete, and its success was uncertain at best. She was technically no closer to securing peace between Ilirya and the Southlands than when she'd set out from King's City, except now Marandir, Commander Bronwen, and Taz were prisoners of the King of Cats. And what about Aeryn's demand for the Death Stone? Asher couldn't begin to think about the future Imari was offering until she had found a solution to all these problems first. There was only one way forward.

She straightened and squared her shoulders. "First things first: we have to get that scepter."

Nyara, like King's City, was a walled city. As Asher and Imari watched it safely from the tree line, its twenty-foot high gray stone walls stretched as far as their eyes could see across the horizon, enclosing the buildings inside like sheep in a pen. More than just the walls, *everything* about the city had been engineered to deter would-be invaders. To capture it, attackers would have to fight every step of the way, always at a disadvantage.

The only way in was through a wide gate facing south that funneled all traffic through a single, easily defended choke point. If enemy soldiers managed to breach the gate, they would still have to fight their way through the entire city to get to the castle on the other side, going street by street exactly as the Northmen had done to reach King Hap's palace in King's City. As Asher had seen then, it was messy, bloody warfare with high casualties on both sides.

Even if attackers managed to reach the castle, that's where their advance would end. The castle's massive, smooth, yellow-hued walls and towers were impossible to scale. With no siege engines, the enemy would be left howling their fury on the outside while the castle's inhabitants remained safe inside. But while the city would have been almost impossible to take in battle, Asher wasn't an army, and she didn't need to conquer an entire city. All she needed to do was get close enough to the king to snatch his scepter from his hands. Not that the task was any easier than conquering the city.

"Are you ready to bring me the Death Stone?" Imari's hood cast her face in shadow and hid her distinctive hair.

Asher's heart pounded. Her palms were damp with sweat, but she had no place to wipe them. Her skin felt too tight for her body. In less than an hour, she would either save Ilirya or condemn it to destruction. It was a heavy responsibility, one she wished she didn't have to bear alone.

"Ride through the main city gate toward the castle. No one will stop you on your way. When you reach the castle gate, tell the guard you're a representative of the Rann queen and you'll be let in," Imari told her.

"You're sure?" Asher couldn't allay the lingering fear that everything would be for nothing if she were turned away at the gate. Then what would she do?

Imari's eyes were flinty. "They'll let you in. The King of Cats won't be able to resist meeting you."

Asher licked her lips. "If I get the Death Stone, how do I escape? They won't let me walk out with it."

Imari gave a coy smile. "Leave that part to me. Once you have the Stone, I'll make sure no one will stop you from leaving."

"How can you promise that?"

It wasn't enough. Asher needed to know specifics. In the unlikely event she was able to get the Stone, she needed to know what would happen next. Losing the Stone after she'd stolen it was just as useless as failing to secure it in the first place.

Imari held up a hand. "I can't tell you everything. If you're caught, I can't have you revealing all my secrets. I'm sure you can understand that. Just trust that I have a plan."

Asher grimaced. So Imari was hedging her bets. Asher wasn't the only one with doubts about her ability to succeed.

"Go now," Imari said. "There is much to do today. By this afternoon, the tyranny of the King of Cats will be no more, and forty years of war between our people will be on its way to an end."

Asher took a deep breath. The time had come. If she couldn't steal the Stone, Ilirya was lost. And if she could…she would worry about Imari and Aeryn's competing demands for it after it was safely away from the king. She nodded at Imari, then urged Cloud into a slow canter through the fields that lay before the city walls, leaving Imari behind her. She carried Ilirya's future on her shoulders alone. She hoped she had the strength and cleverness to succeed.

As Imari had predicted, the guard at the city gate was more interested in staring at Asher than preventing her from entering the city. Asher knew that while her face might pass for a member of one of the five Sarsen tribes, her armor immediately exposed her as an Iliryan to any soldier with experience on the front. Nevertheless, she was allowed to pass through unchallenged. Asher wondered when an Iliryan representative had last entered the city freely. Centuries? Or was she the first?

Cloud walked slowly through the city as Asher gaped at it. It was so much like King's City, and yet so different. The architecture was foreign—the houses were colored bright shades of yellow, pink, and green with triangular, red-orange roofs—but the people were familiar. They were bakers, brewers, and butchers. Carpenters, cartwrights, and chandlers. Under other circumstances, she would have loved to have lingered and learned more about the city's denizens, but now was not the time.

Before she knew it, she found herself in front of the castle. Her stomach lurched, twisting itself in nervous knots. It was an impressive, imposing monument to the wealth and power of the King of Cats. Although not any bigger or more beautiful than the castle in King's City, it nevertheless reminded Asher she was playing a dangerous game. The man who owned a castle like this was not to be underestimated.

Asher looked up. The castle's round keep rose six stories into the air, two stories taller than the curtain walls and towers that formed a defensive perimeter around it. These were for more than just defense, however. Gauzy curtains and the trappings of apartments, storerooms, kitchens, sitting rooms, and armories were barely visible through their narrow windows high above the ground. By Asher's guess, a hundred or more servants, soldiers and administrators must live in the castle in addition to the king himself, filling out its vast spaces. If she managed to wrest the Death Stone away from the king, she wouldn't only be fighting him to escape; she might end up facing all of them, as well.

Asher threw her shoulders back, trying to give herself confidence she didn't feel, and rode forward. When she reached the thick iron gate that protected the castle, she told the guard there, "I'm here to see the king."

The guard, who was sitting outside the gatehouse on a short wooden stool, squinted up at her, the sun in his eyes. His dark iron helmet with bronze inlay reminded her of the shape of a sextant she'd once been shown by a ship's captain in King's City. For a moment, he said nothing, and Asher feared her worst nightmare would come to pass: she would be turned away. Panic began to rise in her chest. What would she do then? How could she save Taz, Commander Bronwen, and Marandir? How could she get the Stone?

Her fear was premature. He stood and barked an order to the gatehouse behind him, and the gate began to rise slowly. The chain clattered as it was wound, reminding Asher of the sound of prisoner chains. Once she was inside that gate, she *would* effectively be the King of Cats's prisoner. She pushed away the thought.

Once the gate was fully up, a woman with short, graying, curly hair and a round face appeared. She wore a heavy green velvet robe and a thick gold chain around her neck. The large silver key fastened to her waist told Asher that she was the castle's chamberlain. She motioned to Asher. "The king has been expecting you."

A frisson ran up Asher's arms. Although she'd anticipated that the king knew who she was—and of course, it had been a key component of Imari's plan—hearing the words still made her uneasy. Was this confirmation he had walked in the Iliryans' dreams? Had someone—the Magus, the Guardian, or even Imari's brother General Zadan—told him, intentionally or unintentionally? Or had he forced the captured Iliryans to tell him about her? What else did he know?

The gate guard appeared at Cloud's side. "If you would dismount, Lady," he said, holding out his hand for Cloud's reins.

Asher dismounted and reluctantly handed them over. She hoped she would see Cloud again, but she didn't know. If the plan failed, she'd likely be locked away in a dungeon forever or killed. She patted him on the nose. If she didn't return, she hoped his next owner would be kind to him.

The chamberlain gave a polite partial bow. "Please come with me."

Asher obliged, following her around the inner bailey and then through a thick metal door in the keep that even a battering ram held by twenty men could never breach. Asher had no time to marvel at the craftsmanship—she thought she saw two cats rampant carved high on the door, among other things—before they entered a large hall. It was smaller than the Great Hall in the castle in King's City, with a very different style. Built of oak and mahogany, the Iliryan Great Hall was stately but warm. The balcony that ringed the room allowed spectators to see royal audiences from all angles, inviting courtiers to be present during events of great importance.

This hall, on the other hand, was cold and without personality. The room was carved entirely of smooth, flawless white marble that stretched endlessly up to a high and vaulted ceiling. Bright, colorful banners with five coats of arms—Asher assumed for the five tribes—hung from the walls, but they were insufficient to counteract the impression that the room was little more than a bland white box. In part, this was because of how astonishingly empty the room was. There were no courtiers producing a chatter of voices and milling of bodies. No heralds or guards. No chairs for spectators and guests.

In fact, there was only one person left in the hall once the chamberlain ducked back outside. Asher froze. There at the end of the short hall, sitting on a simple wooden throne, was a man with a familiar face, the long, rugged brown face from her dreams. The face that didn't belong. The face of the immortal King of Cats.

Until that moment, Asher had forgotten her dream, but now it came back to her in full. The king had been the interloper who asked about Tayanna and turned a cherished memory into a nightmare. Nausea made her mouth water. Discovering the King of Cats had trod through her dreams, picking up her memories and examining them with the same curiosity with which she might have picked up a book in Imari's library, was a devastating blow.

She knew his voice before he even spoke. "Hello, Asher."

Her knees threatened to buckle. A wild desire to run swept over her, then was immediately replaced by despair so heavy she couldn't so much as lift a finger. He knew everything. Without her even knowing, he'd always been one step ahead of her, and now she'd walked right into his trap. Her mouth twitched, searching for words that refused to come. What was left to say? He had won.

He leaned forward in his throne, head cocked slightly. "But you've come alone. Where are your companions?"

Asher clenched her fists but forced herself to remain still. "You know where they are."

"I do," he agreed.

Something glinted at his side, drawing her attention. Was it the Stone? She inched a few steps closer, trying to see better. When she was close enough, she saw it. The scepter, leaning against the throne. It was almost as long as she was tall, and at its top was set a black stone the size of her fist. The Death Stone. Her skin tingled with anticipation. If she could get close enough, maybe—just maybe—she could grab it and then use her sword to fend the king off as she escaped.

She looked around with as much subtlety as she could manage. There were no guards in the room, but that didn't mean there weren't soldiers ready to burst in at any moment. Were there doors hidden behind the banners with soldiers waiting on the other side? Archers poised with arrows notched to shoot precisely through windows? A spell protecting him? After all, what sort of a ruler would allow himself to be in the room with an enemy knight with no protection whatsoever? The king was an oneiromancer, not a war mage. He had no way to defend himself.

The king rested his chin on the heel of his palm, his body relaxed. "Tell me, lady knight, why do the Rann want to end a war they themselves started?"

Asher grimaced. She had grown up hearing how the Southerners launched the first volleys across the border. How the Southerners wouldn't stop until they burned a trail all the way to King's City. She had always been told the Southerners were ruthless invaders who had to be stopped in order to protect Ilirya's helpless citizens. She had been lied to. All of Ilirya had been lied to. They were the aggressors of the war, not its victims.

"Everyone should want an end to war," she said, hoping it sounded diplomatic. It seemed like something Commander Bronwen would have said.

The King of Cats took up the scepter in his hands. When he rolled it between his palms, the facets of the black stone cast squares of dark light all around the room. "For forty years, first Savin and then his son Hap waged war for this." Asher realized he meant the Stone. "If Alea is suing for peace, it can only mean finally a Lamid with some sense has realized the folly of such an effort. I am willing to hear her terms."

Asher's chin jerked. He was open to discussing terms for peace? She was thrown off balance. She had assumed he would laugh at the idea. After all, he'd kidnapped the other Iliryans. What did that say about his willingness to entertain the possibility of peace? But now he wasn't laughing at all. If he was willing to consider peace, what did that mean for her plans to steal the Death Stone?

She tried to think. There was no reason to trust what he said. Imari had warned her he would try to trick her. Perhaps this was a ruse, an effort to distract and befuddle her. She took a few steps forward, still trying to get close to his scepter while she decided what to do. "What would you ask in return for peace?"

He set the scepter down against his throne and rubbed his pointed, beardless chin. "I have lost thousands and thousands of my people in this war. What is a suitable recompense for their lives?"

His words reminded Asher of what Imari's brother, General Zadan, had said. "What will the Rann give for peace? What will the Rann pay for all the lives they have taken?" What would Asher have demanded for Tayanna's life? There was no sum, no object that could ever adequately represent her worth.

Still, Asher had to offer something to the King of Cats. "Gold? Silver? Jewels?" All of these were things Ilirya would happily give for peace. They would give it by the cartful.

The king shook his head, clicking his tongue. "Meaningless trinkets and baubles. I want something the Rann consider invaluable. Something you do not want to give. Something that will repay Sarsenia for all it has suffered."

Asher stepped still closer. Now she was only a few arms' lengths away from him, close enough to see a black freckle beneath his right eye and a chip in his left front tooth. She worked to keep her eyes on him. If she looked at the scepter, he might guess what she meant to do. Her breath was short and tight.

The king said, "Give me Queen Alea herself."

"*What?*" Asher stopped in her tracks. Every part of her recoiled in horror. Give the queen as a hostage? Of all the things the King of Cats could have asked, this was insupportable. It was impossible.

The king smiled, clearly pleased with the shock his terms produced, and played with a silver chain that lay around his neck. "I mean give her in marriage. A union between us would cement peace between our two kingdoms better than any peace treaty ever could. It is fortuitous that we are both unmarried. Indeed, Queen Alea could do no better than marrying a king. It's a far better match than marrying one of her barons."

Asher swallowed the bile rising in her throat. It was out of the question. It was unthinkable. He was asking for Ilirya's willing surrender. If he married Queen Alea, he would gain control over Ilirya almost as effectively as if he'd conquered it with his army. Moreover, so long as he held the Death Stone, he would outlive her and one day become Ilirya's sole regent. Ilirya needed peace desperately, but this was the one price that it would not, could not afford to pay.

Asher made a decision. If there were to be peace between Ilirya and the Southlands, it would be negotiated with a ruler other than the King of Cats. Only one path to peace lay ahead of her. She glanced at the scepter out of the corner of her eye. She still needed to be a few steps closer before she tried to grab it. She said, "The queen will have to decide for herself. Will you guarantee us safe passage back to Ilirya to deliver your terms?"

He flicked his hand. "Do as you must. I have all the time in the world. Although..." his smile made Asher's skin crawl, "I think your army does not."

She took another step closer. "Then shake hands with me to seal this agreement and I'll leave immediately." It was a gamble. Why should a king shake hands with a common knight? But here in the Southlands, she was not simply Lady Asher, she was the representative of Queen Alea herself. She held her breath, hoping for one final stroke of good luck.

The king yawned dramatically to show his boredom. "Fine." He didn't bother to stand.

Asher's heart beat so loud she was certain the king must hear it. The moment had come. It was now or never.

The two of them extended their right hands to shake, but at the last moment, Asher reached down and grabbed the scepter with her left hand. As soon as her fingers wrapped around the cold metal, she jerked her entire body backward and reached for her sword. In a fraction of a second, she was standing in front of the throne with the Death Stone-topped scepter in one hand, her sword in the other. Impossibly, she had done it. She had snatched the Death Stone from the king.

The king gaped at her, frozen in shock. "What is the meaning of this?" His voice was full of disbelief.

Asher took several more steps backward, holding her sword point-first in front of her to discourage him from lunging at her and trying to wrestle it back.

He jumped to his feet, but he was unarmed. He had nothing with which to compel Asher to return his scepter.

"Did Alea send you to steal the Stone? If so, she's as much a fool as her brother and father. It can't leave Sarsenia."

"No," a familiar female voice said from behind Asher. "She stole it for *me.*"

Asher spun a quarter turn. Imari was at the back of the hall, rapidly striding forward. Her hood had fallen back, revealing her distinctive almost white hair. She looked every bit the White Queen of the Walakai.

"What are you doing here?" Asher and the king said the words simultaneously, their voices blending into one. Whereas Asher's tone was one of surprise, however, the king's was accusatory.

Asher realized with shock that Imari had refused to tell her what would happen after she secured the Stone because she had planned to be there herself to collect it. She never intended for Asher to leave the castle grounds with it. But how had she known exactly when to make her appearance? *Spies everywhere.* The chamberlain must have been her spy. How else could she have gotten into the castle and then the hall without being detected? Who else had she co-opted among the king's courtiers?

The king must have been asking himself the same question. His dark eyes traveled back and forth between Asher and Imari, furious. "I see now. The White Queen has been plotting, plotting, and you were all too happy to help her. I wonder, did she tell you how she murdered her own father to take his throne? Ambitious little creature, isn't she?"

Imari didn't blink. "The tyranny of the king is at an end. Give me the scepter and we'll rid the world of him once and for all." Her voice was sharp as a knife. Asher was taken aback by the cold ruthlessness in her eyes.

The king kept his attention focused on Asher. "What lies might she have told you to win you to her side? Did she tell you I kidnapped your companions? That I'm holding them in my dungeons, torturing them to amuse myself? I've been in their dreams. I know where they are. When were you going to tell her that *you* have them in your dungeon, Imari, daughter of Canth?"

Chapter 12

Everything hurts. Existence itself is excruciating. Every breath Asher takes is a betrayal. A betrayal by her body, a betrayal by the world, a betrayal by justice. Why is she alive when Tayanna is dead? A single spirit shared by two bodies, when the flame was snuffed both should have been extinguished. But she's still here and now every second is a cruel reminder that the world will never again be filled by Tayanna's presence. The world will forevermore be empty.

Asher had been told that grief came in waves, a seemingly endless ocean of pain, but this is no wave. It is a gaping, yawning emptiness in Tayanna's exact shape, and that emptiness is swallowing her whole. What is she supposed to do now? How can she go on?

When Taz leaves her side to get food or bathe, she doesn't notice. She doesn't notice that he has stayed with her for weeks, sleeping on a pile of blankets on her floor and bringing her food she can hardly force herself to chew much less swallow. She doesn't know how many days she's been in bed or when she last bathed, either. Time has lost all meaning. All she knows, all she can think about, is that Tayanna is never coming home. Never again will she hear Tayanna's voice or feel her touch, and every time she remembers that, it's all she can do not to scream and scream until her raw, hoarse voice is reduced to a soundless wail.

She wants to wake up from this terrible, terrible dream. It can't be real. It can't be. It's too awful, too painful to be real. But she's trapped in the nightmare, unable to escape, and Taz's eyes tell her this is how life will be now. Hollow.

Most days, not even water can pass around the hard knot in her throat. Maybe she'll thirst or choke to death. She doesn't care. It would be better than this meaningless existence to which she's been condemned. There's no future anymore. Only a vast and incalculable period of wakefulness in which Asher is acutely aware of her loss, followed by brief periods of sleep.

She would happily die and rejoin Tayanna, but Death won't take her. She is being punished with the worst possible punishment: life. No bargaining, no wishing, and no desperate longing will reunite her with Tayanna. The thread that bound them in life has been cut forever.

THE HAIR ON ASHER'S ARMS stood up. No. It couldn't be. Imari couldn't have her companions. He was lying, trying to turn her against Imari. He would do or say anything to get the Death Stone back. Of course Imari didn't have the Iliryans. Asher would have suspected. She couldn't have been so close to them without sensing, without knowing…right?

She turned to Imari, looking for the rebuttal she knew must come. Imari would never let such ridiculous slander stand. She would rebuke the king, casting aside his ridiculous aspersion with all the scorn it was due. The White Queen was glaring at the king, her jaw flexed and her eyes burning. But, to Asher's horror, she said nothing. Why wasn't she denying the charge?

The longer the silence lingered, the more Asher began to panic. There were, she saw now with dread, too many unexplained, fortuitous coincidences that she'd been too exhausted to identify. Why had Imari's people been present exactly when the king's soldiers were ambushing the Iliryans in their camp, for example? A place that was, moreover, not on Walakai land. And of course, how could Cloud have walked tens of miles in completely foreign territory to find her?

Her body trembled, drained to collapse by the magnitude of Imari's duplicity. Asher had been so blinded by fear, fatigue, and confusion that she had missed or ignored every warning sign. She had seen Imari as her savior when she should have seen her as her captor. What a fool she'd been. She clenched her teeth together. She never should have trusted Imari. She should never have let her guard down. Commander Bronwen would never have made such a stupid mistake.

The king took a cautious step forward. "I suppose she promised you something you wanted desperately. Something you wanted enough to blind you to who she really is. Did she promise you peace? She must have said all the right words about wanting nothing but harmony and friendship between the Rann and the Sarsen to win you to her side."

He sneered at the White Queen, a superior, cruel expression made worse by the thinness of his lips. "All lies. She craves power and will stop at nothing to get it. Give her the Stone and she will use it not for peace, but to empower the Sarsen army. She will stream over the border and take your kingdom, too."

Asher's eyes widened. The king barked a short, caustic laugh. "Do you think it's coincidence her brother is the leader of my army? No, I've read her 'secret' missives to him. She has an eye on the lands north of the border. She wants *both* our kingdoms. Such is the ambition of the 'White Queen.'"

Imari's mouth twitched. Her pale face was flushed a soft pink. "Your desperate words won't save you. She won't believe your lies. She knows you're a tyrant who would do anything and say anything to get the Stone back. All tyrants are the same."

He glowered. "You would know, cut from the same cloth as you are. But at least I am honest. Everything I have told her is the truth. I'm sure everything *you* have told her is lies."

Asher's mind reeled. Truth, lies, how could she distinguish between them? Her mind fixed on the most immediate, most devastating accusation. "Why did you take them, Imari? Why did you lie to me?"

Imari held out a beseeching hand toward her, her face contrite. "I'm sorry. I should have told you. I should never have hidden it from you. I took them before I knew you. And then when I did…how could I tell you? You would have thought me a monster. You wouldn't have understood."

That was true.

"Where are they?"

"Safe in my castle. I never hurt them. I protected them, just like I did you. Listen to me: nothing has changed. Give me the Stone, and I'll give you everything you want: the peace you want and your friends safely back in your hands. Don't you see? The King of Cats will never give you peace. *I* will."

The King of Cats snorted, crossing his arms. "How could anyone trust such hollow promises? She's lied to you, manipulated you, and imprisoned your companions. Did she touch you? Therein lies her mage gift. What emotions were even your own and which did she give to you?"

Asher's knees were weak. Every blow fell more heavily than the last. How many more could she stand?

He reached out a hand. "Return the Stone to me and I will have her suitably punished and your cohorts returned to you as a demonstration of my good will."

"Don't listen to him," Imari warned. "He'll never let you leave Sarsenia alive. The King of Cats doesn't forgive and doesn't forget. Do you think he'll pardon you for stealing the Death Stone from him in his very throne room? He'll make an example of you so that no one ever dares try again. If you give him the Stone, you'll die. And with you, all your hopes for peace."

Asher looked back and forth between the two Southerners, trapped between them. Imari, pale and haughty, her young face full of fiery, righteous anger. The King of Cats, dark and intense, a crouched mountain cat waiting for the moment to pounce. What should she do? To whom should she give the Stone? Who was more likely to give her peace? Would either? Or was all hope lost no matter her choice?

There was another option too. She could keep the Stone from both of them and await Aeryn's arrival, if indeed she came. But if she gave the Stone to Aeryn, she was guaranteeing Ilirya's fall. There would be no peace. Could she make that sacrifice?

She'd have to decide soon. The two rulers were creeping closer to her, crowding her as they itched to snatch the scepter from her fingers. It was all too much. She had no way of knowing who was lying and who was telling the truth. It was possible, perhaps even probable, that both were lying. How could she decide between them?

"*Tayanna*."

The name cut through the air like a falling axe blade. It was a magic word, a spell, that caused the air and everything in the room to freeze, caught in a moment in time. Asher turned her head so quickly to look at the King of Cats it gave her whiplash.

He dropped his voice, saying words meant only for her ears to hear. "Return the Stone to me and I will give you that which you desire most of all: Tayanna."

Asher stared at him, unable to speak.

His eyes glowed intensely, peeling back her skin and staring into her deepest desires. "I know what she means to you. I can feel it in your dreams. She can be yours once more."

His words struck her like a lance through the heart, a reminder of all she had lost. But what did he think he was offering? The past could not be rewritten. She shook her head. "Tayanna is dead."

The king pointed with a long brown finger at the black gem atop the scepter Asher was holding, drawing her eyes to it. "That stone is called the *Death Stone* for a reason. With it, I can bring even the dead back to life. I swear it. I am stronger even than Death himself. Give me the Stone and you can have your lover back."

In an instant, all the air was sucked out of the room. Asher couldn't breathe. Her legs began to shake, threatening to collapse beneath her. Her heart beat erratically. Everything she had felt since learning about Tayanna's death, every agonizing emotion returned to her at once. It took every ounce of strength left in her not to crumple to the ground.

It wasn't only Tayanna who had died that day; it was Asher as well. She'd been forever maimed, a part of herself amputated and lost forever. Though she had been forced to bandage the wound and keep living, she would never be whole again. Now the King of Cats was offering her the one thing in life she wanted more than anything else: Tayanna back. She had dreamed of this exact impossibility countless times. If she gave him the Stone, could this fantasy become real? She didn't know. Aeryn had called the Stone powerful and said that with it, the King of Cats could defy even Death. But was it enough to pull someone from the Eternal Realms?

She took a shuddering breath. What wouldn't she give for Tayanna back? What mountain wouldn't she climb, what ocean wouldn't she swim across to see the face she loved more than any other? If the King of Cats was right, she would be able to touch and hold Tayanna again. She would hear her laugh and smell her perfume. She would have her best friend back, the other half of her soul. She would have a second chance at the life they'd dreamed of. How could she turn down the opportunity for more time with the light of her life? All it would take was returning the Stone to the king.

She wanted Tayanna back so badly she physically ached. Every cell in her body called out for its missing twin. Unconsciously, her hand swung the scepter in the king's direction. His fingers twitched, wanting to seize it from her hand. At the last minute, she realized what she was doing and pulled it back, cradling it to her chest with trembling hands.

She needed to think. If she gave him the Stone in return for Tayanna, what would become of Ilirya? In the best case, he would marry Queen Alea and then take her kingdom over after she died. In the worst case, the queen would reject his terms and Ilirya would fall to the Northmen. Both options were devastating to Ilirya. To give him the Stone would therefore be a supreme act of selfishness. It went against everything she'd been taught as a knight.

Then again, a devious, venal voice in her head whispered, *no one would have to know about this part of the bargain*. The only witnesses to the scene unfolding in the great hall were her, the king, and Imari. All the Iliryans needed to know was that she had done her best to achieve peace under impossible conditions. She would carry the king's terms—peace in return for marriage—to Queen Alea, and it would fall to her to accept or refuse. Asher would have done her duty to Ilirya and would be blameless for whatever happened next.

Then again, there was no guarantee he would honor any of his promises even if he could bring Tayanna back. What if Imari was right and he intended to kill her instead as punishment for stealing the Stone? His vow to revive Tayanna could be nothing but a ploy to return the balance of power in his favor. Once he had the Stone back, Asher would be entirely at his mercy.

The room erupted in a flash of light so bright Asher was momentarily blinded. When she was able to see once more, Aeryn stood in front of her, between Imari and the king. With her ghostly white eyes and black clothes offset against the gleaming white marble of the room, she presented a striking, otherworldly figure. She reached out a pale white hand to Asher. "You've done it!" Her voice was elated. "Give me the Death Stone and we'll finish this. The world will be safe."

"What is this?" the king exclaimed.

He had taken a step backward, throwing his hands up defensively. Imari's eyes widened with surprise. She reached her hand inside her cloak, suggesting she carried a weapon there—something small, a dagger, perhaps—although she didn't draw it. Asher, too, was stunned by Aeryn's arrival, but when the initial shock wore off, she clutched the scepter even more tightly to her body, shielding it.

Aeryn cocked her head. "What are you doing? I told you, it must be taken off the mortal plane."

Asher's mind whirled feverishly. Aeryn had some strange and unexplained relationship with Death. If it was possible to bring back Tayanna, Aeryn might know. Asher had to find out. She held the scepter aloft. "Can the Death Stone be used to bring back the dead?"

Aeryn's black eyebrows knit together in confusion. "Death never relinquishes what it has taken. You know that."

"She doesn't know what the Stone can do." The king's voice was an urgent hiss in Asher's ear, a worm that burrowed its way into her mind. "I can do it. Tayanna can be yours once more. With the snap of my fingers, you can behold her again."

A look of suspicion passed across Aeryn's face. Her eyes narrowed. "What has he promised you if you return the Stone to him?"

"He says he can bring back Tayanna."

It didn't matter she'd never mentioned Tayanna to Aeryn. The deep, aching longing in her voice was enough to convey Tayanna's importance. Asher licked her lips, her mouth dry. What if the king *could* do exactly what he said? Was she really willing to give up the chance to see Tayanna again, even knowing the risks?

"Shades." Aeryn's voice was hard, and the word as it fell from her mouth dripped with disgust. "He can't raise the dead. Only Death could do that. But I suppose it's possible he could summon a shade."

"What's a shade?"

"Shades are exactly as they sound: shadows of the person they were in life. Unfilled outlines. Don't be deceived by him. *If* he can summon a shade, whomever he's promised to pull from the Eternal Realms will come back as nothing more than a voiceless silhouette, not the person you loved. No mortal power can pull the dead back among the living." She glared at the king. "And using the Stone to steal a shade from Death would only make the imbalance between the worlds worse."

Her eyes softened as they returned to Asher. "Whoever you've lost is gone forever. I'm sorry."

"She's wrong. I can do it. I can defeat even Death himself."

The king was inching ever closer. Asher could almost feel his breath upon her. Desperation shone from his eyes. She took a step away from him.

The vows she made on the day of her knighting returned to her. "Being a knight requires sacrifice and hardship. It requires selflessness. Do you vow to defend this kingdom and protect her citizens, putting the good of Ilirya above all else from now on? To always place concern for the welfare of others over concern for yourself?" She had so vowed and been enrolled in the knighthood. To give the King of Cats the Stone in return for a chance to see Tayanna again would be to abandon that vow. She could no longer call herself a knight.

Imari stomped her foot impatiently, perhaps feeling forgotten in the discussion of the Stone's dominion over death. "Enough of this! *I* am the only one who will give you peace. That's why you're here, isn't it? To save your precious Ilirya? Give me the Stone, and I promise to establish peace with the Rann immediately."

"It wasn't terribly peaceful of you to take her companions prisoner," the king taunted.

Imari's nostrils flared and her face darkened. She drew herself up, chin held high. "Very well. Deny me that Stone and the Walakai will kill all the Rann prisoners. You'll be left with nothing. No peace, no friends. And then the King of Cats will kill you too. Not a single Rann will straggle home to tell the tale of your failure."

Asher's stomach pinched. Taz. Commander Bronwen. Marandir. She had been so overcome by the possibility of seeing Tayanna again she'd completely forgotten them. Now she realized why the White Queen had taken them: she'd anticipated the need to use them for leverage against Asher. The White Queen had been telling the truth when she told Asher the kidnapper had taken them to act as bargaining chips. Only, it had been she who had taken them, not the King of Cats.

Asher's world was falling to pieces all around her. If she didn't give Imari the Stone, she would condemn her companions to death. Having lost Tayanna, could she live without Taz, too? She didn't think so. She had promised to always be there for him. She couldn't be his executioner. The guilt and loss would be too much for her to bear.

And the blatant, repellant ruthlessness of her threats aside, Imari was right; Asher's mission was to obtain peace on the best terms possible for Ilirya. Between Imari and the king, Imari was offering better terms: peace with no conditions. At least, on the face of it. But neither of them was trustworthy, and what if the king was right that Imari planned to use the Stone against Ilirya? Turning the Stone over to her could be worse for Ilirya even than returning it to the king.

The king reached out his shaking hand. "Give me the Stone and I will raise your Tayanna for you. I swear she will not be a shade. You will have everything you ever wanted."

The first tear rolled down Asher's cheek. It wasn't fair. It wasn't fair to dangle Tayanna before her like this. She would do anything to see Tayanna one more time, give anything no matter the cost. But what was the king asking in return? For Ilirya itself. At best, he was asking her to betray her kingdom and every piece of herself.

If she gave him back the Stone, Jazmen and Henrek would have died for nothing. *Tayanna* would have died for nothing. She would be betraying every soldier who had given their life to protect Ilirya. Ilirya might not fall to the Northmen, but it would fall nevertheless. If the king *could* return Tayanna to the land of the living, what would she say if she found out her life had been traded for the lives of thousands of Iliryan soldiers and Ilirya's sovereignty? She would never forgive Asher. It was anathema to everything she was as a person, everything Asher loved about her.

"Their promises will mean nothing if the Stone isn't taken out of the mortal plane," Aeryn said, breaking into her thoughts. "This isn't a game of playing kingmaker to the Southerners; it's a matter of saving the entire world. Can't you see? This is about more than the war between Ilirya and the Southlands."

So said Aeryn. But what evidence had she presented of it other than mysterious words and a strange new power? As much as Asher trusted Aeryn, at that moment she was just one more voice laying claim to the Stone. A claimant, moreover, whose motives and patron were unclear. If Asher gave Aeryn the Stone, she was dooming Ilirya to further war with the

Southlands and because of that, its ruin. Aeryn would take the Stone, and the King of Cats would take out his fury on Ilirya.

The weight of the decision she faced was dragging Asher deep, deep into a bottomless ocean. She was drowning. Trust Imari and hope she would fulfill her promise of immediate peace and the return of her companions but never know whether the king could revive Tayanna. Trust the King of Cats and hope he would fulfill his promise of giving her Tayanna and the possibility of a bitter peace. Trust Aeryn and possibly save the world at the cost of everything else: the fall of Ilirya, the lives of her companions, and any hope of ever seeing Tayanna again outside the Eternal Realms.

Each contradicted the other and argued for their own, exclusive veracity. Each claimed to be her best and only option. Asher's head rang. She was so, so tired. How could she possibly choose between them? How could she give up Tayanna? But how could she turn her back on her duties as a knight? Was the greater good the protection of the entire world or was it only Ilirya's people?

Imari, Aeryn, and the King of Cats all stared at her, waiting. Each expected, no doubt, to be her selection. Two of them would be disappointed. Asher was crying freely now. Having mourned Tayanna's death once already, she was now facing the prospect of having to do it a second time, and she wasn't sure she was strong enough. She wanted so badly to see her again that even though her mind told her not to believe the king, her heart cried out for the chance to see what might happen.

She pictured Tayanna's hands on her face, her sparkling eyes looking into hers. She imagined Tayanna's arms wrapping around her back, holding her close. It was too much to ask to give that up. It was too much to ask for her to keep living, knowing she would never have those things again. She'd rather die.

She screamed, an ear-piercing, sky-shattering cry that was ripped from the very depths of her soul. Then in one swift move, she dashed the Death Stone against the ground, shattering it. She wasn't clever like the knight commander. She couldn't distinguish between the lies and the truths of the King of Cats and the White Queen. Let them fight between themselves for control of the Southlands. Let them scheme and plot and conspire. She wanted none of it.

In the meantime, Ilirya would have to hope the destruction of the Stone would weaken the Southerner army enough to bring about a reprieve. Perhaps the Magus and the Guardian would even order their troops to stand down once they heard the king had lost the source of his power. If fighting died down enough that the Iliryan army could shift some of its troops north, it might be sufficient to deter the Northmen. It was a long shot, perhaps even impossible, but it was hope.

The reaction to Asher's decision was instant. Imari lunged toward the scepter but froze when she saw it was too late. Black pieces of crystal skittered across the floor in every direction. Her face filled with horror. The Stone was destroyed. She would never have it. Asher thought with some satisfaction that whatever her plans for it, they were ruined.

The king, meanwhile, was silent, and for good reason. To Asher's alarm, he had begun to…crumble. His legs dissolved beneath him, and his torso melted down to the floor, his arms receding into the sleeves of his tunic. Like the sun-baked mud of Rath, his face cracked and disintegrated, his clothing collapsing onto the ground all around him. All that remained of the dread King of Cats was the clothing he wore and the narrow gold circlet that had once adorned his head. The magic that had kept him alive almost twice as long as a mortal man was gone, and death, having been kept at bay for well over a century, rushed forward to claim him. He disappeared without even uttering a peep and with him any hope that Tayanna would ever be returned to the mortal plane.

"*What have you done*?" Aeryn's voice was full of indescribable horror.

Asher dropped the scepter, now without its crowning gem, to the ground. It rolled away from her, clanking against the white marble floor. She was too weak and emotionally drained to reply. Her scar burned like liquid lightning, painful enough she had to resist doubling over. Asher had given up everything for a glimmer of hope that Ilirya might still achieve some sort of peace. Whatever happened next, she'd taken the route she thought was most likely to end the war. She had fulfilled her duties as a knight, regardless of the personal cost.

A black mist rose from the shards of the Stone. It seemed to be thickening as it wafted toward the ceiling. Aeryn's voice was high and agitated. "You've done the worst possible thing! You've released the Dark Magic from the Stone into the world!"

Asher barely heard her. Her legs, already shaky, gave out completely, and she sank to her knees on the floor. It was over. The King of Cats was gone and his instrument of power destroyed. And it had cost her the one thing she couldn't bear to give: Tayanna. All the emotions that had overwhelmed her so long ago when Taz appeared at her door bearing news of Tayanna's death now returned, dashing her to the ground and piling upon her, smothering her. Her lungs couldn't draw breath. She was suffocating. She choked, a sob caught in her throat.

She stared blankly at the ruined, sharp-edged pieces of the Death Stone around her. Tayanna was gone forever. The only hope for her return lay scattered in shards. No horse would ever carry her home. No knock would ever signal her return. Asher had condemned herself to a lifetime of hollowness. She was as broken as the Death Stone itself.

Aeryn moaned softly, her hands pressed over her mouth. "The damage… the damage you've done… gods help us."

Asher couldn't rouse herself to care. She didn't have the capacity left to worry about what the Stone's destruction might mean beyond undercutting the White Queen and the King of Cats. All she knew, all she could understand, was that the Stone was destroyed, the king was dead, and Tayanna would never again walk the earth. If Asher never moved from this spot and her legs became tree roots and her body its trunk, forever destined to remain in that same spot where she'd crumbled, she wouldn't care.

The light that filled the room alerted Asher to the opening of a Gate behind Aeryn. It sparkled like sunlight on snow, sending flashes of white across the walls. Aeryn rubbed her face, which seemed to have aged years in the space of a few minutes. When she spoke, her voice was tinged with an infinite lassitude. "You have no idea what you've done. How could you, Asher? How could you have done such a terrible thing?"

Asher had no will to argue, to defend herself. She just wanted all of it to be over. The weight of having to decide Ilirya's future had been too heavy. It was too much for her to bear. Now all she wanted was to be left alone.

Aeryn shook her head. She opened her mouth as though to speak, then closed it. Without saying anything more, she stepped backward through the Gate and was swallowed by it.

Only Asher and Imari were left in the throne room. Asher closed her eyes, trying to block out the world around her. She had reached the end of the road, and there was no place left to go. She bowed her head, waiting for the floor to open up and swallow her whole. Instead, a soft, unexpected breeze lifted her hair.

"Ash."

That voice. She'd hear it in a screaming windstorm. She'd hear it whispered a mile away. It was a voice that had sung her to sleep and murmured her awake a thousand times. She opened her eyes.

There, standing before her, was Tayanna. There were the dark, dancing eyes she knew so well. The thin, pink lips. The long, black hair parted down the center that finished in a thick braid down her back. Her full battle armor gleamed as if she were standing in a bright ray of sunshine even though she stood in the shadow of the wall. She looked no different from the last time Asher saw her. Tears of joy and longing immediately sprang to Asher's eyes, making Tayanna blur and swim before her.

"My brave girl." Tayanna's voice was like music. It carried notes of pity and empathy. Asher couldn't believe she was hearing it again.

"Tayanna?" Asher's voice was small and child-like. "I've missed you so much." Her mouth twisted as she remembered the endless months of bottomless grief. Her longing now was visceral. It struck her like a heavy blow to the chest. She wanted to reach out, to touch Tayanna, but she was too weak. She couldn't raise her arms.

Tayanna's voice was sympathetic. "I know." Her face said she understood exactly what Asher had been through and she regretted all of it.

This wasn't real. It couldn't be, and Asher knew it. And yet she wanted it to be real. She wanted it so much it hurt. But if the only way to see Tayanna again was in a delusion, it was better than never seeing her again. She wouldn't try to stop the hallucination.

"I don't want to go on anymore. It's too hard." Her voice was plaintive.

"You're strong. You can do it. You *will* do it. You have so much more to do in this world. You've grown so much over the last few weeks. You're not who you were when your journey began." Tayanna smiled. "I'm so proud of you."

She knelt so that her eyes were level with Asher's. "You need to go now. You need to get up. Your friends need you. And Ilirya will need you, too. Darker days are yet to come. You must go fight the coming Darkness."

She started to shimmer, her body becoming translucent enough that Asher could see the wall with its banners behind her. Asher reached out, her fingers grasping as though she could stop the illusion from disappearing. As though her need for Tayanna could keep the vision tethered to the hall indefinitely. "No! Don't leave me! Not again. Stay with me. Please, stay."

Tayanna's smile turned sad. "Be strong for me. If you can face down a dragon, you can face anything. The time has come to become the great knight you're meant to be. Don't let yourself become lost searching for me. I'm always right here. We'll meet again one day, but first you have a world to help save, starting with the White Queen's prisoners."

Asher blinked and Tayanna was gone. She stared numbly at the spot where she'd been, not bothering to try to understand what she'd seen. Whether she'd just seen some kind of a vision or merely a hallucination didn't matter. She'd gotten to see Tayanna one last time. A tiny crack in her soul was healed.

She heard a sound to her left and forced herself to look. Imari had bent down to pick up the gold scepter. She held it in her hands, her face as dazed as Asher felt. What would she do next? Would she use the king's death to immediately claim dominion over all the Southlands, or would she have to fight the other four tribes for control? Asher couldn't guess. All she knew for sure was that whatever Imari did, it would be without the Death Stone.

She drew her sword. Tayanna was right. She had friends to save and a kingdom in peril to which to return. There wasn't a moment more to waste. She announced, "I'll collect my companions from your castle, and we'll depart the Southlands. If you were honest about desiring peace, send word through your brother at the border."

She didn't wait for Imari to respond. Still holding her sword in front of her, she ran out of the great hall, back the way the chamberlain had led her, and called for the unwitting gate guard to bring her horse. She was in a race against time. If she didn't reach Imari's castle before the ripples from what had just occurred in the great hall reached it, they would likely never leave the Southlands alive.

Chapter 13

Tayanna laughs as Asher nuzzles into her neck, tickling her. "Ash, listen." She pushes Asher back and sits up on her elbow. "No, listen. I've been ordered to the front again."

Asher collapses, sighing. "How long this time?"

"I don't know. But the war can't go on forever. I believe that. One day, we'll have peace. And you'll be part of that."

Asher rode faster than she ever had in her life. The lives of Taz, Marandir, and Commander Bronwen depended on it. At every moment, she expected to be challenged. By the Southerners walking in the city, by the soldiers at the gate leaving the city, and even by the farmers on the road back to Walakia. But no one did. News, normally faster than a gust of wind, had not yet spread about the death of the King of Cats. So far, she was outrunning it. That would change quickly.

When she reached the White Queen's castle, breathless and anxious, it was as though she'd stepped through a Gate into another time. Everything was as peaceful and idyllic as when she left it that morning. The chaos swirling in her mind was unmatched by the calmness of the castle grounds. She rode into the stable courtyard and leapt from Cloud's back, tying him loosely to a stable door. She didn't know how much time she had before a message might reach the castle bearing orders from the White Queen to stop the absconders. A few minutes was all she needed.

She grabbed the arm of a passing servant, remembering at the last moment to appear as dignified and collected as she could. "Where are the prisoners?"

The man squinted at her suspiciously and said nothing. Asher recognized he had little reason to trust her. She was, after all, an Iliryan, and the prisoners she was seeking were too. She did her best to smile disarmingly. "Imari has asked me to retrieve them. I've just come from the capital."

When he still looked uncertain, Asher crossed her arms and tapped her foot. "Give me your name. If you refuse to assist me, I will inform Imari of your intransigence."

The man winced. He raised his arm and pointed at a door on the side of the castle. "That's the Hole."

Asher raised her chin, mimicking a look she'd seen plenty of Iliryan noblewomen give. Not bothering to thank him, she crossed the courtyard and opened the door he'd indicated. On the other side was a short wooden staircase that led down into a small, dark room lit only by a small, ground-level window. Asher peered inside, not wanting to step into a trap. When her eyes adjusted, she saw there were two cells, one on each side of the room.

Her heart skipped a beat. There they were! Dark as it was, she could see three shapes in the cell on the left. She looked around. Where was the key that would open their cell? If it was on the castle bailiff's keychain, how would she ever get it? And if it was here, why hadn't Marandir used his power to escape the cell and get it? But she was in luck. A set of keys that could only go to the cells was hanging on a ring at the top of the staircase. She grabbed the keys and flew down the stairs.

Crying out to get her companions' attention, she jabbed the first key into the lock. It fit. She turned it, and the padlock dropped with a heavy metallic thud against the stone floor. Marandir and Taz, standing in the cell, stared at her, eyes wide and mouths agape. Their faces were tired and haggard, their clothes stained and wrinkled. Asher realized for the first time how much weight they had all lost during their expedition. Commander Bronwen didn't move from where she lay on a wood plank in the cell, her red hair loosely falling around her. If she was asleep, even the clatter of Asher's feet on the ground and her rattling at the door was insufficient to wake her.

Asher threw the door open. "Come on! Let's get out of here!"

"You're alive!" Taz's voice was exhilarated.

"You're here!" Marandir exclaimed at the same time. "Is the guard gone?"

Asher looked back toward the door. If there was normally a guard, he would no doubt be back soon. "We have to move quickly. We don't have much time. I'll explain everything later. Grab the commander."

Gently and with great care—although moving as quickly as they could—the two men lifted her in their arms, carrying her like a child between them. Her head lolled backward, and her body was limp as a doll. She did not wake. Asher didn't have time to worry about how badly her condition had deteriorated. They were all getting out together.

She ran back up the stairs and checked the courtyard. It was empty. She motioned for them to follow. "This way."

They ran out the door and to the stables. If any of the servants they saw moving around the castle at a distance noticed them, they didn't seem to care. The Iliryans passed through the castle grounds unchallenged.

Asher hadn't checked to see if the other Iliryan horses were in the stable, hidden away in some part Imari had kept her from noticing. It didn't matter. If they weren't, the Iliryans would steal whatever horses they had to. She pointed to the stalls. "Go and tack up a horse," she told Taz. "You'll find everything you need in the tack room here at the end of the barn."

Everything, that is, but their weapons. Asher suspected their swords were now part of Imari's personal collection. They would have to leave unarmed. Taz and Marandir set Commander Bronwen down, leaning her against the stable wall, and in the blink of an eye, Taz disappeared inside.

Asher laid a hand on Marandir's arm, holding him back when he started to follow Taz. "You must go as quickly as possible back to Ilirya."

His face was instantly full of concern. "What? But what about Nyara? What's happened?"

"The King of Cats is dead."

His eyes widened. "And our petition for peace?"

Asher shook her head in answer. "I don't know what will happen next. I hope the Magus and the Guardian will advocate for peace with whoever follows, but…all I know is the Southerners are weakened. Whoever replaces the King of Cats will not share his power. His magic is broken. Hopefully it will be enough for us to have a chance at changing the battlefield."

Marandir lowered his head, his shoulders slumping. Asher felt a flicker of guilt. Had she done the wrong thing? Could she have done something else? Was he disappointed in her?

Marandir said nothing more, however, and in a moment, he transformed into a light brown bird so small it could fit in her hand. Asher recognized the form as a great snipe. He leapt into the air and began to wing away, heading north toward Ilirya. Asher didn't know how long it would take him to reach the border and then King's City, but she hoped it would only be a few days. The Iliryans needed to know there would be no instant peace. But that even so, not all hope was lost. The army could still stand down as a new ruler was installed on the Southerner throne.

She jogged down the line of stalls, looking at the horses inside. Finally, she caught sight of Ever's white and yellow flank. So Imari *had* taken all the Iliryan horses. Stifling a cheer, she raced back to the tack room and grabbed his tack. As she saddled him, she saw Taz lead Fleet from another stall. They would have to leave Marandir's horse Crow behind in the Southlands.

Taz waited to help her hoist Commander Bronwen into her saddle. Trying to position the unconscious commander would be like maneuvering two lumpy sacks of potatoes, and it would take both of them to do it. Asher put Ever's reins over his neck and walked back to where the knight commander was slumped against the wall. She knelt and put her left arm under the commander's legs and her right arm behind her back to lift her.

The commander's eyelids fluttered open. "What's going on?" Her voice was disoriented and groggy.

Asher's heart was racing now. It was just her and Taz left to protect the commander. Every passing minute put them into more danger. How long had it been since she'd left Nyara? Depending on what Imari was doing, an order could come at any time to capture them. Nor was the White Queen the only danger. At any moment, the prison guard could realize his charges had escaped and confront them. With only two of them, they wouldn't be able to fight their way free.

Trying her best to sound calm, Asher said, "We're leaving the Southlands, Commander. It's time to go home."

Commander Bronwen's hand flopped weakly onto Asher's arm. Her blue eyes bored into Asher's. "No." Her voice was hard as iron. "Not until we have achieved peace."

It was one of her rare moments of lucidity. This was the knight commander talking, as aware and keen as she'd ever been. Asher swallowed the wave of emotions that rose up in her throat. Commander Bronwen had deserved far better than to end her journey imprisoned in the White Queen's castle. She had deserved to face the King of Cats herself, to decide what was best for Ilirya. *She* would have found a way to guarantee peace.

Asher didn't have time to explain to the commander what had happened. They needed to escape. Hoping to appease Commander Bronwen so she would mount, Asher nodded. "Yes, we have peace."

The knight commander's eyes peered into hers, searching. Asher couldn't stand their scouring intensity. She looked away.

"You're lying." There was no doubt in Commander Bronwen's voice.

Asher winced. They didn't have time to discuss the issue. She said quickly, "The King of Cats is dead. At least two of the Southerners' five tribal leaders prefer peace to war. If peace is at all possible, we have done the best we could to achieve it. I swear it. Now we must go."

Commander Bronwen scrutinized her face for long seconds more, and Asher worried she would demand they stay until peace was certain and a treaty was signed. It was, after all, what she had vowed to do. Without a peace treaty, the mission was a failure. Would the commander accept failure? Finally, Commander Bronwen broke off her examination. Her eyes flickered to their surroundings, taking in Taz and the three horses. "Are we fleeing?"

"Yes. We need to leave *now*." Asher placed an urgent emphasis on the final word. She hoped Commander Bronwen would understand the direness of the situation from her tone.

Commander Bronwen nodded. Taking this as consent, Asher lifted her from the ground and carried her to Ever's side. Asking him to kneel, she lifted the commander onto the saddle. Taz grabbed Commander Bronwen's right leg from his side and helped maneuver her into place. The two quickly buckled her legs to the saddle, then mounted their own horses.

Asher said, "We're in Walakia, close to the border with the Maji. If we ride hard, we can reach it in a few hours."

"Will we be chased?" A fierce and warlike light glimmered in Commander Bronwen's eyes.

"We may be." Asher looked around the yard. She half expected armed soldiers to come bursting into the stables. She didn't believe Imari would let them leave the Southlands alive, not if she could help it. The White Queen wasn't the type to forgive the foiling of her plans.

"Then I'll stay."

Asher gawped at the commander. "What?"

Commander Bronwen sat as straight in her saddle as she could. Her face had a bluish hue to it. Purple bags were etched beneath her eyes. Still, she was strong and determined.

"I will lead the pursuers in the wrong direction while you escape."

"Commander, no!" Taz and Asher objected simultaneously.

"We can all go together. We can outrun them," Asher said.

The knight commander looked over her two knights. "A commander's job is to ensure all the members of her squadron return home safely. If the pursuers follow me rather than you, it will buy you time. Enough, hopefully, to escape them completely. Enough for you to make it home."

Asher shook her head. "No, Commander—"

"As Knight Commander of Ilirya, I order you to return without me." Commander Bronwen's voice was hard with resolve. It brooked no objection.

Asher looked at Taz. Ordinarily, there was no contradicting the commander's orders, but this was a special circumstance. Could they tie Ever to Cloud's saddle and flee? Asher was willing to try.

Commander Bronwen's voice softened. "Let us not pretend any future awaits me in Ilirya. I will not make it back to the border. My time has come. I can lead the Southerners for at least a little while before they realize they have been deceived. That time might be the difference between escape and capture for you. Now, no more delay. This is my last order as knight commander. *Go*!"

It was undignified to cry in front of the knight commander, but Asher didn't care. This expedition to the Southlands had taken everything from her. All she could hope was that somehow all the sacrifices that had been made would one day be rewarded. And that somehow, they would be enough to save Ilirya. Her voice barely a whisper, she said the only thing she could. "Strength and honor, Commander."

Commander Bronwen smiled at her, the brave, valiant knight commander of Ilirya. "Duty and queen."

Taz and Asher wheeled their horses, clattering away over the cobblestones and out of the castle grounds. In the immediate term, they needed to put enough distance between themselves and the White Queen that she would give up pursuit. But in the longer term, they would have to find a way to recross the Hollow Lands and the Southerner line controlled by Imari's brother if they were to get back to Ilirya. The way home was no less treacherous than the journey outbound had been. Asher didn't know how, but she was determined to find a way to make it back.

She looked one last time over her shoulder at the retreating castle. Far away, she could still make out the figure of the knight commander, waiting for her final ride.

Asher picked up a stick and poked at the small fire she'd built. They needed its warmth and light, but too large and it might give them away to any Walakai still pursuing them. She said, "If we're on Maji lands now, the Guardian must know. At any moment, his warriors could come for us." She paused. "If there are any in the area, that is. If there aren't, it may take a little longer."

But then she frowned, catching herself. Maybe the Guardian *didn't* know. Imari had said his exceptional warging power had been derived from the Death Stone. Now that it was shattered, how much had he been weakened? Could he detect them at all? From how far away? She hoped he could. Since they'd fled the White Queen's castle with only the clothes on their backs and the saddles on their horses, they would need food and water soon. Neither she nor Taz had the energy to hunt.

Taz's face was pinched and gray. The flickering yellow firelight revealed deep hollows carved into his cheeks. Sorrow, loss, and fatigue had drained the life from his body; weariness bleached the blue from his eyes. In the space of a few weeks, the lighthearted boy with whom she had grown up had been replaced by a somber, melancholy adult. Would she see her old friend again? Would the light return to his eyes?

He nodded listlessly in response to her patter, and a pang of dismay coursed through her heart. She wished she could give him energy and hope, but she had none to spare. She tried to smile at him. "At least we're safe now." Unless the White Queen's hunters crossed into Maji lands to chase them. Unless the Guardian turned on them in retribution for the destruction of the Death Stone.

The corners of Taz's mouth pulled down. "I've been thinking. I understand why you didn't give the Death Stone to the King of Cats or the White Queen, because obviously they were lying to you and didn't really want peace, but why didn't you give it to Aeryn?"

Asher threw her stick into the fire, watching as it smoldered. "If I gave it to Aeryn, there would have been no hope for peace. She would have taken it and then the King of Cats would never have agreed to peace, out of spite." She reflected for a moment. "Well, now I know he might have dissolved when she took it, but I didn't then."

She pulled her knees to her chest and wrapped her arms around them. "Everything we did, our trip here, would have been for nothing. All I wanted was to give Ilirya a chance. I thought if I broke the Stone, it would shatter the Southerners' power, too, and Ilirya would have a hope of surviving."

Taz bit his lip. In a quiet voice, he asked, "Do you think he really could have brought Tayanna back? Or was that just another lie?"

Asher closed her eyes. That was a question whose answer she would never know. She remembered what Commander Bronwen had said when told that if she traveled to the Southlands she would die. "A soldier fulfills her duty, no matter the cost." Asher understood what that meant now in a way she hadn't before.

She said, "It doesn't matter." It had cost her everything, but she had done what she thought was best for Ilirya because the greater good for her people was more important than her individual need to have Tayanna back. Before they embarked for the Southlands, she wouldn't have believed she would give up the chance to see Tayanna again, but now she realized this was what had to happen. It had been the right thing to do. No matter how much it hurt.

"What happens now?"

"We find the Guardian and tell him what happened. Then we hope. In the meantime, Marandir will go to General Oran and the queen and let them know what happened. They can decide what to do next."

"Do you think the Guardian and the Magus will withdraw their troops and stop fighting?"

Asher thought of the dignified Maji and the fiery Isenii. She hoped so. She shrugged. "The King of Cats is dead. Who knows what will happen now? But if they can, I think they will."

"What about the Dark Magic that was released from the Stone?"

Asher winced, remembering the black smoke that curled up from the stone shards and the look of horror on Aeryn's face. She rocked her body back and forth. She had a bad feeling, one she couldn't shake. "I don't know. I guess I hoped it would dissolve once the Stone was broken. I couldn't worry about both peace for Ilirya and what the Dark Magic might do."

Unexpectedly, her scar began to ache. She rubbed it, remembering what it meant for her future. Now wasn't the time to tell Taz about the Dark Magic infection. They had a long journey ahead of them to get back to Ilirya, and if they didn't make it, the wound wouldn't matter anyway. There was no use worrying him.

A clap of thunder echoed overhead, reverberating around them. Although it sounded far away, the tremors shook the leaves of the trees around them and rattled the branches that had been stacked together in their fire. Asher frowned, peering up into the darkness above as though she could see whatever storm was brewing there. When the daylight had faded, there hadn't been any clouds in the sky. How had a storm moved into the area so quickly?

Taz stood, his hand on the hilt of his sword, looking around. "Something doesn't feel right."

Asher felt it too. She rose to her feet as a sense of foreboding swept over her. "I don't think that was thunder."

Far away, a gash appeared in the sky over the sleeping city of Nyara. From it, hundreds of dark and formless shapes spilled out into the night and through the streets of the city.

In the bright white space between life and death, Death's Champion stood before Lymon, one of the black-winged servants of Death. Her dark head was bowed, concealing her pale face and mist covered eyes. Mortals could not pass between the world of the living and the dead. Every trip Aeryn took stripped more and more of her mortality from her. She was wearing away like cloth washed too many times.

"I'm sorry. I failed. Asher smashed the Death Stone before I could stop her. The Dark Magic was released into the world." She grimaced. She knew instinctively that the consequences for Asher's mistake would be terrible and far-reaching, even if she didn't know exactly what they would be.

Lymon shook his head. "I know. So much Dark Magic released into the mortal realm has rent multiple tears in the fabric of the world. The veil between the mortal and divine planes is disintegrating. We will do what we can here to contain the damage, but the effects are escalating by the minute. The Darkness is pressing in on all sides."

Aeryn shivered, unnerved by the strain in Lymon's voice. Unbeknownst to mortals, Dark Magic was tied to a malevolent, semi-living entity that was somehow both a place and a thing that Lymon called "the Darkness." According to Lymon, the Darkness was the source of the ills that plagued the Southlands, like the dragon the Iliryans had killed and the monsters in Sarsenia's southern seas. Separate from the mortal and divine planes, the Darkness was always trying to spread into both using power siphoned from Death. Even the gods were threatened by the Darkness.

Lymon said the Darkness had never been able to secure a toehold in either the mortal or the divine realm, but Aeryn got the sense from Lymon's words that with the destruction of the Death Stone, this might be about to change. But what did that mean for the two planes? Her skin prickled. She had saved Ilirya from the conspiracy to bring the One God into their world, but the danger now might be greater yet because it threatened not just Ilirya, but their entire world. *And* that of the gods.

"What will happen next? Can the Darkness be stopped?"

"We cannot see how this will end. Dark Magic clouds our view of the future. You must go back to the mortal plane and do what you can to stop the spread of the Darkness there. It will be a bitter fight on many fronts. You will need whatever allies you can rally to your side. You cannot defeat it alone."

Aeryn bit her lip. "What if it can't be stopped?"

Lymon didn't answer, and Aeryn was glad. Some things, she didn't want to know. He touched her on the head, and burning magic poured from his hand into her veins. The scalding heat as it tore through her was almost unbearable. She ground her teeth together, refusing to cry out. To fulfill her missions to counter the Darkness, she was lent some of Death's power, but it came at a high cost: pieces of her humanity. More of her essence was chipped away from her with every magical infusion. No mortal could have accepted that power and lived. It was only possible because Aeryn was already dead.

At Ilirya's northern border, a snow-dusted army stirred in the night, creeping closer to a string of unsuspecting villages. In the falling snow, they looked like moving snowdrifts, invisible to the sentries napping at their posts. The Iliryan soldiers had been warned to be on the lookout for a Northman invasion in hasty messages sent from the capital, but they had grown complacent. It had been over a century since the Northmen had come marching over the border. They balled up the orders and cast them into the fire. The soldiers wouldn't live to regret their mistake.

In Prabst, black-robed creatures opened their eyes in the mortal realm for the first time and felt for the life forces of the humans sleeping around them. They were hungry.

Other Books from Ylva Publishing

www.ylva-publishing.com

Daughter of Fire: Conspiracy of the Dark

(Destiny and Darkness series – Book 1)

Karen Frost

ISBN: 978-3-96324-267-0
Length: 195 pages (76,000 words)

In an isolated land of ice and snow, a girl finds she has the rare gift of fire. It's raw and exciting, but sets her apart. Aeryn is taken to train as a mage at a university. There, she meets a healer in training, Lyse, whose beauty draws her in. But there's also darkness all around that could threaten whole kingdom.

A compelling fantasy novel, part one of the Destiny and Darkness series.

Daughter of Fire: The Darkness Rising

(Destiny and Darkness series – Book 2)

Karen Frost

ISBN: 978-3-96324-300-4
Length: 181 pages (71,000 words)

Aeryn, a young mage with the gift of fire, draws around her a group of fellow students and allies to protect their world from a sinister plot. At her side is the beautiful healer, Lyse. In front of her is nothing but awful choices. Can Aeryn protect a kingdom she may not even want to save?

This conclusion to Conspiracy of the Dark is a thrilling fantasy novel in the Destiny and Darkness series.

About Karen Frost

Karen Frost is an armchair pop culture pundit and blogger whose articles have been spread internationally by actresses, production companies, directors, and news outlets. She loves YA high fantasy and wants to introduce more lady knights and mages in the literary world, particularly if they're LGBT. She lives just outside of Washington, D.C, but has an active imaginary life in which she lives in a cabana on a beach instead.

CONNECT WITH KAREN

Website: www.karenfrostbooks.com

Destiny's Choice

ISBN: 978-3-96324-392-9

Also available as e-book.

Published by Ylva Publishing, legal entity of Ylva Verlag, e.Kfr.

Ylva Verlag, e.Kfr.
Owner: Astrid Ohletz
Am Kirschgarten 2
65830 Kriftel
Germany

www.ylva-publishing.com

First edition: 2020

Credits
Edited by Miranda Miller and Amber Williams
Cover Design by Grit Richter | Coverdesign und mehr
Print Layout by Streetlight Graphics

www.ingramcontent.com/pod-product-compliance
Ingram Content Group UK Ltd.
Pitfield, Milton Keynes, MK11 3LW, UK
UKHW041830200726
13854UKWH00002BA/915